No Tomorrow

Also by Luke Jennings

Fiction
Breach Candy
Atlantic
Beauty Story
Codename Villanelle

Non-Fiction
Blood Knots: A Memoir of Fishing and Friendship
The Faber Pocket Guide to Ballet (with Deborah Bull)

Children's Fiction
Stars (with Laura Jennings)
Stars: Stealing the Show (with Laura Jennings)

No Tomorrow

Luke Jennings

JOHN MURRAY

First published in Great Britain in 2018 by John Murray (Publishers)
An Hachette UK Company

1

© Luke Jennings 2018

The right of Luke Jennings to be identified as the Author
of the Work has been asserted by him in accordance with
the Copyright, Designs and Patents Act 1988.

A CIP catalogue record for this title is available from the British Library

ISBN 978-1-473-67656-5
ANZ/SA Trade Paperback ISBN 978-1-473-67657-2
Ebook ISBN 978-1-473-67659-6

Typeset in Sabon MT by Hewer Text UK Ltd, Edinburgh
Printed and bound by CPI Group (UK) Ltd, Croydon, CR0 4YY

John Murray policy is to use papers that are natural, renewable
and recyclable products and made from wood grown in sustainable
forests. The logging and manufacturing processes are expected to
conform to the environmental regulations of the country of origin.

John Murray (Publishers)
Carmelite House
50 Victoria Embankment
London EC4Y 0DZ

www.johnmurray.co.uk

For N, B, R & L as ever.

I

Cruising through Muswell Hill on his carbon-framed bike, his hands resting lightly on the alloy handlebars, Dennis Cradle feels a pleasing exhaustion. It's a longish ride from the office to his north London home, but he's made good time. It's something that he would hesitate to confide to his colleagues or his family, but Dennis sees himself as the upholder of certain values. The hard cross-town ride satisfies the Spartan in him. Cycling keeps him lean and mean, and, incidentally, looking pretty damn *sportif* in his form-fitting Lycra shorts and tactical-fabric jersey, given that he's going to be forty-eight next birthday.

As the director of D4 Branch at MI5, responsible for counter-espionage against Russia and China, Dennis has reached a level of seniority where he can, if he wishes, get chauffeured home in one of the Service's fleet of anonymous, mid-range vehicles. Tempting of course, status-wise, but a slippery slope. Let the fitness go, and it's all over. Before he knows it, he'll be one of those paunchy old shags propping up the Thames House bar, nursing his Laphroaig and complaining about how much better things were before the fembots in HR took over.

Cycling helps keep Dennis in touch. Keeps his ear to the street and the blood racing through his veins. Which is where he needs it, given Gabi's raging libido. God, he wishes he was going home to her right now, rather than to Penny, with her diet-drained body and her incessant fault-finding.

As if on cue, as he glides the final hundred metres, the 'Eye of the Tiger' theme from *Rocky III* kicks in on the Bluetooth player in his cycling helmet. As the big chords punch home, Dennis's heart begins to pound. In his mind, Gabi is waiting for him on a king-size bed in the master cabin of a superyacht. She's naked, except for a pair of fluffy white tennis socks, and her gym-toned legs are invitingly parted.

Then, incomprehensibly, a steel-strong hand grabs his arm and wrenches him to a halt, the bike skidding to the ground beneath him. Dennis opens his mouth to speak, but is silenced by a vicious short-arm punch to the gut.

'Sorry, squire. Need your attention.' Dennis's captor is fortyish, with the features of a well-groomed rat, and smells of stale cigarette smoke. With his spare hand, he removes Dennis's cycle helmet and drops it on the fallen bike. Dennis writhes, but the grip on his arm is unyielding.

'Stand still, yeah? Don't want to hurt you.'

Dennis groans. 'What the *fuck* . . .?'

'I'm here for a friend, squire, who needs to talk to you. About Babydoll.'

The remaining colour drains from Dennis's face. His eyes widen with shock.

'Pick the bike up. Put it in the back of the vehicle. Then get into the front seat. Do it now.' He releases Dennis, who looks around him with dazed eyes, noting the elderly white Ford Transit van and the pasty-faced youth with the lip-piercing at the wheel.

2

Opening the van's rear door, his hands trembling, Dennis turns off the helmet's Bluetooth sound-system, which is now playing 'Slide It In' by Whitesnake. He hooks the helmet over the handlebars and loads the bike into the van.

'Phone,' Ratface says, following the demand with a stinging slap that leaves Dennis's ears ringing. Shakily, Dennis hands it over. 'OK, into the passenger seat.'

As the van pulls out into the traffic, Dennis tries to remember the Service capture and interrogation protocols. But suppose this lot *are* the sodding Service, and part of some internal investigation team? They'd have to have gone to the DG to authorise turning over someone of his rank. So who the *fuck*? Could they be hostiles? SVR, perhaps, or CIA? Just say nothing. Take each moment as it comes. *Say nothing.*

The drive takes less than ten minutes, with the Transit van weaving in and out of the rush-hour traffic. They cross the North Circular Road, and then pull in to the car park of a Tesco superstore. The driver selects a bay at the furthest point from the store's entrance, brings the van quietly to a halt, and switches off the ignition.

Dennis sits there, his face the colour of raw pastry, staring through the windscreen at the boundary fence. A faint fuel haze rises from the traffic on the North Circular. 'Now what?' he asks.

'Now we wait,' says the voice of Ratface behind him.

Further minutes pass, and then a ringtone sounds. Grotesquely, it's a laughing duck.

'For you, squire.' From the back seat, Ratface passes him a cheap plastic phone.

'Dennis Cradle?' The voice is low, with a tinny electronic twang. Voice-changer, he notes subconsciously.

'Who is this?'

'You don't need to know. What you need to know is what we know. Let's start with the big one, shall we? That in return for betraying the Service, you've accepted the best part of fifteen million pounds, and parked it in an offshore account in the British Virgin Isles. Do you have any comment to make about that?'

Cradle's world contracts to the windscreen in front of him. His heart feels as if it's been packed in ice. He can't think, let alone speak.

'I thought not. So let's continue. We know that earlier this year you took possession of a three-bedroom apartment in a building named Les Asphodèles in Cap d'Antibes on the French Riviera, and that last month you bought a forty-two-foot motor yacht named *Babydoll*, presently moored at the Port Vauban marina. We also know about your association with twenty-eight-year-old Ms Gabriela Vukovic, currently employed by the fitness club and spa at the Hotel du Littoral.

'At present neither MI5 nor your family know about any of this. Nor do the Metropolitan Police or the Inland Revenue. Whether that state of affairs continues is up to you. If you want us to remain silent – if you want to retain your freedom, your job and your reputation – you need to tell us everything, and I mean *everything*, about the organisation that's been paying you. Short-change us, hold a single fact back, and you will spend the next quarter-century in a Belmarsh Prison cell. Unless you die first, obviously. So what do you say?'

The faint drone of traffic. Somewhere in the distance, the sound of an ambulance alarm. 'Whoever you are, you can fuck yourself,' Dennis says, his voice low and unsteady. 'Assault and kidnapping are crimes. Say whatever you want to whoever you want. I don't give a shit.'

'You see, here's the problem, Dennis,' the tinny voice continues. 'Or maybe I should say, here's *your* problem. If we send a report to Thames House, and there's an investigation and a prosecution and all that sort of thing, it will be assumed that you've talked to us, and the people who are paying you all that money – and fifteen mill is a *lot* – will be forced to make an example of you. You'll be dealt with, Dennis, and it'll be nasty. You know what they're like. So really, you don't have a choice. There's no bluff to call.'

'You haven't the first idea what you're talking about, have you? I may have concealed certain things from my wife and my employers, but having an affair isn't a crime, at least it wasn't when I last checked.'

'No, it isn't. But treason is, and that's what you'll be charged with.'

'You've got no grounds whatever to charge me with anything of the sort, and you know it. This is just a cheap attempt at blackmail. So whoever you are, like I said, go fuck yourself.'

'OK, Dennis, here's what's going to happen. You're going to get out of that van in five minutes' time, and ride your bike home. You might want to pick up some flowers for your wife; they've got some very reasonably priced roses at the petrol station. Tomorrow morning a car will pick you up at your house at 7 a.m. and drive you to Dever Research Station in Hampshire. Your deputy at Thames House has been informed that you will be spending the next three working days there, attending a counter-terrorism seminar.

In the course of that time, you will also, in another part of the station, be privately interviewed about the subjects we've discussed. No one else there will be aware of this, and there will be no outward sign of any break in your usual duties. Dever, as I'm sure you know, is listed as a government secret asset, and is completely secure. If these interviews go well, which I'm sure they will, you will be free to go.'

'And if I say no?'

'Dennis, let's not even begin to think about what happens if you say no. Seriously. It would be a total shit-storm. Penny, for a start. Can you imagine? And the kids. Their dad on trial for treason? Let's not even go there, OK?'

A long silence. 'You said 7 a.m.?'

'Yes. Leave it any later and the traffic will be impossible.'

Dennis stares into the hazy twilight. 'OK,' he says.

Laying the phone on her desk, Eve Polastri exhales and closes her eyes. The tough, authoritative character she's been playing for Dennis Cradle is nothing like her own, and face to face with him she wouldn't have been able to keep up the mocking tone, not least because he seemed so stratospherically senior to her when she worked at MI5. But with that final 'OK', he's effectively conceded his guilt, and if he'll almost certainly be shocked to see her sitting opposite him tomorrow, it won't be anything she can't handle.

'Neatly played,' says Richard Edwards, removing the headphones through which he's been listening to Dennis and Eve's conversation, and settling back into the Goodge Street office's least uncomfortable chair.

6

'Team effort,' says Eve. 'Lance scared the hell out of him, and Billy drove like an angel.'

Richard nods. The head of MI6's Russia desk, Richard is technically Eve's employer, although he's an infrequent visitor to the office, and her name is not on any official Security Services personnel list. 'We'll give him tonight to meditate on his situation, ideally in the presence of that short-tempered wife of his. Tomorrow you can set about stripping him to the bone.'

'You think he'll be there at 7 a.m.? You don't think he'll cut and run tonight?'

'No. Dennis Cradle may be a traitor, but he's not a fool. If he runs, he's finished. We're his only chance, and he'll know that.'

'No chance he'll . . .'

'Kill himself? Dennis? No, he's not the type. I've known him since we were at Oxford together, and he's a ducker and diver. The sort who thinks you can sort out any problem, no matter how tricky, over a decent bottle of wine in a good restaurant, preferably on someone else's expense account. He'll tell us what we need to know, and he'll keep quiet about it. Because scary though our people can be, the lot he's betrayed us to have got to be infinitely more so. Any suggestion he's compromised, they'll shut him down straight away.'

'With prejudice.'

'With extreme prejudice. They'd probably send your lady friend to do it.'

Eve smiles, and the phone in her bag vibrates. It's a text from Niko, asking when she's going to be home. She answers eight o'clock, although she knows that her actual arrival time is likely to be at least eight thirty.

Richard stares through the office's single, long-uncleaned window. 'I know what you're thinking, Eve. And the answer is no.'

'What am I thinking?'

'Wring Cradle out, then use him as bait. See what swims up out of the deep.'

'It's not a wholly bad idea.'

'Murder's always a bad idea, trust me, and murder's what it would amount to.'

'Don't worry, I'll stick to the plan. Dennis will be back in the arms of the lovely Gabi before you can say full-blown mid-life crisis.'

Rinat Yevtukh, leader of Odessa's Golden Brotherhood crime network, is frustrated. Venice, he's been assured, is more than a city. It's one of the high citadels of Western culture, and perhaps the ultimate luxury destination. But somehow, standing at the window of his suite at the Danieli Hotel in his complimentary dressing gown and slippers, he can't quite engage with the place.

Partly, it's stress. Kidnapping the Russian in Odessa was a mistake, he sees that now. He'd assumed, quite reasonably, that the thing would play out in the usual way. A flurry of back-channel negotiations, a cash sum agreed on, and no hard feelings on either side. In the event, some lunatic chose to take the whole thing personally, leaving Rinat with six men and the hostage dead, and his house in Fontanka shot to pieces. He has other houses, obviously, and men are easily enough replaced. But it's all extra work and, at a given point in your life, these things begin to take their toll.

The Doge's Suite at the Danieli is reassuringly luxurious. Winged cherubs disport among candy-floss clouds in the ceiling fresco, portraits of Venetian aristocrats hang from walls shining with gold damask, antique carpets cover the floors. On a side table stands a metre-high, multicoloured glass statuette of a weeping clown, bought in a Murano factory that morning and destined for Rinat's Kiev apartment.

Katya Goraya, Rinat's twenty-five-year-old lingerie model girlfriend, is sprawled barefoot across a rococo chaise longue. Dressed in a Dior crop top and Dussault thrashed jeans, Katya is gazing at her phone, chewing gum, and nodding her head to a Lady Gaga song. At intervals she sings along, insofar as the chewing gum and her limited English permit. There was a time when Rinat found this endearing, now he just finds it annoying.

'Bad Romance,' he says.

Unhurriedly, her expensively augmented breasts straining against the lacy fabric of her top, Katya removes her ear-buds.

'Bad Romance,' Rinat repeats. 'Not Bedroom Ants.'

She looks at him blankly, then frowns. 'I want to go back to Gucci. I've changed my mind about that bag. The pink snakeskin one.'

There's nothing Rinat wants to do less. Those superior San Marco shop assistants. All smiles until they've got your money, and then you might as well be dogshit.

'We need to go now, Rinat. Before they close.'

'You go. Take Slava with you.'

She pouts. Rinat knows that she wants him to come because if he does, he will pay for the bag. If the bodyguard takes her it will come out of her allowance. Which he also pays for.

'You want to make love?' Katya's gaze softens. 'When we get back from the shop I'll fuck you up the ass with the strap-on.'

Rinat shows no sign of having heard her. What he really wants is to be somewhere else. To lose himself in the world beyond the gold silk curtains, where afternoon is shading into evening, and gondolas and water taxis are drawing pale lines across the lagoon.

'Rinat?'

He closes the bedroom door behind him. It takes him ten minutes to shower and dress. When he returns to the reception room, Katya hasn't moved.

'You're just leaving me here?' she asks, incredulous.

Frowning, Rinat checks his reflection in a silvered octagonal mirror. As he closes the door of the suite behind him, he hears the sound, not unimpressive in its way, of a twenty-kilo Murano glass clown shattering on an antique terrazzo floor.

In the hotel's top-floor bar, it's blessedly quiet. Later it will be thronged with guests, but for now there are just two couples, both sitting in silence. Installing himself on the terrace, Rinat leans back in his chair, and through half-closed eyes watches the soft rise and fall of the gondolas at their moorings. Soon, he muses, it will be time to leave Odessa. To get his money out of Ukraine and into a less volatile jurisdiction. For the last decade sex, drugs and human trafficking have proved themselves the ultimate gilt-edged trifecta, but with new players like the Turkish gangs moving in, and the Russians cracking down hard, the game is changing. The wise man, Rinat tells himself, knows when to move on.

Katya has her gaze set on Miami's Golden Beach, where for less than $12 million, including bribes to the US Citizenship and Immigration Services, you can get a luxury waterfront home with a private dock. Rinat, however, is increasingly of the opinion that life might be less stressful without Katya and her incessant demands, and the last few days have got him thinking about Western Europe. About Italy in particular, which appears to take a relaxed view of crimes of moral turpitude. The place is classy – the sports cars, the clothes, the fucked-up old buildings – and Italian women are unbelievable. Even the shop-girls look like movie stars.

A grave young man in a dark suit materialises at his elbow, and Rinat orders a malt whisky.

'Cancel that. Make the gentleman a Negroni Sbagliato. And bring me one too.'

Rinat turns, and meets the amused gaze of a woman in a black chiffon cocktail dress, who is standing behind him.

'You are, after all, in Venice.'

'I am,' he concurs, a little dazedly, and nods to the waiter, who silently withdraws.

She looks out over the lagoon, which shimmers like white gold in the dusk. 'See Venice and die, is what they say.'

'I'm not planning to die yet. And I haven't seen much of Venice, except the inside of the shops.'

'That's a pity, because the shops here are either full of tourist trash, or the same as those in a hundred other cities, except maybe more expensive. Venice is not about the present, Venice is about the past.'

Rinat stares at her. She really is very beautiful. The amber gaze, the oblique smile, the whole artfully expensive look of her. Belatedly, it occurs to him to offer her a chair.

'*Sei gentile*. But I'm interrupting your evening.'

'Not at all. I'm looking forward to that drink. What was it again?'

She sits, and with a whisper of silk tights, which Rinat does not fail to appreciate, crosses her knees. 'A Negroni Sbagliato. It's a Negroni, but with sparkling wine instead of gin. And at the Danieli, *naturalmente*, they make it with champagne. For me, the perfect drink at sunset.'

'Better than a single malt whisky?'

A faint smile. 'I think so.'

And so it proves. Rinat is not an obviously handsome man. His shaved head resembles a Crimean potato, and his handmade silk suit cannot disguise his brutal build. But wealth, however acquired, has a way of commanding attention, and Rinat is not unused to the company of desirable women. And Marina Falieri, as he learns her name to be, is nothing if not desirable.

He can't take his eyes off her mouth. There's a faint scar on the bow of her upper lip, and the resultant asymmetry lends her smile an equivocal quality. A vulnerability that speaks, quietly but insistently, to the predator in him. She is flatteringly interested in everything he has to say, and in response he finds himself holding forth freely. He tells her about Odessa, about the historic Cathedral of the Transfiguration, where he is a regular worshipper, and about the magnificent Opera and Ballet Theatre, to which, as an enthusiastic patron of the arts, he has contributed millions of roubles. This account of himself, if wholly fictional, is richly and convincingly detailed, and Marina's eyes shine as she listens. She even persuades him to teach her a couple of phrases in Russian, which she repeats with endearing inaccuracy.

And then, all too soon, the evening is over. She has to attend an official dinner in Sant'Angelo, Marina explains apologetically. It will be dull, and she wishes she could stay, but she's on the steering committee of the Venice Biennale, and . . .

'*Per favore, Marina. Capisco,*' Rinat says, discharging his entire stock of Italian with what he hopes is a gallant smile.

'Your accent, Rinat. *Perfezione*!' She pauses, and smiles at him conspiratorially. 'It's not possible, by any chance, that you're free for lunch tomorrow?'

'Well, as it happens, I am.'

'Excellent. Let's meet at eleven at the hotel's river entrance. It will be my pleasure to show you something of . . . the *real* Venice.'

They rise, and she's gone. Four empty cocktail glasses stand on the white linen tablecloth, three of his and one of hers. The sun is low in the sky, half obscured by oyster-pink cirrus clouds. Rinat turns to beckon for the waiter, but he's already standing there, as patient and unobtrusive as an undertaker.

In the bus, moving at a snail's pace up the Tottenham Court Road, the only person to give Eve a second glance is an obviously disturbed man who winks at her persistently. It's a warm evening and the interior of the bus smells of damp hair and stale deodorant. Opening the *Evening Standard*, Eve flicks through the news pages and the descriptions of parties and serial adultery in Primrose Hill, and settles pleasurably into the property section.

There's no question of her and Niko being able to afford any of the living spaces so seductively laid out there. All those Victorian warehouses and industrial units reimagined as fabulous, light-filled apartments. All those panoramic river-views framed in steel and plate glass. Nor, in any real sense, does Eve covet them. She's entranced by them because they're deserted, and not quite believable. Because they serve as the imagined backdrops to other lives that she might have led.

She reaches the one-bedroom flat that she and Niko rent shortly after eight forty-five, and pushing past the accretion of footwear, bicycle accessories, Amazon packaging and fallen coats, follows the smell of cooking to the kitchen. The table, which holds an unstable pile of maths textbooks and a bottle of supermarket Rioja, is laid for two. A hissing sound and a tuneless whistling from the bathroom tell her that Niko is in the shower.

'Sorry I'm late,' she calls out. 'Smells delicious. What is it?'

'Goulash. Can you open the wine?'

Eve has just taken the corkscrew from the drawer when she hears a frantic clicking sound on the floor behind her, and turns to see two substantial animal forms hurtling through the air and landing on the table, sending the textbooks flying. For a moment she's too shocked to move. The Rioja rolls from the table and smashes on the tiled floor. Two pairs of sage-green eyes watch her quizzically.

'*Niko*.'

14

He saunters damply out of the bathroom, a towel round his waist, slippers on his feet. 'My love. I see you've met Thelma and Louise.'

She stares at him. When he steps over the widening lake of Rioja and kisses her, she doesn't move.

'Louise is the clumsy one. I expect it was her that—'

'Niko. Before I fucking *kill you* . . .'

'They're Nigerian dwarf goats. And you and I are never buying milk, cream, cheese or soap again.'

'Niko, listen to me. I'm going to the off-licence, because I've had a bitch of a day, and every drop of alcohol we have is there on the floor. When I get back I want to sit down to your goulash, and a nice bottle of red wine, possibly two, and relax. We won't even mention those two animals on the table, because by then they will have vanished as if they'd never existed, OK?'

'Er . . . OK.'

'Excellent. See you in ten minutes.'

When Eve returns with another two bottles of Rioja, the kitchen has had a superficial but adequate makeover, there are no goats in sight, and Niko is fully dressed. With a simultaneous lifting and plummeting of her heart Eve notes that he smells of Acqua di Parma, and is wearing his Diesel jeans. Neither of them has ever put it into words, but Eve knows that when Niko wears these particular jeans and that cologne after 6 p.m., it's to signal that he's romantically inclined, and would like the evening to end with them making love.

Eve has no equivalent of Niko's sex jeans, as she calls them. No fuck-me shoes or flirty dresses, no lace and satin lingerie. Her work wardrobe is anonymous and utilitarian,

15

and she feels silly and self-conscious wearing anything else. Niko regularly tells her that she's beautiful, but she doesn't really believe him. She accepts that he loves her – he says so too often for it not to be true – but why he should do so is wholly mysterious to her.

They talk about his work. Niko teaches at the local school, and has a theory that less well-off teenagers, who do all their shopping with cash, are much better at mental arithmetic than richer kids who have been given credit cards.

'They call me Borat,' he says. 'Do you think that's a compliment?'

'Tall, eastern European accent, moustache . . . Kind of inevitable. But you're wonderful with them, you know that.'

'They're good kids. I like them. How was your day?'

'Weird. I phoned someone using a voice-changer.'

'Actually to disguise your voice, or for fun?'

'To disguise it. I didn't want the guy to know I was a woman. I wanted to sound like Darth Vader.'

'I'm not even going to begin to imagine that . . .' He looks at her. 'I think you'd like the girls. Truly.'

'Which girls?'

'Thelma and Louise. The goats. They're very sweet.'

She closes her eyes. 'Where are they now?'

'In their house. Outside.'

'They have a house?'

'It came with them.'

'So you've actually bought them. They're permanent?'

'I've done the maths, my love. Nigerian dwarfs give the richest milk of all breeds, and they only weigh about seventy-five pounds fully grown, so they eat the least hay. We'll be completely self-sufficient for dairy products.'

'Niko, this is the arse end of the Finchley Road, not the fucking Cotswolds.'

'Also, Nigerian dwarfs are—'

'Please stop calling them that. They're goats, period. And if you think I'm getting up every morning – or any morning, for that matter – to milk a pair of goats, you're insane.'

In answer, Niko gets up from the table, and goes out onto the tiny paved area that they call the garden. A moment later Thelma and Louise come bounding joyfully into the kitchen.

'Oh God.' Eve sighs, and reaches for the wine.

After the meal Niko does the washing-up, then takes himself to the bathroom to freshen up the Acqua di Parma, wash his hands, and run his wet fingers through his hair. When he returns he finds Eve fast asleep on the sofa, a spoon in one hand and an ice-cream tub trailing from the other. Thelma is lying contentedly at her side, and Louise is standing with her forelegs on the sofa, scouring the tub for the last of the melting Chocolate Chip with a long, pink tongue.

Rinat Yevtukh has dressed carefully for his morning rendez-vous, and after some thought has selected a Versace polo shirt, raw silk slacks and Santoni ostrich-skin loafers. A solid-gold Rolex Submariner completes the impression of a man who espouses quiet good taste, but is by no imaginable means to be fucked with.

Marina Falieri keeps him waiting underneath the iron-work canopy of the Danieli's river entrance for half an hour. Two bodyguards in tightly fitting suits lounge behind him, surveying the narrow canal with bored eyes. Katya's vindictive mood has not abated, but has been tempered by the promise of a photo-spread in Russian *Playboy*, and perhaps even the cover. Such a thing is by no means within Rinat's gift, but he will cross that bridge when he comes to it. Meanwhile, Katya is safely ensconced in the hotel's hair-dressing salon, undergoing a revitalising treatment involving white truffle essence and pulverised diamonds.

Shortly after eleven thirty, an elegant white *motoscafo* launch swings beneath the low, balustraded bridge and draws up at the hotel jetty. Marina is at the wheel in a striped T-shirt and jeans, her dark hair swinging around her shoulders. She's also wearing – and this Rinat finds unaccountably sexy – soft leather driving gloves.

'So.' She raises her sunglasses. 'Ready to see *la vera Venezia*?'

'Very much so.' Stepping onto the varnished mahogany afterdeck in his new loafers, Rinat teeters for a moment. As the bodyguards move reflexively forward, he lurches into the cockpit beside Marina, placing a heavy hand on her shoulder for balance.

'Excuse me.'

'No problem. Those your boys?'

'They're on my security staff, yes.'

'Well, you should be quite safe with me.' She smiles. 'But you're welcome to ask them along if you'd like to.'

'Of course not.' Rinat addresses the two men in fast idiomatic Russian, ordering them to keep an eye on Katya, and to tell her that he is lunching with a business associate. A man, obviously. Not this *devushka*.

18

The men smirk and withdraw.

'I'm definitely going to learn Russian,' Marina says, manoeuvring the launch beneath the road bridge. 'It sounds such an expressive language.'

Skilfully, she threads a path between the gondolas and the other river traffic, and steers an unhurried southern course past the island of San Giorgio Maggiore and the eastern curve of the Giudecca. As the *motoscafo* noses through the unruffled surface of the lagoon, its 150-horse-power engine carving a pale wake behind them, she tells Rinat about the palaces and churches that they pass.

'So where exactly do you live?' Rinat asks her.

'My family has an apartment next to the Palazzo Cicogna,' she says. 'The Falieri were originally from Venice, but our principal residence is now in Milan.'

He glances at her gloved left hand, curled lightly round the wheel. 'And you're not married?'

'I was close to someone, but he died.'

'I'm sorry. My condolences.'

She opens up the throttle. 'It was very sad. I was there when he passed away. I was devastated. But life goes on.'

'Indeed it does.'

She turns to him and pushes up her sunglasses so that, for a moment, he's caught in her amber gaze. 'If you look behind you, in that cold-box, you'll find a shaker and some glasses. Why don't you pour yourself a drink?'

He retrieves the ice-frosted shaker and a tall glass. 'Can I give you one?'

'I'll wait until we get to the island. You go ahead.'

He pours, drinks and nods appreciatively. 'This is . . . very good.'

'It's a limoncello cocktail. Perfect, I always think, for a morning like this.'

'Delicious. So tell me about this island we're going to.'

'It's called the Ottagone Falieri. It was once a fortification, built to protect Venice from invaders. One of my ancestors bought it in the nineteenth century. We still own it, even though no one goes there any more, and it's pretty much a ruin.'

'It sounds very romantic.'

She gives him a veiled smile. 'Let's see. It's certainly an interesting place.'

They're holding a steady course now. The Giudecca is far behind them; ahead Rinat can see only grey-green water. The limoncello is creeping through his veins with glacial slowness. He feels, for the first time in as long as he can remember, at peace.

The fortification looms, quite suddenly, out of the haze. Walls of cut stone, and above them a few sparse treetops. Soon, a jetty becomes visible. Tied up to it is another, smaller motor launch, with a black-painted hull.

'We have company.'

'I asked someone to come ahead with the lunch,' Marina says, as if this is the most natural thing in the world.

Rinat nods. Of course. Everything about this woman charms and impresses him. Her unusual beauty, which over the last couple of hours he has had considerable opportunity to examine at close range. Her easy familiarity with wealth. Old-money wealth, of the kind that doesn't need to proclaim itself, but nevertheless makes its presence felt with unambiguous force. It's not enough to be rich, Rinat knows. You have to be connected, to know the secret signs by which

20

real insiders recognise each other. Insiders like Marina Falieri.

Katya, it's increasingly clear, has to go.

Marina ties up the *motoscafo*, and as they make their way along the sun-bleached planking of the jetty, Rinat hears a faint clinking sound. There are steps built into the wall, and at the top is an octagonal compound, perhaps a hundred metres from end to end. At one extremity are the ruins of a brick and tile building, shadowed by stunted pines. Elsewhere the ground is rough scrub, quartered by a pathway. At the end of the compound furthest from the steps, a strongly built young woman with cropped hair is wielding a pickaxe, swinging it steadily at the stony ground. In her bikini top, military shorts and combat boots, she cuts an unusual figure. As Rinat watches, the woman turns, briefly meets his gaze, drops the pick, and saunters towards the ruined building.

Ignoring her, Marina leads Rinat to a table covered by a white cloth at the centre of the compound. At either side of the table is an ironwork garden chair. 'Shall we?' she asks.

They sit. Beyond the stone wall there is no land in sight, just the vast stillness of the lagoon. Behind him, Rinat hears the rattle of a tray. It's the pickaxe woman, with chilled wine and mineral water, antipasti and tiny, exquisite pastries. A faint sheen of sweat covers her muscled body, and her calves and combat boots are dusty.

Marina ignores her, and smiles at Rinat. 'Please. *Buon appetito.*'

Rinat tries to swallow a forkful of mortadella, but for some reason his appetite has deserted him, and he feels mildly nauseated. He forces himself to chew and swallow. Soon the steady clinking of the pickaxe resumes.

'What's she doing, exactly?' His voice sounds distant, disembodied.

'Oh, just some gardening. I like to keep her busy. But let me pour you some of this wine. It's a local Bianco di Custoza, I'm sure you'll like it.'

Wine, local or otherwise, is the last thing that Rinat feels like, but politeness compels him to tender his glass. He can hardly hold it steady as she pours. Sweat is running down his face and back; the horizon shimmers and sways. Some still-observant part of him notes that the clinking of the pickaxe has been replaced by the steady, rhythmic thudding of a spade. He tries to drink some mineral water but gags, and regurgitates the wine and mortadella onto the table-cloth. 'I'm . . .' he begins, and slumps back heavily in his chair. His heart is racing, and his arms and chest have started to prickle and burn as if fire-ants were creeping beneath his skin. He claws at himself, panic rising in his chest.

'That sensation's called paraesthesia,' Marina explains in Russian, sipping her wine. 'It's a symptom of aconitine poisoning.'

Rinat stares at her, his eyes widening.

'It was in the limoncello. In less than an hour you'll die of either heart failure or respiratory arrest, and looking at you right now my money's on heart failure. Until then you can expect—'

Twisting convulsively in the ironwork chair, Rinat vomits for a second time and then voids his bowels, not silently, into his ivory silk slacks.

'Exactly. And as for the rest, I won't spoil the surprise.' Turning, she waves to the other woman. 'Lara, *detka*, come over here.'

Lara lays down the spade and walks unhurriedly over. 'I've pretty much finished digging out that grave,' she says, and after some thought selects one of the pastries from the box. 'Oh my God, *kotik*, these are so good.'

'Aren't they heaven? I got them from that *pasticceria* in San Marco where we had the cream cake.'

'We must go back there.' Lara glances at Rinat, who has fallen off his chair and is convulsing on the ground, blow-flies buzzing around his soiled slacks. 'How long till he's actually dead, do you think?'

Marina wrinkles her nose. 'Half an hour or so? It'll be good to get him in the ground. That smell's really putting me off my lunch.'

'It is a bit rank.'

'On the other hand we could save his life if he tells us what we need to know. I've got an antidote for the aconitine.'

Rinat's eyes widen. '*Pozhaluysta*,' he whispers, tears and vomit streaking his face. 'Please. Whatever you need.'

'I'll tell you what I need right now,' says Lara thoughtfully, selecting another pastry. 'I've had this tune going round and round in my head all morning, and it's literally driving me crazy. *Dada dada dada dada da dadadada . . .*'

'*Posledniy raz*,' whispers Rinat, agonisedly contracting into a foetal position.

'Oh my God, that's right. How totally embarrassing. My mum used to sing along to that song. I bet yours did too, *detka*.'

'To be honest, she didn't have much to sing about. Unless you count terminal cancer.' The tip of her tongue flicks to the scar on her upper lip. 'But we're wasting Rinat's last precious minutes.' She crouches down so that she's directly in his line of sight. 'What I need from you, *ublyudok*, is answers, and I need them fast. One lie, one fucking hesitation, and you can shit yourself to death.'

'The truth. I swear it.'

'OK then. The man you kidnapped in Odessa. Why did you take him?'

'We were ordered by the SVR, the Russian secret—'

'I know who the fucking SVR are. Why?'

'They called me in to one of their centres. Told me—' He's racked by another spasm, and a bubble of yellowish drool forms on his lips.

'Clock's ticking, Rinat. What did they tell you?'

'To . . . take that man Konstantin. Take him to the villa in Fontanka.'

'So why did you do what they asked?'

'Because they . . . Oh my God, *please* . . .' His hands claw at his arms and chest as the paraesthesia renews its assault.

'Because they?'

'They . . . they knew things. About *Zolotoye Bratstvo*, the Golden Brotherhood. That we'd sent girls from Ukraine to Turkey, Hungary, Czech Republic for sex work. They had interviews, documents, they could have destroyed me. Everything I'd—'

'And the SVR interrogated this man Konstantin at your house in Fontanka?'

'Yes.'

'Did they get the answers they wanted?'

24

'I don't know. They questioned him but they . . . Oh God . . .' He retches, spits bile, and his bladder empties. The smell, and the furious buzzing of the blowflies, intensifies. On the other side of the table Lara helps herself to a third pastry.

'They . . .?'

'They made me keep away. All I heard was one question that they kept shouting at him. "Who are the *Dvenadtsat*, the Twelve?" '

'Did he tell them?'

'I don't know, they . . . They beat him up pretty badly.'

'So he talked, or not?'

'I don't know. They kept asking this same question.'

'So who or what are the Twelve?'

'I don't know. I swear it.'

'*Govno*. Bullshit.'

He retches again, tears streaming down his cheeks. '*Please*,' he whimpers.

'Please what?'

'You said . . .'

'I know what I said, *mudak*. Tell me about the Twelve.'

'All I've heard is rumours.'

'Go on.'

'They're supposed to be some kind of . . . secret organisation. Very powerful, very ruthless. That's all I've heard, I swear.'

'What do they want?'

'How the fuck would I know?'

She nods, her expression thoughtful. 'So how old were those girls? The ones the Golden Brotherhood sent to Europe?'

'Sixteen, minimum. We don't do—'

'You don't do kids? What are you, a feminist?'

Rinat opens his mouth to answer but convulses, his back arching upwards so that, for a moment, he is supported on his hands and feet like a spider. Then a foot is planted on his chest, forcing him agonisingly to the ground, and the woman he knows as Marina Falieri pulls off her raven-black wig and removes her amber contact lenses. 'Burn these,' she tells Lara.

Undisguised, she looks very different. Dark blonde hair, and ice-grey eyes of a fathomless blankness. Not to mention the silenced CZ automatic pistol in her hand. Rinat knows it's the end, and somehow, with this knowledge, the pain recedes a degree or two. 'Who are you?' he whispers. 'Who the *fuck* are you?'

'My name is Villanelle.' She points the CZ at his heart. 'I kill for the Twelve.'

He stares at her, and she fires twice. In the sultry midday air the suppressed detonations sound like the snapping of dead wood.

It doesn't take long to drag Rinat to the prepared grave and bury him. It's a hot and unpleasant task, and Villanelle leaves it to Lara. Meanwhile she loads the table, chairs and remains of lunch into the *motoscafo*. When she returns, it's with a fuel can. She takes off her T-shirt and jeans, soaks them in gasoline, and places them on the fire that Lara has built, on top of the smouldering remains of the wig.

When Lara has finished burying Rinat, Villanelle orders her to take off her shorts and bikini top. The clean-up takes the best part of an hour, but eventually the clothes have all been burned, the ashes picked through, and all surviving buttons, studs and clips thrown in the lagoon.

'There's a bucket in the boat,' Villanelle murmurs, staring out over the water.

'What for?'

'Take a guess?' She indicates the pungent traces of Rinat's bodily fluids.

Finally, she's satisfied, and they go down to the jetty, change into new clothes that Lara has brought, untie the boats from their moorings, and set off on a north-easterly course. The Venice Lagoon is shallow, with an average depth of ten metres, but there are declivities of more than twice this. Not far from the island of Poveglia, the *motoscafo*'s depth-finder indicates that they are passing over just such a drop-off, and Villanelle takes the opportunity to drop the metal table and chairs, the pickaxe and the spade overboard.

In the eighteenth and nineteenth centuries Poveglia was a quarantine station for the crews of ships harbouring the plague. In the early twentieth century it was home to a mental institution where, Venetians say, patients were subjected to sinister experiments. Now abandoned, and reputed to be haunted, the island has a desolate look about it, and tourist craft rarely venture there.

A narrow canal, overhung by foliage, divides Poveglia into two halves. Here, out of sight of any passing vessel, the two women moor the launches. Under Villanelle's critical eye, Lara wipes every surface of the *motoscafo* clean with an anti-DNA Erase spray, and then removes the drain plug, and joins Villanelle in the second launch. It takes twenty minutes for the *motoscafo* to slip quietly beneath the water and come to rest on the floor of the canal.

'She'll be found,' Villanelle says. 'But not immediately. We should go to the hotel. We're supposed to be sisters, right?'

'Yes, I told them I was picking you up from Marco Polo airport.'

'Wouldn't I have luggage?'

'In the locker.'

Villanelle inspects the calfskin Ferragamo bags. 'So who are we?'

'Yulia and Alyona Pinchuk, co-owners of MySugarBaby. com, a dating agency based in Kiev.'

'Nice. Which am I?'

'Yulia.'

Villanelle settles back against the cream leather passenger seat of the launch. 'Let's go. We're done here.'

In the restaurant of the Hotel Excelsior on the Lido, Villanelle and Lara are sipping pink Mercier champagne, and eating iced *frutti di mare* from a tiered silver stand. The room, a pillared Moorish fantasia in shades of white and ivory, is not quite full; it's late in the season and the summer crowd has moved on. There's an animated buzz of conversation, nevertheless, frequently interrupted by laughter. Beyond the terrace, indistinct in the dusk, is the lagoon, its surface a shade darker than the sky. There's not a whisper of a breeze.

'You did well today,' says Villanelle, spearing a langoustine with her fork.

Lara touches the back of her hand to Villanelle's warm shoulder. 'Thank you for mentoring me, *kroshka*. This whole work experience has been incredibly valuable. I've learned so much. Seriously.'

'You're certainly starting to dress more stylishly. Not so *lesbiskoye porno.*'

Lara smiles. In her silk-chiffon dress, with her cropped hair and bared, muscular arms, she looks like some mythical goddess of war.

'Do you think they'll be sending you out on solo actions soon?' Villanelle asks.

'Possibly. The problem is my languages. Apparently I still speak English like a Russian, so they've got me a temporary position as an au pair.'

'In England?'

'Yes. Somewhere called Chipping Norton. Have you been there?'

'No, but I've heard of it. It's one of those dirty-money suburbs like Rublyovka, full of bored housewives snorting cocaine and fucking their tennis coaches. You'll love it. What does the husband do?'

'He's a *politik.* A Member of Parliament.'

'In that case you'll probably have to get him to lick your pussy for *kompromat.*'

'I'd rather lick yours.'

'I know, *detka*, but work is work. How many kids?'

'Twin girls. Fifteen.'

'Well, be careful. Try not to hit them, or not so that it shows. The English are sensitive about that.'

Lara gazes into the oyster shell in her hand, lets a single drop of Tabasco fall into the brine, and watches the oyster's tiny convulsion. 'I wanted to ask you something. About today.'

'Go on.'

'Why did you have to do that whole poison thing? When you had the gun?'

'You think I should have just threatened to shoot him if he didn't talk?'

'Why not? Much easier.'

'Think. Play the scenario out in your mind.'

Lara pours the oyster down her throat and gazes out into the soft dusk. 'Because it's a stalemate game?'

'Exactly. They're tough, these old-school *vory*, even shit-sacks like Yevtukh, and in that world, face is everything. You can threaten to kill a guy like that if he doesn't talk, but if he says go fuck yourself, what then? If you kill him, you don't get his story.'

'How about you shoot him through the hand or the foot, somewhere super-painful but not life-threatening, and tell him you'll do the other one if he doesn't talk?'

'That's smarter, but if you're after the truth, you don't want your subject in shock from a gunshot wound. People say very weird things when they're traumatised. The whole point about the poison-antidote play is that it takes the game to him. He's the one with the hard choice, not you. He may or may not believe you, and by the way there's no known antidote for a lethal dose of aconitine, but he knows that his only chance of survival is to talk. If he stays silent he definitely dies.'

'Checkmate.'

'Exactly. It's all in the timing. You've got to let the poison do its work so that it, and not you, is exerting the pressure. In the end he'll be so desperate you won't be able to shut him up.'

*

Much later, they're lying in bed. A faint night breeze is agitating the curtains.

'Thank you for not killing me today,' Lara murmurs into Villanelle's hair. 'I know you considered it.'

'Why would you say that?'

'Because I'm beginning to understand how you work. How you think.'

'So how do I think?'

'Well, let's say, just for the sake of argument, that you shot Rinat, like you did, and then you shot me, and you put both bodies on the boat and blew it up . . .'

'Go on.'

'When the police investigate the explosion, they'd find the remains of Rinat and a woman. And then when they talked to people at Rinat's hotel they'd find out that he left by boat this morning with a woman.'

'OK.'

'So they'd assume that my remains were that woman's. And that there had been some kind of fatal accident.'

'And why would I go to all this trouble, *detka*?'

'Well, the police wouldn't look for you, because they'd think you were dead. And I really would be dead. The only person who knows who you are. The only person who knows that you used to be Oxana Vorontsova from Perm.'

'I'm not going to kill you, Lara. Truly.'

'But you thought about it.'

'Maybe for a second or two.' She turns to face Lara so that they are eye to eye, mouth to mouth, breathing each other's breath. 'But not seriously. You're soon going to be a fully-fledged soldier for the Twelve. They wouldn't be very pleased if I blew you into little pieces, now would they?'

'Is that the only reason?'

'Mmm . . . I'd miss all this.' She runs her hand down Lara's hard belly, her fingertips stroking the warm skin.

'You're so beautiful,' Lara says, after a moment. 'I look at you, and I can hardly believe you're so perfect. Yet you do such . . .'

'Such?'

'Such terrible things.'

'So will you, trust me.'

'I'm a soldier, *kroshka*. You said so yourself. I'm built to fight. But you could have any life you want. You could walk away.'

'There's no walking away. And I wouldn't if I could. I like my life.'

'Then you'll die. Sooner or later the Englishwoman will find you.'

'Eve Polastri? I want her to find me. I want to have some fun with her. I want to roll her under my paw like a cat with a mouse. I want to prick her with my claws.'

'You're mad.'

'I'm not mad. I like to play the game. And to win. Polastri's a player too, that's why I like her.'

'Is that the only reason?'

'I don't know. Maybe not.'

'Should I be jealous?'

'You can if you want. Doesn't make any difference to me.'

Lara is silent for a moment. 'You never have any doubts? About any of this?'

'Should I have?'

'That moment before you pull the trigger. When the target's already dead, but doesn't know it. And then when

32

you close your eyes at night, there they all are. All the dead people, waiting for you . . .'

Villanelle smiles, kisses Lara's mouth, and slips her hand between her legs. 'They're gone, *detka*. All of them.' Her fingers begin a delicate dance. 'The only person who's waiting for you is me.'

'You never see them?' Lara whispers.

'Never,' says Villanelle, sliding her fingers inside her.

'So do you ever feel . . . anything about them?' Lara asks, moving against Villanelle's hand.

'Sweetie, please. Shut the fuck up.'

They're almost asleep when, half an hour later, a phone stars to vibrate on the bedside table.

'What is it?' asks Lara dreamily, as Villanelle reaches across her.

'Work.'

'You're fucking kidding me.'

Villanelle plants a kiss on the tip of her nose. 'No rest for the wicked, *detka*. You should know that by now.'

2

If Dennis Cradle is surprised to see Eve when she collects him from his house, he conceals it well. The car is an eight-year-old VW Golf from the MI6 vehicle pool, smelling of stale air-freshener, and Cradle takes his place in the passenger seat without a word. As they drive away Eve switches on the Radio 4 *Today* programme, and they both pretend to listen to it.

Cradle remains silent for the duration of the journey to Dever. Initially, Eve reads this as a desperate attempt to assert some sort of authority, given that when she worked at MI5 he was considerably her senior. And then a darker interpretation of his manner strikes her. He's not saying anything because he knows exactly what she's doing here, and so does the organisation he works for. In which case, how much else do they know about her? And for that matter, about Niko? At the thought that her husband might be the object of hostile surveillance, and possibly worse, Eve feels a twisting, agonising guilt. There is no way of avoiding the fact that she's brought this situation on herself. Richard would have understood if she had decided to step down after Simon Mortimer was murdered in Shanghai; indeed, he encouraged her to do so. But she can't, and won't, let go.

In part, it's a desire for answers. Who is the unnamed woman who has carved such a bloody trail through the shadowlands of the intelligence world? Who are her employers, what do they want, and how have they achieved such terrifying power and reach? The mystery, and the woman at the heart of the mystery, speak to a part of Eve that she's never really explored. Could she herself ever be transformed into someone who acts as her target does? Who kills without hesitation or pity? And if so, what would it take?

The traffic is heavy leaving London, but Eve is able to make up time on the motorway, and it's just after quarter to nine when she takes the slip road signposted 'Works Access Only'. The road leads through sparse woodland to a steel gateway set into a high chain-link fence topped with razor-wire. In front of the gate is a guardhouse, where an armed military police corporal checks Eve's security pass before nodding her through the gate towards the cluster of low, weather-stained brick buildings that comprise the former government research station. As Eve drives into the car park, she sees half a dozen tracksuited figures running laps of the fenced perimeter. Others, carrying automatic weapons, saunter between the dilapidated buildings.

At the reception block, Eve and Cradle are met by a trooper from E Squadron, the Special Forces unit based at the camp. Casting an eye at Eve's pass, he beckons them to follow him. The interview room is at the end of a strip-lit underground corridor. It's minimally furnished and there are no CCTV cameras in evidence. A trestle table holds an electric kettle, a half-full bottle of mineral water, two stained mugs, a packet of biscuits and a box holding tea bags and sachets of sugar and powdered milk. The room is colder than Eve would have liked, and the air-conditioning gives off a faint, shuddering whirr.

'Shall I be mother?' asks Cradle drily, approaching the trestle table.

'Whatever,' says Eve, seating herself in a dusty plastic chair. 'I haven't got time to waste here, and neither have you.'

'Are we observed? Overheard? Recorded?'

'I'm assured not.'

'I suppose that will have to do . . . Christ, these biscuits must be six months old.'

'Ground rules,' says Eve. 'You lie, prevaricate or bugger me around, the deal's off.'

'Fair enough.' He pours the mineral water into the kettle. 'Milk, one sugar?'

'Do you understand what I just told you?'

'Mrs Polastri. Eve. I've been conducting tactical questioning sessions for over a decade. I know the rules.'

'Good. Let's start at the beginning, then. How were you approached?'

Cradle yawns, unhurriedly covering his mouth. 'We were on holiday, about three years ago. A tennis camp, near Málaga. There was another couple there from Holland, and Penny and I started playing regularly with them. They told us that their names were Rem and Gaite Bakker, and that they came from Delft, where he was an IT consultant and she was a radiographer. In retrospect I doubt that any of that was the case, but I had no reason not to believe it at the time, and we became quasi-friends, in the way that you do on holiday. Going out for meals together, and so on.

Anyway, one evening Penny and Gaite went with some of the other wives on a girls' night out – flamenco, sangria, all that – and Rem and I went to a bar in the town. We talked about sport for a bit, he was a big Federer fan, and then we got onto politics.'

'So what did you tell this man Rem that you did for a living?'

'I gave him the standard, non-specific Home Office line. And inevitably, for a time, we got stuck into the immigration question. He didn't push the politics, though. I think we ended the evening talking about wine, which he knew a lot about, and as far as I was concerned it was just one of those pleasant, setting-the-world-to-rights-type evenings that happen on holiday.'

'And then?'

'And then, a month after we went back home, Rem emailed me. He was over in London for a couple of days, and he wanted me to meet a friend of his. The idea was that the three of us would go to a wine club in Pall Mall, where the friend was a member, and try out a couple of rare vintages. He mentioned, I recall, Richebourg and Echezeaux, which were quite some distance out of my orbit on a Thames House salary, even as a deputy head of section. Did you say you wanted milk and sugar?'

'Black's fine. So how did you feel about him getting back in contact like this?'

'I remember thinking, in an English kind of way, that it was slightly overstepping the mark. That going out for a drink on holiday was one thing, but pursuing the acquaintanceship afterwards quite another, even though we'd gone through the motions of swapping email addresses. At the same time I have to admit that the thought of drinking truly great Burgundy just once in my life was too good a chance to pass up, so I said I'd go.'

'In other words, they played you perfectly.'

'Pretty much,' says Cradle, handing her one of the mugs. 'And when I got there, I can tell you, I was glad I went.'

'So who was the friend?'

'A Russian, Sergei. A young guy, about thirty, incredibly polished. Brioni suit, flawless English, perfectly accented French to the sommelier, charming as the day is long. And on the table, unbelievably, three glasses and a bottle of DRC.'

'And what's that, when it's at home?'

'Domaine de la Romanée-Conti. The finest, rarest and without question the most expensive red Burgundy in the world. This was a 1988, with a list price of around twelve K. I practically fainted.'

'That was your price? The chance to drink some expensive wine?'

'Don't be judgemental, Eve, it doesn't suit you. And no, that wasn't my price. That was just the handshake. And good though the wine was, and when I say good I mean sublime, I didn't feel myself compromised in the slightest, and in the normal course of events I would've happily thanked Rem and Sergei, shaken hands and never seen either of them again.'

'So what was abnormal about that evening?'

'The conversation. Sergei, if that was really his name, had a grasp of global strategy that you rarely encounter outside the better think-tanks and the higher echelons of government. When someone like that dissects and lays out the issues, you listen.'

'It sounds as if he knew exactly who you were.'

'After listening to him for a few minutes I had no doubt of that. Or that he and Rem were important players in the intelligence world. The whole thing was very fluent, and I was curious to see what the offer would be.'

'You knew there'd be an offer?'

'Of some kind. But they didn't lead with the money, and . . . well, you can choose to believe this or not, but it wasn't about that. The money, I mean. It was about the idea.'

'The idea,' says Eve flatly. 'You're telling me that this was nothing to do with apartments in the south of France, or twenty-something Serbian gym instructors sunning themselves on yachts, or anything like that. You're saying that this was about conviction.'

'Like I said, you can choose to believe me or not.'

'So who's Tony Kent?'

'No idea.'

'He was the fixer behind the scenes. He paid you, basically, though he tried very hard to cover his tracks.'

'Whatever you say.'

'Are you sure? Tony Kent. Think.'

'I'm completely sure. I was told nothing I didn't need to know. No one was giving out names, I promise you.'

'And you're telling me that you believed in this cause of theirs? Seriously?'

'Eve, listen. Please. You know, and I know, that the world's going to hell. Europe's imploding, the United States is led by an imbecile, and the Islamic south is moving north, dressed in a suicide vest. The centre cannot hold. As things stand, we're fucked.'

'That's how it looks to you, is it?'

'That's how it is, period. Now you might say that the West's loss is the East's gain, and that while we tear ourselves apart they make hay. But long-term, that's not how it works. Sooner or later, our problems become their problems. The only way that we retain any kind of stability, the only way that we all *survive*, is if the major powers co-operate. I don't just mean through trade agreements or political alliances, I mean actively working as one to impose and protect our values.'

'These values being, specifically?'

He leans forward on his chair. His eyes meet and hold hers. 'Look, Eve. We're alone here. No one's watching, no one's listening, no one knows or gives a shit what we're talking about. So I'm asking you to see sense. You can be on the side of the future, or you can lock yourself into the burned-out wreck of the past.'

'You were going to tell me about those values.'

'I'll tell you what's been proven not to work. Multiculturalism, and lowest-common-denominator democracy. That's had its day. It's over.'

'And in its place?'

'A new world order.'

'Engineered by traitors and assassins?'

'I don't consider myself a traitor. And as for assassins, what do you think E Squadron's for? Every system needs its armed wing, and yes, we have ours.'

'So why did you kill Viktor Kedrin? I'd have thought his political philosophy was right up your street.'

'It was. But Viktor was also a drunk with a taste for very young girls. Which would have got out, sooner or later, and tainted the message. This way he's a martyr, tragically slain for his beliefs. I don't know if you've been to Russia lately, but Viktor Kedrin is everywhere. Posters, newspapers, blogs . . . Dead, he's far more popular than he ever was when he was alive.'

'Tell me the name of the woman.'

'Which woman?'

'The assassin who killed Kedrin on my watch, and killed Simon Mortimer, and God knows how many others besides.'

'I have no idea. You'll have to speak to someone from Housekeeping.'

A second later, without conscious thought, Eve has unholstered her automatic pistol and is pointing it at Cradle's face. 'I said don't fuck with me. What's her name?'

'And I told you I don't know.' He regards her steadily. 'I also suggest you put that thing away before you cause an accident. I'm worth a great deal more to you alive than dead. Imagine the explaining you'd have to do.'

She lowers her arm, furious at herself. 'And you'd do well to remember the conditions under which you're sitting here talking to me, rather than under arrest for treason. You're going to tell me the names of all your contacts, and how and when you communicated with them. You're going to tell me what services you performed for them, and what information you passed them. You're going to describe who paid you, and how. And you're going to give me the names of every single member of the Security Services, and indeed anyone else, who has betrayed his or her country to this organisation.'

'The Twelve.'

'What?'

'That's what it's called. The Twelve. *Le Douze. Dvenadtsat.*'

There's a peremptory knock at the door and the trooper who brought them to the interview room leans in. 'Boss has a message for you, ma'am. Can you come up?'

'Wait here,' she tells Cradle, and follows the trooper up to ground level, where a compact, moustached officer is waiting for her.

'Your husband called,' he tells her. 'Says you need to get back home, there's been a break-in.'

Eve stares at him. 'Did he say anything else? Is he OK?'

'I'm afraid I don't have that information. Sorry.'

She nods, and fumbles for her phone. The call goes straight to Niko's message service, but moments later he calls her back. 'I'm at the flat. The police are here.'

'So what happened?'

'All pretty strange. Mrs Khan, over the road, saw a woman climbing out of our front room window – completely brazen, apparently, not trying to hide what she was doing at all – and dialled 999. First I knew of it was when a couple of uniformed cops came to the school and picked me up. Nothing's missing, as far as I can tell, but . . .'

'But what?'

'Just get back here, OK?'

'I'm assuming the woman got away?'

'Yes.'

'Any description?'

'Young, slim . . .'

Eve knows. She just knows. Minutes later, she's driving southwards on the A303, with Cradle in the passenger seat. She dislikes the physical closeness, and the faint but cloying smell of his aftershave, but she definitely doesn't want him lurking behind her.

'I'm empowered to make you an offer,' he says, as they pass Micheldever service station.

'You make me an offer? Are you fucking kidding me?'

'Look, Eve. I'm not sure what your present status is, or exactly which department you now work for, but I do know that it wasn't very long ago that you were in a junior liaison post at Thames House, earning chicken-feed. Public service its own reward, and all that bollocks. And I'm betting things haven't greatly changed. Financially, at least.'

'Shit!' Eve brakes hard to avoid a Porsche that has swerved into the slow lane to overtake her on the inside. 'Nice driving, arsehole!'

'Imagine, though. Suppose you had a few million banked, so that when the time was right, you and your husband could give up work and slip away to the sunshine. Spend the rest of your life travelling first class. No more cramped flats or crowded tubes. No more endless winters.'

'Worked brilliantly for you, didn't it?'

'It will do, in the end. Because I know that you're smart enough to realise that you need me. That the ship of state isn't sinking, it's sunk.'

'You seriously believe that?'

'Eve, what I'm suggesting isn't treasonable, it's common sense. If you really want to serve your country, join us and help create a new world. We're everywhere. We're legion. And we will reward you . . .'

'Oh God, I don't believe this.' A police motorcycle, blue lights flashing, is growing larger and larger in her rear-view mirror. Eve slows down, hoping that the motorcycle will race past, but it swings in front of her, and the uniformed officer indicates with a waving arm that she pull in on the hard shoulder.

As Eve does so the officer halts in front of her, pulls the powerful BMW bike onto its stand, saunters over, and peers through the driver-side window.

Eve lowers the window. 'Is there some problem?'

'Can I see your licence please?' A woman's voice. The visor of her white helmet reflecting the sunlight.

Eve hands her the licence, along with her Security Services pass.

'Out of the car, please. Both of you.'

'Seriously? I'm travelling to London because there's been a break-in at my house. You're welcome to check with the Met. And I strongly suggest you take another look at that pass.'

'Right away, please.'

'Oh, for heaven's sake.' Slowly, not attempting to disguise her frustration, Eve climbs out of the car. Traffic races past, terrifyingly close.

'Hands on the bonnet. Legs apart.'

That not-quite-identifiable accent, unusual in a police officer. Doubt is beginning to enter Eve's mind now. Expert hands pat her down, take her phone, and unholster the Glock. She hears the faint click of the magazine release, and then feels the pistol replaced. This, Eve knows with sick certainty, is no police officer.

'Turn round.'

Eve does so. Notes the lean female form in the high-visibility jacket, leather trousers and boots. Watches as the woman's hands lift her visor to reveal a flat, ice-grey gaze. A gaze that she has encountered once before. On a busy street in Shanghai, the night that Simon Mortimer was found with his head all but hacked from his body.

'You,' Eve says. She can hardly breathe. Her heart is slamming in her chest.

'Me.' She removes her helmet. Underneath it she's wearing a Lycra face-mask that conceals all her features except those frozen grey eyes. Lowering the helmet to the ground she beckons to Cradle, who walks over. 'Let the VW's tyres down, Dennis, and put the car key in your pocket. Then wait over by the motorcycle.'

Cradle looks at Eve, smiles, and shrugs. 'Sorry,' he says. 'I'm afraid you lose this round. We look after our own, you see.'

'I see,' says Eve, trying to steady herself.

The woman takes her by the upper arm, leads her away a few paces, and examines her features as if trying to commit them to memory. 'I've missed you, Eve. Missed your face.'

'I wish I could say the same.'

'Don't be like that, Eve. Don't be bitter.'

'Are you going to kill Cradle?'

'Why? Do you think I should?'

'It is what you do, isn't it?'

'Please. Let's not talk about that. We meet so rarely.' She raises her hand and touches a finger to Eve's face, and as she does so Eve is dumbfounded to see that she is wearing the bracelet that she lost in Shanghai.

'That's . . . that's *mine*. Where did you get it?'

'From your room at the Sea Bird Hotel. I climbed in one night to watch you sleep, and I just couldn't resist it.'

Eve stares at her, blank-faced. 'You . . . watched me sleep?'

'You looked so adorable, with your hair all over the pillow. So vulnerable.' She loops an errant tress behind Eve's ear. 'You should take more care of yourself, though. You remind me of someone I used to know. The same pretty eyes, the same sad smile.'

'What was her name? What's *your* name?'

'Oh, Eve. I have so many names.'

'You know my name but you're not going to tell me yours?'

'It would spoil things.'

'Spoil things? You broke into my fucking house this morning, and you're worried that you'll spoil things?'

'I wanted to leave you something. A surprise.' She shakes the bracelet on her wrist. 'In return for this. But now, although I'm really loving our chat, I have to go.'

'You're taking him?' Eve nods at Cradle, who is loitering by the motorcycle, twenty paces away.

'I have to. But we must do this again, there's so much I want to ask you. So much I have to tell you. So *à bientôt*, Eve. See you soon.'

As they fly along the country roads, the trees and hedgerows still vivid in the early autumn sunlight, Cradle feels a profound lightening of spirit. They've come for him, as they always promised they would if he was blown, and now they're going to take him somewhere safe. Somewhere the Twelve's word is the rule of law. It will mean never seeing his family again, but sometimes you have to make sacrifices. In the case of Penny, that sacrifice is not so arduous. And the kids, well, he's given them a first-class start in life. Fee-paying north London schools, skiing holidays in the Trois Vallées, godparents well-placed in the City.

He wasn't expecting a woman to come for him, but he certainly isn't complaining, given what he's seen of this one. She certainly put that Polastri bitch in her place. And what genius to send her in the guise of a traffic-cop.

They ride for almost an hour, before stopping by a bridge over a river outside the Surrey town of Weybridge. The woman pulls the BMW onto its stand, then removes her helmet and jacket, tugs off her face-mask, and shakes out her hair. Taking off his own, borrowed, helmet, Cradle stares at her appreciatively.

He considers himself something of a connoisseur of the female form, and this one scores highly. The dark blonde hair sweaty, but nothing he can't work with. The eyes a bit frozen and weird, but that mouth suggesting whole realms of sexual possibility. The tits? Sweet as apples beneath the tight T-shirt. And what man didn't feel a stirring in his Calvins at the sight of a girl in leather trousers and biker boots? Dressed like that, she has to be up for it. And he is, effectively, a single man again.

'Let's walk,' she says, glancing at the BMW's satnav. 'The rendezvous for the next stage of your journey is up this way.'

A path leads from the road down to the side of the River Wey. The water is dark olive, the current so slow that the surface looks still. The banks are shadowed by trees, and overgrown with cow-parsley. At intervals, narrowboats and barges lie motionless at anchor.

'So where am I going?'

'I can't tell you that.'

'Perhaps, if we meet again . . .' he begins.

'Yes?'

'Bite of dinner? Something like that?'

'Perhaps.'

They continue along the sun-splashed path, passing no one, until arriving at a broad weir-pool fringed with bull-rushes and flag-iris.

'This is the rendezvous,' she says.

Cradle looks around him. The river, its waters moving smoothly towards the rushing weir, has the keen, indefinable smell of such places. Mud, vegetation and rot. There's a timelessness about the scene that reminds him of his childhood. Of *The Wind in the Willows*, of Ratty, Mole and Toad. And that chapter he never quite understood: 'The Piper at the Gates of Dawn'. Cradle is pondering this enigma when a police-issue baton, swung with extreme force, connects with the base of his skull. He pitches almost noiselessly into the river. His half-submerged body hangs there for a moment, and then, as Villanelle watches, begins its inexorable drift towards the crest of the weir, where it is immediately drawn deep underwater. She stands there, imagining his body turning and turning in the vortex, far beneath the glassy surface. And then she holsters the baton, and unhurriedly makes her way back along the path.

By the time Lance drops her off at her house, Eve is exhausted. She's also furious, apprehensive, and faintly nauseous from the nicotine smell of Lance's car. There's a horrendous conversation with Richard still to be had – he's coming by the office at 6 p.m. – but the most shaming admission that Eve has had to make is to herself. How easily, how effortlessly and contemptuously, she has been played. How naive she has been. How utterly unprofessional.

She should have known, from Cradle's bullish manner, that he had sounded some sort of alarm, and expected to be exfiltrated. Rather than congratulating herself on having uncovered his treachery, she should have been expecting precisely the sort of audacious manoeuvre that had been mounted against her. How could she have been so ill-prepared? And then there's that surreal encounter on the A303, which has left her shot through with emotions she can't begin to define.

So she's in no mood for Niko's hostility when he lets her into the flat. 'I rang you four and a half hours ago,' he tells her, pale-faced with suppressed tension. 'You said you'd be here by midday, and it's nearly three.'

She forces herself to breathe. 'Look, I'm sorry, Niko, but explanations are going to have to wait. If you've had a bad day, trust me, I've had a worse one. Since we spoke I've had my car keys and my phone stolen, and I've spent an hour beside a busy main road, trying to wave down a car so that I could get help. And that's just the start of it. So just tell me, without getting angry, what's going on.'

Niko compresses his lips, and nods. 'As I told you on the phone, Mrs Khan reported seeing a young woman climbing out of our window at about ten thirty this morning, and rang the police. Two police officers called round at the school, picked me up, and drove me here. They were obviously taking the whole thing quite seriously, because there was a forensics person waiting outside when we got back. Perhaps they've got our address on file because of your old job at MI5, who knows? Anyway, they went through the flat with me, room by room, and the forensics woman did her stuff on the door handles and the front room window and various other surfaces, looking for fingerprints, but she found nothing. She told me the intruder must have been wearing gloves. She'd undone the window lock, but nothing else had been disturbed, as far as I could see, and nothing taken.'

'Thelma and Louise?'

'Fine, just chilling outside. They made a big impression on the cops, as you can imagine.'

'They left, these cops?'

'Ages ago.'

'So how do they think the intruder got in?'

'Through the front door. They had a close look at the lock and they reckon she picked it. Which makes her a professional, not some teenager looking for phones and laptops.'

'Right.'

'So . . . do you have any idea who she might be?'

'I don't know any professional burglars, no.'

'Please, Eve, you know what I mean. Is this something to do with your work? Was this woman looking for something specific? Something . . .' His voice trails off, and then, as she watches, a darker suspicion takes hold. 'Was this . . . *that woman*? The one you were after? Probably still are after? Because, if so . . .'

She meets his stare calmly.

'Tell me the truth, Eve. Seriously, I need to know. I need you, just this once, not to lie.'

'Niko, truthfully, I have absolutely no idea who this was. Nor is there any reason whatsoever to connect this with my work, or the investigation you were talking about. Do you know how many break-ins were reported in London last year? Almost sixty thousand. *Sixty thousand.* That means that statistically—'

'Statistically.' He closes his eyes. 'Tell me about statistics, Eve.'

'Niko, please. I'm sorry you think I lie to you, I'm sorry some burglar broke into our house, I'm sorry we don't have anything worth stealing. But this is just some random fucking London event, OK? There *is* no explanation. It just . . . happened.'

He stares at the wall. 'Maybe the police will—'

'No, the police won't. Especially if she didn't take anything. They'll log it, and it'll go in the files. Now let me have a look round the place, and make sure nothing's missing.'

He stands there, breathing audibly. Finally, slowly, he bows his head. 'I'll make some tea.'

'Oh, yes please. And if there's any of that cake left, I'm starving.' Stepping behind him, she puts her arms around his waist and lays her head against his back. 'I'm sorry, I've really had the most horrendous day. And this just makes it worse. So thank you for coping with the police and everything, I honestly don't think I could have managed.'

Opening the back door, she smiles as Thelma and Louise come bounding towards her and nose inquisitively at her hands. They really are very hard to resist. On the far side of the wall bordering the tiny patio there's a drop of some twenty metres to the overground railway track. Its proximity to the line, the letting agent explained to them when they moved in, was the reason that the flat was cheaper than others in the

51

area. Eve no longer hears the trains; their rattle and thrum has long been subsumed into the ambient noise that is London. Sometimes she sits out here and watches them, soothed by the ceaselessness of their coming and going.

'When did we last spend a weekday afternoon together?' Niko asks, handing her a cup of tea with a slice of cake balanced on the saucer. 'It seems like for ever.'

'You're right, it does,' she says, staring out towards the dim, urban horizon. 'Can I ask you something?'

'Go on.'

'About Russia.' She takes a bite of cake.

'What about it?'

'Have you ever heard of anything or anyone called the Twelve?'

'The poem, you mean?'

'What poem?'

'*Dvenadtsat. The Twelve*, by Aleksandr Blok. He was an early twentieth-century writer who believed in the sacred destiny of Russia. Pretty crackpot stuff. I read him at university, during my revolutionary poetry phase.'

Eve feels a coldness at the back of her neck. 'What's it about?'

'Twelve Bolsheviks pursuing some mystical quest through the streets of Petrograd. At midnight, as far as I remember, and in a snowstorm. Why?'

'Someone at work today referred to an organisation called the Twelve. Some political group. Either Russian, or Russian-connected. I'd never heard of it.'

Niko shrugs. 'Most educated Russians would know the poem. There's nostalgia for the Soviet era right across the political spectrum.'

'What do you mean?'

'That a group calling itself after Blok's midnight ramblers could be of almost any complexion from neo-communist to outright fascist. The name doesn't tell you much.'

'So do you know where I could . . . Niko?'

But Thelma and Louise are butting at his knees and bleating for his attention.

Tea in hand, Eve goes through the flat. It's a small place, and although it's crammed with stuff, mostly Niko's, it doesn't look like anything has been moved or stolen. She visits the bedroom last, checking under pillows and in drawers, and paying particular attention to her modest stock of jewellery. She's furious at the theft of her bracelet, and still can't begin to process the knowledge that a professional killer broke into her Shanghai hotel room while she slept. Imagining that woman staring at her with those flat, affectless eyes, and perhaps even touching her, makes her feel faint.

'*You looked so adorable, with your hair all over the pillow . . .*'

Eve opens the wardrobe and flips through her dresses, tops and skirts, sliding the hangers along one by one. And comes to a disbelieving halt. On a shelf with her belts, gloves and a straw hat from the previous summer is a small package wrapped in tissue paper, which she has definitely never seen before. After pulling on one of the pairs of gloves, she carefully lifts the package, weighs it in one hand, and unwraps it. A dove-grey box bearing the words Van Diest. Inside, on a pillow of grey velvet, an exquisite rose gold bracelet, set with twin diamonds at the clasp.

For several heartbeats, Eve stares. Then, twitching off her left glove, she slips her wrist into the bracelet and snaps the clasp into place. The fit is perfect, and for a moment, languidly extending her arm, she thrills to the look and the delicate weight of it. In the folds of tissue paper, its corner just visible, is a card. The note is handwritten.

Take care, Eve – V

Eve stands there, the bracelet on her wrist, the card in her gloved hand, for a full minute. How should she interpret those words? As flirtatious concern, or outright threat? On impulse, she lowers her face to the card, and detects expensive, feminine scent. Her hand shaking, she replaces the card in the box, possessed by emotions she can't immediately identify. Fear, certainly, but an almost stifling excitement, too. The woman who chose that beautiful, feminine object and wrote that message is a murderer. A stone-cold professional assassin whose every word is a lie, and whose every action is calculated to unsettle and manipulate. To meet her gaze, as Eve did just hours ago, is to look into a heart-freezing void. No fear, no pity, no human warmth, only their absence.

Just metres away on the patio, talking enraptured nonsense to the goats – the *goats* – is the best and kindest man that Eve has ever known. The man into whose warm body, familiar but still mysterious, she moulds herself at night. The man whose unaccountable love for her has no horizon. The man to whom she now lies with such fluency that it's almost second nature.

Why is she so stirred by this lethally dangerous woman? Why do her words cut so deep? That cryptic V is no accident.

It's a name, if only a partial one. A gift, like the bracelet. A gesture at once intimate and sensual and profoundly hostile. Ask and I will answer. Call and I will come for you.

How have the two of them locked themselves so inescapably into each other's lives? Could it be that, in some bizarre way, V is reaching out to her? Raising her arm, Eve touches the smooth gold to her cheek. What can this lovely, luxurious object have cost? Five thousand pounds? Six? God, she wanted it. Couldn't she perhaps just not say anything? Now that she's committed herself to a completely unprofessional course of action by unwrapping the thing in the first place, and quite possibly compromising forensic evidence, wouldn't it be easier to just . . . keep it?

With a flush of shame and regret, she removes the bracelet and places it back in its box. Fuck's *sake*. She's reacting precisely as her adversary wants her to. Falling for the most blindingly obvious temptation, and personalising the situation in a completely irrational fashion. How egotistical and delusional, to think that she, Eve, is the object of this V person's affection or desire. The woman is without doubt a narcissistic sociopath, and attempting to undermine Eve through passive-aggressive taunting. To think otherwise, even for an instant, flies in the face of everything Eve has ever learned as a criminologist and an intelligence officer. She takes a carrier bag from the floor of the wardrobe and stuffs the box, card and tissue inside with a gloved hand.

'Anything?' Niko calls out from the kitchen.

'No,' she says. 'Nothing.'

On the Eurostar, no one takes much notice of the young woman in the black hoodie. Her hair is greasy, her pallor unhealthy, and there's something indefinably dirty about her. She's wearing scuffed black motorcycle boots, and her insolent posture suggests that she might use them on anyone rash enough to approach her. To the middle-aged couple sitting opposite her, working their way through the *Daily Telegraph* cryptic crossword, she's exactly the type of person that makes train travel so unpleasant. Unwashed. No consideration whatever for those around her. Forever on her phone.

'Give us another clue,' the husband murmurs.

'Thirteen across: "Eliminate a flock of crows",' says his wife, and they both frown.

Villanelle, meanwhile, having disabled the location tracker on Eve's phone and read all her disappointingly boring texts and emails, is thumbing through her photographs. Here's Niko, the *Polskiy* asshole, in the kitchen. Here's an Eve selfie at the optician's, trying on new glasses (please, angel, not those frames). Here's another of Niko with the goats (and what the fuck is with those animals, anyway? Do they mean to eat them?). And then there's a whole series of celebrity portraits, which Villanelle guesses Eve has snapped from magazines so that she can show her hairdresser. Who's this one? Asma al-Assad? Seriously, sweetie, that look is *so* not you.

Looking up, Villanelle sees from the high-rise blocks and graffiti-tagged walls that the train is entering the outer Parisian suburbs. Pocketing Eve's phone and taking out her own, she rings her friend Anne-Laure.

'Where have you been?' Anne-Laure asks her. 'I haven't seen you in an age.'

'Working. Travelling. Nothing interesting.'

'So what are you doing this evening?'

'You tell me.'

'The prêt-à-porter shows start tomorrow, and tonight some of the younger designers are having a party on my friend Margaux's boat at the Quai Voltaire. It'll be fun, everyone will be there. We could dress up and have dinner at Le Grand Véfour, just the two of us, and go on to the party afterwards.'

'That sounds nice. Margaux's cute.'

'Are you up for it?'

'Definitely.'

The train is pulling into the Gare du Nord. Emboldened by their incipient arrival, the middle-aged couple look at Villanelle with frank dislike.

'That crossword clue,' she says to them. ' "Eliminate a flock of crows". Did you work out the answer?'

'Er, no,' the husband says. 'We didn't, actually.'

'It's "murder".' She flutters her fingers. 'Enjoy Paris.'

'Run me through that again,' says Richard Edwards. An intelligence officer of the old school, he is a vaguely patrician figure with thinning hair and a velvet-collared overcoat that has seen better days. 'You say you were stopped by a person you thought was a police officer on a motorcycle.'

He, Eve, Billy and Lance are sitting in the Goodge Street office. A strip light casts a sickly glow. At intervals, there's a muted rumbling from the Underground station beneath them.

'That's right,' says Eve. 'On the A303 near Micheldever. And I'm pretty sure it was a real police uniform and bike.

The shoulder number and the plates both check out. They belong to a Road Policing Unit of the Hampshire Constabulary.'

'Not easy to nick, I wouldn't have thought,' says Billy, leaning back in the computer chair that almost seems part of him, and absently fingering his lip-piercing.

'Unless you've got someone inside that particular force.'

'Lance is right,' says Richard. 'If they've penetrated MI5, then they're certainly going to have people in the police.'

They look at each other. Eve's earlier exhilaration is now just a memory. What possessed me? she wonders. This whole situation is a catastrophe.

'OK, so this woman searches you, takes your phone and the ammunition clip from your Glock, and gets Dennis Cradle to pocket your car keys and deflate your tyres. You and she then have the conversation that you've described to me, in the course of which you notice that she's wearing a bracelet that belonged to you.'

'The bracelet was my mother's, and this woman told me she stole it from my hotel room in Shanghai.'

'And you never mentioned to her that you'd been to China.'

'Obviously not.'

Richard nods. 'So then she gives Cradle her spare crash-helmet, and drives him away on the motorcycle.'

'That's about the long and the short of it, yes.'

'You then manage to wave down a car, borrow a phone, and ring Lance, who collects you in his car and drives you home. You get there at about 3 p.m., at which point you learn of the break-in at your house which took place at around 10.30 a.m.'

'No. I already knew about that. My husband rang to tell me. That's why I was driving home early from Dever with Dennis Cradle.'

'Of course, yes. But there was no sign of anything having been disturbed, or taken from your home?'

'No, nothing disturbed or taken. But this Van Diest bracelet, and the note, had been placed in my wardrobe.'

'I suppose there's no way of knowing where the bracelet was bought?'

'I've checked with the company,' Eve says. 'There are sixty-eight Van Diest boutiques and concessions world-wide. It could have come from any one of them. It could have been bought over the phone or online. I suppose it's a line of enquiry, but—'

'And there's absolutely no doubt in your mind that the woman who broke into your house, and the woman who stopped you on the A303 and abducted Cradle, were the same person?'

'None. The whole thing with the bracelets is very much her style. She'd have calculated that if she was seen climbing out of my flat, and the police were rung, there was a good chance that a message would get to me within an hour or so. She'd guess that I'd drive Cradle straight back to London, and that would give her enough time to get up to the A303 to intercept us. It'd be tight, but it could be done, especially on a police motorcycle.'

'OK, let's assume that you're right, and that this woman who signs herself V is the one we've been dealing with all along. The one who killed Kedrin, Simon Mortimer and the rest of them. Let's further assume that she works for the organisation that Cradle talked about, the one he said was called the Twelve. We still haven't answered either of the two key questions. One, how did she know that we were onto Cradle? And two, what has she done with him?'

'In answer to the first question, I got the strong impression that Cradle had contacted the Twelve himself. He probably had some kind of emergency number, and believed that if he was compromised he'd be pulled out, like an agent in the field. In answer to the second question, she's killed him. I've no doubt about that whatsoever. It's what she does.'

'Which means—' Richard begins.

'Yes. We've got a senior MI5 officer dead, a serious amount of explaining to do, and no lead of any kind. We're back where we were post-Kedrin, and it's entirely my fault.'

'I don't accept that.'

'I do. I rode Cradle far too hard in that phone call to the van. I never thought he'd let his people know we were onto him. What did he think they were going to do? Did he really believe he'd live happily ever after?'

'I listened to your conversation with Cradle. We all did. And you handled him fine. The truth is, he was in serious trouble with those people from the moment we identified him, however we played it.'

Without warning, the overhead strip light cuts out, plunging them all into dimness. Lance takes a broom from the stationery cupboard behind the printer, then taps the handle sharply against the fluorescent tube, which flickers for a moment and then comes back on again. No one comments.

'So what about MI5?' Eve asks Richard.

'I'll handle them. Let them know about the south of France property and the boat and the rest of it. Say we're not sure who was paying Cradle off, but that someone was, big-time. Explain that we questioned him, which they'll find out sooner or later, and that he did a runner. That way, the whole thing becomes their problem. And when he turns up, which he will – dead or alive but probably dead, as you say – they'll shut down the story in the usual way.'

'So we carry on?' asks Eve.

'We carry on. I'll get a forensics person I can trust onto that bracelet and the note. Also, I'm going to have people watching your flat round the clock until further notice, unless you and your husband would prefer to move into a safe house.'

'Niko would literally go ballistic. Please not that.'

'OK. For the time being not. What else have we got?'

'I'm still on the Cradle money-trail,' says Billy. 'And that goes to some seriously weird places. I'm also in contact with GCHQ about the Twelve, and hoping that someone, somewhere, has let something slip. If Cradle knew that name, so do others.'

'Lance?'

The rodent features sharpen. 'I might go and sniff around the Hampshire Constabulary HQ in Eastleigh. Buy pints for a few coppers. Ask about borrowed bikes and uniforms.'

'I just want to get something clear,' Eve says, walking to the window and staring out at the traffic on Tottenham Court Road. 'Is the purpose of this unit still to identify a professional assassin? Or are we now trying to acquire intelligence on what appears to be an international conspiracy? Because I'm beginning to sense mission-creep.'

'First and foremost, I want our killer,' says Richard. 'Kedrin was killed on our turf and I need a scalp to give Moscow. Also, this woman killed Simon Mortimer, one of our own, and that I won't have. But it's becoming increasingly clear that if we want her, we're going to have to acquire some understanding of the organisation she works for. And the more we see and hear of them, the more formidable a force they appear. But there's got to be a way in. A tiny corner you can unpick. Like, for example, this woman's interest in you.'

Lance grins horribly, and stares into space.

Eve looks at him wearily. 'Please, whatever's on your mind, don't share it.'

'You must admit, the situation's got honey-trap written all over it.'

'Lance, I'm sure you're a great field agent, but you're a seriously tragic human being.'

'You know what they say, Eve. Old dogs. New tricks.'

'Seriously, people,' says Richard. 'What's she saying with this bracelet? What's the message here?'

'That she's in control. That she can drop into my life any time she chooses. She's saying I've got your measure, and compared to me you're a loser. She's saying I can give you all the things you want – the intimate, feminine, super-expensive things – but can't have. It's a woman-to-woman thing.'

'Manipulative lady,' murmurs Billy knowledgeably, hunching into his Megadeth hoodie.

'That's an understatement,' says Eve. 'But I've been watching her, too. She's been getting more and more reckless, especially in her dealings with me. That motorcycle

62

cop caper, for example. Somewhere along the line she's going to go too far. And then we'll have her.'

Lance nods at the carrier bag holding the bracelet. 'Maybe we don't really need to go out looking for her. Perhaps, if we just sit tight, she'll come to us.'

Richard nods. 'I don't like it, but I'm afraid you're right. That said, I think we need to acknowledge that we've turned a dangerous corner here. So full counter-surveillance measures, please. Remember your tradecraft. Eve and Billy, listen to Lance and be guided by him. If he tells you that a situation smells bad, you walk away.'

Eve glances at Lance. He looks sharp and alert, like a ferret about to be slipped into a rabbit-hole.

'Meanwhile, Eve, I'll have a word with the CO at Dever. Ask him to set up a detail to watch your flat. You probably won't see much of them, but they'll be there if you need them. Can we get a photofit of this V woman?'

'It's difficult. I got a split-second glance at someone I thought was her in Shanghai, and today she had this Lycra mask on under her helmet so that I could only see her eyes. But I could try.'

'Excellent. We're going to watch, and we're going to wait, and when she comes, we're going to be ready.'

3

The man sits, ankles crossed, in a carved oak armchair upholstered in emerald silk. He is wearing a charcoal suit, and his blood-red Charvet tie strikes a dramatic note in the muted surroundings of the hotel suite. Frowning thoughtfully, he removes his tortoiseshell spectacles, polishes them with a silk handkerchief, and replaces them.

Villanelle glances at him, swallows a mouthful of vintage Moët et Chandon, and turns her attention to the woman. Seated beside her husband, she has dark eyes and hair the colour of summer wheat. She is, at a guess, in her late thirties. Villanelle places her champagne flute on a side table, beside an arrangement of white roses, then takes the woman's slender wrists and draws her to her feet. For a few moments they dance together, the only sound the murmur of the evening traffic in the Place de la Concorde.

Softly, Villanelle's lips brush those of the other woman, and her husband shifts appreciatively in his chair. One by one, Villanelle undoes the half-dozen buttons of the woman's pleated shift dress, which falls soundlessly to the floor. The woman's hands move towards Villanelle's face, but Villanelle gently forces them down: she wants total control here.

Soon the woman is naked, and stands there tremulous and expectant. Closing her eyes, Villanelle runs her hand over the woman's hair, inhales her scent, explores the soft curves of her body. As her fingers move downwards she hears herself breathing a long-unspoken name, murmuring half-remembered endearments in Russian. The years and her surroundings fall away, and once again she is in the flat on Komsomolsky Prospekt, and Anna is there, smiling her sad smile.

'Tell her she's a dirty bitch,' says the man. '*Une vraie salope.*'

Villanelle opens her eyes. Catches sight of herself in the overmantel mirror. The slicked-back hair, the raking cheekbones, the permafrost gaze. She frowns. This isn't working for her. The woman whose legs she's parting is a stranger, and her husband's pleasure is repulsive. Abruptly, Villanelle disengages, and wipes her fingers on the roses, scattering the floor with petals. Then she walks out of the suite.

From the taxi, she watches as the illuminated shopfronts of the rue de Rivoli glide past. It's as if she's in a silent film, detached from her surroundings, disconnected from experience and sensation. She's felt like this for a couple of weeks now, since coming back from England, and it worries her, although the worry itself is something vague, something she can't quite bring into focus.

Perhaps it's a delayed reaction to the killing of Konstantin. Villanelle is not given to self-pity, but when you're ordered to kill your handler, who not only discovered and trained you but is also your friend, insofar as such things are possible, it's disconcerting. She's only human, after all.

Now that Konstantin is gone, Villanelle misses him. His judgements could be brutal, he castigated her again and again for her recklessness, but at least he cared enough to make them. And he valued her. He appreciated just how rare a creature she was, with her unblinking savagery and her incapacity for guilt.

As an assassin for the Twelve, Villanelle has always accepted that she will never see the organisation's grand plan, never be told more of the story than she needs to know. But she's also aware, because Konstantin repeatedly told her so, that her role is vital. That she's more than just a trained killer, she's an instrument of destiny.

Anton, Konstantin's replacement, has so far failed to give Villanelle the impression that he thinks of her as more than an employee. He dispatched the kill orders for Yevtukh and Cradle in the usual way, via innocuous-looking stegano-graphically encrypted emails, but he didn't thank her afterwards, as Konstantin always did, which Villanelle considers just plain rude. Not even the fun she's having with Eve makes up for the fact that Anton is shaping up to be a thoroughly unsatisfactory handler.

The taxi draws up to the kerb in the Avenue Victor Hugo. Villanelle's scooter is parked opposite the club where she met the couple. The club's still open, and the lamps flank-ing the entrance still dimly glowing, but she doesn't give the place a second glance. Rocking the scooter off its stand, she kick-starts the engine and glides unhurriedly into the traffic.

Villanelle doesn't go straight back to her apartment, but heads for La Muette. For ten minutes she threads the narrow streets, her gaze flickering between her wing mirror and the vehicles ahead of her, all senses alert. She varies her speed, pretends to stall at a green traffic light, and at one point, deliberately drives in the wrong direction down the tiny, one-way Impasse de Labiche. Finally, satisfied that she is not being followed, she turns westwards to the Porte de Passy, and the building where she lives.

After parking the Vespa in the underground car park beside her silver-grey Audi, she takes the lift to the sixth floor, and climbs a short flight of stairs to the entrance of her rooftop apartment. She's about to disarm the electronic locking system when she hears a faint, distressed mewing from the stairs behind her. It's a kitten, one of several belonging to the building's housekeeper, Marta, who lives on the fifth floor. Carefully scooping up the tiny creature, Villanelle strokes and calms it before ringing Marta's bell.

The housekeeper is effusive in her thanks. She's always liked the quiet young woman from the *sixième étage*. She's clearly extremely busy, judging by how often she's away, but she always finds a smile for Marta. She's a caring person, unlike so many of her generation.

When all the niceties have been observed, and the other kittens and their mother admired and cooed over, Villanelle returns to the sixth floor. Locking the door of the apartment behind her, she is finally enfolded in silence. The apartment, with its walls of faded sea-green and French blue, is spacious and restful. The furniture is mid-twentieth century, worn but stylish, with several pieces by the designer Eileen Gray. There's a scattering of minor post-Impressionist paintings which Villanelle has never examined, but whose presence she tolerates.

No one ever visits her here. Anne-Laure is under the impression that Villanelle lives in Versailles, and works as a currency trader. Her neighbours in the building know her as a courteous but distant figure, often absent. Her service charges and property taxes are paid from a corporate account in Geneva, and in the unlikely event that anyone were to investigate this, they would find themselves drawn into a web of front companies and cut-outs so complex as to be effectively impenetrable. But no one has ever done so.

In the kitchen Villanelle prepares a plate of yellowtail sashimi and buttered toast, then takes a bottle of Grey Goose vodka from the freezer and pours herself a double measure. Seating herself at a table in front of the long, east-facing plate-glass window, she gazes at the glittering city spread out below her, and thinks about the games she'd like to play with Eve. This is precisely the sort of reckless behaviour Konstantin was always warning her about. It leads to mistakes, and mistakes get you killed. But what's the point of a game if the stakes aren't high? Villanelle wants to shatter Eve's protective shell and manipulate the vulnerable being inside. She wants her pursuer to know that she's been out-thought and outplayed, and to witness her capitulation. She wants to own her.

Equally importantly, Villanelle wants a new assignment. Something more demanding than bread-and-butter kills like Yevtukh and Cradle. She wants a well-protected, high-status target. A really challenging set-up. It's time to show Anton just how good she is.

Flipping open the laptop on the kitchen counter, she opens the homepage of an innocuous-looking social media account, and posts an image of a cat wearing sunglasses.

Anton's tradecraft, she's discovered, often takes a surprisingly sentimental turn.

Three days after his abduction on the A303, Dennis Cradle is found dead by National Trust volunteers, who are removing a fallen tree from a weir pool on the River Wey. Brief notices appear in the local papers, and the finding of Weybridge Coroner's Court is death by misadventure. The victim, it is reported, was a Home Office employee who may have been suffering from amnesia. He appeared to have fallen into the river, struck his head on a rock or other hard surface, lost consciousness, and drowned.

'Obviously our killer didn't make it look too much like murder,' says Richard Edwards, when he visits the Goodge Street office on the evening of the inquest. 'But I'm guessing Thames House had to call in a few favours to get that result.'

'I knew she'd kill him,' says Eve.

'It did always look probable,' Richard admits.

'But didn't Cradle tell you he was authorised to try and recruit you?' asks Lance. 'Wouldn't the Twelve have let that play out?'

'Whatever they told him, I doubt they believed he could pull it off,' says Eve. 'The speed with which they deployed V suggests that they decided to kill him the moment he signalled he'd been compromised.'

'Poor bugger,' says Billy, reaching for a half-eaten Cornish pasty.

'Poor bugger nothing,' says Eve. 'I'm sure it was him who blocked me when I requested police protection for Viktor Kedrin. He personally enabled that murder.'

'So let me just run through where we are now,' says Richard, laying his coat over Eve's desk, and pulling up a chair. 'Stop me if I make any unfounded assumptions, or you want to add anything.'

The others make their own seating arrangements beneath the strip light's sepulchral glow. Taking a bite from his pasty, Billy coughs crumbs over his knees.

'Fuck's sakes,' murmurs Lance, wrinkling his nose. 'What's in that thing? Dogshit?'

Leaning forward, Richard steeples his fingers. 'While at MI5, Eve identifies a series of murders, apparently by a woman, of prominent figures in politics and organised crime. The motive for the murders is unclear. Viktor Kedrin, a controversial Moscow activist, comes to give a talk in London, and when Eve requests protection for him, she is blocked by a superior, whom we may reasonably assume to have been Dennis Cradle. Kedrin is duly murdered, and as a consequence of his death Eve is dismissed from MI5. It's probably Cradle, once again, who engineers this.

'A Chinese People's Army hacker is killed in Shanghai, reportedly by a woman. Eve and Simon Mortimer share intel with Jin Qiang, who returns the compliment by providing evidence that a multimillion-pound payment has been made by a Middle Eastern bank to one Tony Kent. Jin clearly knows more than he's letting on, and lo and behold, when we investigate Kent, we discover that he's an associate of Dennis Cradle.

'While Eve and Simon are in Shanghai, Simon is murdered. We're not sure why, but possibly to intimidate Eve. We know that the woman who signs herself V was in Shanghai at the time, as she later produces a bracelet she stole from Eve's hotel room there.

'Investigation of Dennis Cradle shows that he is being paid huge sums by an unknown source. We confront him, and he tells Eve of the existence of a covert but rapidly growing organisation named the Twelve, and attempts to recruit her, apparently having been given the green light to do so. In other words, he has contacted the Twelve to tell them he has been compromised. Their actual intention, however, is to kill him, which they duly do.'

'Query,' says Lance, dropping tobacco into a cigarette paper and beginning to roll. 'Why do they, the Twelve, let Cradle try to recruit Eve? And in doing so, tell her so much about the organisation?' He licks the paper and places the cigarette behind his ear. 'Why don't they tell him to stall? Standard resistance to questioning?'

'I've asked myself the same question,' says Eve. 'And I think it's because they know Cradle's not stupid. If they tell him to stall, he'll suspect that they mean to kill him, and he'll cut and run. If they give him a specific job to do – turning the situation round and recruiting me – he'll think they trust him. Which'll give them time to get their killer, V, in place. And when it comes down to it, how much did he tell me about the Twelve? How much did he even know? A couple of names which are certainly false. Some vague stuff about a new world order.'

'I think Eve's right,' says Richard. 'Dennis was always a pragmatist, never an idealist. They recruited him because they needed a senior desk officer in MI5, and whatever he might have told Eve, it would have been the money that he went for, not the ideology. People like Dennis don't change horses at this stage of their career.'

'The thing that really clicked for me,' Eve says, 'was Cradle saying that Kedrin was killed to turn a liability into a martyr. That confirms what we already know, that their methods are completely ruthless, but it also tells us that Kedrin's vision was basically the same as theirs. A world dominated by an alliance of hard-right – or as they prefer to put it, "traditionalist" – Eurasian powers led by Russia.'

'I agree,' says Richard. 'And that squares with what we know about the rise of nationalism and identity politics in Europe. That it's being skilfully mobilised and massively funded by parties we can't identify, but suspect to be Russian.'

'Are we talking official Kremlin policy?' Billy asks, wiping his fingers on his jeans and stuffing the wrapper of his pasty in his pocket.

'Unlikely. In today's Russia, the people you read about in the papers and see on TV are mostly figureheads. The real power-players move in the shadows.'

Villanelle hunches into her down jacket as the Super Puma helicopter circles the marine platform. Rain flurries wash the windscreen and, in the sea below, heavy waves rear and fall.

'Going in to land now,' the pilot tells her, and she gives him a thumbs-up, removes her headset, and grabs her rucksack.

They touch down, the helicopter rocking in the gale-force wind, and Villanelle jumps out and swings her pack onto her back. The rain lashes her face, and she has to lean into the wind as she runs head-down across the platform deck. Anton, a lean figure in a reefer jacket and submariner's sweater, gives her a cursory glance and beckons her through a white-painted steel door. As he swings it shut behind her the sound of the roaring wind is muted a degree or two. Villanelle stands there, expectant, rain dripping from her nose.

The platform, some ten miles east of the Essex coast, is one of five built in the Second World War to protect the North Sea shipping lanes. Known as Knock Tom, it originally consisted of an anti-aircraft emplacement supported by reinforced concrete towers. After the war the anti-aircraft platforms were allowed to fall into disrepair. Three of the five were eventually demolished, but Knock Tom passed into private hands. Its present owner is the Sverdlovsk-Futura Group, a company registered in Moscow. SFG have undertaken extensive reconstruction of Knock Tom, and the former gun deck now holds three freight containers that have been converted into offices and a dining unit. The support towers have been divided into living quarters accessed by a vertical steel ladder. Following Anton, Villanelle climbs downward past a humming generator room and into a concrete-walled cell furnished with a bunk bed and a single chair.

'In the office in ten?' Anton says.

Villanelle nods, drops her pack, and hears the door close behind her. The room smells of corrosion, and the bedclothes are damp, but of the sea beyond the windowless concrete walls she can hear nothing. Somehow, Knock Tom is perfect for Anton. It's exactly the sort of remote and brutally functional setting in which she's always imagined him, and for a moment she wishes she'd brought something wildly inappropriate to wear – a hot pink Dior tulle dress, perhaps – just to annoy him.

He's waiting for her at the top of the ladder. As they cross the platform deck to the containers, Villanelle looks out over the churning grey sea. The desolation of it makes her think, unexpectedly, of Anna Leonova. She hasn't seen or spoken to her former teacher for a decade, but when she remembers her it's with a sadness that nothing and no one else has ever made her feel.

'I like this view,' Anton tells her. 'It's so indifferent to human activity.'

'Are we alone?'

'There's no one here except you and me, if that's what you mean.'

The shipping container housing the office is surmounted by a steerable microwave antenna. The only link, Villanelle guesses, to the world beyond the waves. The interior is frugal but well-appointed. On a metal desk are a laptop, a satphone and an anglepoise lamp. A wall-mounted unit holds electronic hardware and several shelves of charts and maps.

Anton motions Villanelle to a leather-upholstered chair, pours them both coffee from a cafetière, and seats himself behind the desk.

'So, Villanelle.'

'So, Anton.'

'You're bored of routine actions like the Yevtukh and Cradle jobs. You feel it's time you moved to the next level.'

Villanelle nods.

'You've contacted me to request more complex and demanding work. You think you've earned it.'

74

'Exactly.'

'Well, I applaud your keenness, but I'm not sure that I agree. You're technically adept, and your weapons skills are good, but you're reckless, and your judgement's often questionable. You're sexually profligate, which I don't give a shit about, but you're indiscreet, which I do. Your fixation on the MI6 agent Eve Polastri, in particular, leads you to ignore the very real problems that she and her team could cause us. And cause you.'

'She won't give us any problems. I keep an eye on her so that I can keep up with what she knows, but she really doesn't have any idea what's going on.'

'She found out about Dennis Cradle. And she's not going to go away. I know her type. On the outside disorganised, but inside sharp. And patient. Like a cat watching a bird.'

'I'm the cat.'

'You think you are. I'm not so sure.'

'She's vulnerable, because of the asshole husband. I can manipulate her.'

'Villanelle, I warn you. You've already killed her deputy. You threaten her husband, and she will unleash hell. She won't rest until you're laid out on a mortuary slab.'

Villanelle looks up, considers a facetious response, meets Anton's level gaze, and decides against it. 'Whatever.'

'Whatever indeed. As you will have calculated, I haven't brought you here for the pleasure of your company. I have a mission for you, if you want it.'

'OK.'

'It's important, but it's dangerous. You won't be able to afford any mistakes.'

The tip of her tongue touches the scar on her upper lip. 'I said OK.'

He regards her with fastidious distaste. 'Just for the record, I'm not attracted to promiscuous women.'

Villanelle frowns. 'Should I care?'

Eve's phone rings when she's walking out of the office to pick up a sandwich for lunch. It's Abby, her contact at the Metropolitan Police Forensics Laboratory in Lambeth. With encouragement from Richard, Abby has fast-tracked the analysis of the Van Diest bracelet.

'Do you want the good news or the bad?' Abby asks.

'Bad.'

'OK. We performed a tape-lift on the bracelet and the card, but found no extractable DNA. No hairs, no epithelial cells, nothing we could use.'

'Shit.'

'Not even that. Sorry.'

'The card?'

'Again, nothing. Gloves worn, I'd guess. I sent a copy on to graphology.'

'Any joy with the perfume?'

'We tried. It's possible to identify the compounds in commercially produced fragrances using gas chromatography and mass spectrometry, but you have to have an adequate sample, which we didn't here. So no joy.'

'I thought you said there was some good news.'

'Well.' Abby pauses. 'I did find one interesting thing.'

'Go on.'

'A flake of pastry, almost invisible, caught in a fold of the tissue paper.'

'What kind of pastry?'

'I sent it for analysis. There were traces of vegetable oil, vanilla essence, confectioner's sugar. But there was something else, too. Grappa.'

'That Italian firewater? Like brandy?'

'Exactly. So I put all these ingredients together and did a search. And came up with something called *galani*. They're fried pastries, flavoured with grappa and vanilla and dusted with confectioner's sugar. A speciality of Venice.'

'Oh my God, thank you. Thank you.'

'There's more. The Van Diest jewellery boutique in Venice is in Calle Vallaresso, at the eastern end of Piazza San Marco. Three doors down is a small, very expensive *pasticceria* called Zucchetti, specialising in guess what?'

'Abby, you are a fucking genius. I owe you so massively.'

'You do. But bring me back a box of *galani* from Zucchetti and we're square.'

'You're on.'

'The target,' says Anton, 'is Max Linder. Have you heard of him?'

'Yes. I've read a couple of profiles.'

'Franco-Dutch political activist and media celebrity, twenty-nine. Gay, but nevertheless a figurehead for the extreme right, with a huge following in Europe, especially among young people. Looks like a pop star, and believes, among other things, that the obese should be put in labour camps and sex offenders guillotined.'

'And why exactly do you want me to kill him?'

'Some of what he says makes sense. His worldview is, overall, not so very different from ours. But Linder is also a

Nazi, and Nazism is a problematic brand, discredited on so many levels, and that's an association we do not need. In fact it could really damage us.'

'You said the job would be dangerous.'

'Linder is aware that he has enemies. He's accompanied, everywhere he goes, by a praetorian guard of ex-military types. Security is always tight, and there's invariably a heavy police presence at events he attends. That's not to say that it's impossible to kill him. It's never impossible, there's always a way. The problem is getting away with it.'

'Have you got any ideas? I assume you've been thinking about this for some time.'

'We have. Next month Linder is going to a mountain hotel in Austria called the Felsnadel, high above the snow-line in the High Tauern. He goes there every year with a group of friends and political associates. It's a luxury place, designed by some famous architect or other, and you can only get in and out by helicopter. Linder considers it safe enough to stay there without bodyguards. He's booked the whole hotel for his guests for several days.'

'So how do I get in?'

'A week from today, one of the hotel's service team is going to contract a vomiting bug that will require her hospitalisation. The agency in Innsbruck that provides their staff will send a replacement.'

'Me.'

'Correct.'

'And do you want me to kill everyone in sight, or just Linder?'

'Just Linder will be fine. It's a personality cult. Eliminate him, and the movement will wither away.'

'So what's my exit plan?'

'That'll be up to you to improvise. We can get you in there, but we can't guarantee to get you out.'

'Nice.'

'I thought you'd like it. In the other office I've got maps, a floor-plan of the hotel, and detailed files on Linder and everyone else we think is going to be there. How you kill him is up to you, but I'll need a full list of supplies and weaponry before you leave here. Bear in mind that you'll be expected to present yourself at the heliport with a single suitcase or bag which will certainly be searched and X-rayed, and cannot exceed ten kilos in weight.'

'Understood. And now I'm hungry. Is there any lunch?'

'Waiting for you in the other office. I assume you're not a vegetarian?'

On her way home, Eve picks up half a dozen duck breasts, fennel and a large tiramisu from Sainsbury's in the Tottenham Court Road. New neighbours have moved in opposite them, and, rather wildly, Eve has asked them to dinner, telling Niko that 'they look very nice'. What this supposed niceness actually boils down to is that the husband, Mark, is moderately good-looking and the wife – was her name Maeve, Mavis, Maisie? – has a highly covet-able black Whistles coat. To make up numbers, Eve has invited Niko's friends Zbig and Leila. It will be an interest-ing and sophisticated evening, she tells herself. Six young (well, youngish) professionals from diverse backgrounds and walks of life exchanging informed opinions over home-cooked food and cleverly chosen wine.

With a flash of apprehension, as she's sitting on the bus,

it occurs to Eve that the Maeve, Mavis, Maisie person might be vegetarian. She doesn't *look* vegetarian. When Eve met her she was wearing court shoes with little gilt snaffles, and surely no one owning shoes like that has ever been vegetarian. And the husband, Mark. He does something in the City, so is surely a carnivore.

Niko's home on time, for once. He tends to hang about at school, giving unofficial coding and hacking classes in the IT room, and teaching the science club how to make miniature volcanoes out of vinegar and baking powder. But today he's busily peeling potatoes at the sink, and leans back to give Eve an over-the-shoulder kiss as she comes in.

'I've fed the girls,' he tells her. 'I've given them extra hay to keep them busy.'

'Can we give them those potato peelings?'

'No, potato peel contains solanine, which is harmful to goats.'

She puts her arms round his waist. 'How do you know these things?'

'Urban Goat Forum.'

'Sounds like a porn site to me.'

'You should see LondonPigOwners.com.'

'Pervert.'

'I wasn't deliberately searching for it. It just came up on the screen.'

'Of course it did. Have you got the wine?'

'Yes. White in the fridge. Red on the table.'

When she's put the potatoes and fennel in the oven to roast, Eve goes outside onto the patio, where Thelma and Louise nibble affectionately at her fingers in the fading light. Despite her misgivings, Eve has grown very fond of them.

Zbig and Leila arrive at eight o'clock on the dot. Zbig's an old friend of Niko's from Cracow University, and Leila is his girlfriend of several years' standing.

'So what's new?' Zbig asks them. 'Are you doing anything next week, for half-term?'

'We were thinking of going up to the Suffolk coast for a couple of days,' Niko says. 'It's wonderful at this time of year. No crowds. We've even found someone to goat-sit Thelma and Louise.'

'What do you do there?' asks Leila.

'Walk. Look at seabirds. Eat fish and chips.'

'Catch up on your love life?' Zbig suggests.

'Maybe even that.'

'Oh my God' says Eve, her heart plummeting. 'The roast potatoes.'

Niko follows her to the kitchen. 'The potatoes are fine,' he tells her, glancing into the oven. 'What is it really?'

'Next week. I'm really sorry, Niko. I have to go to Venice.'

He stares at her. 'You're not serious.'

'I am serious. It's already booked.'

He turns away. 'Jesus, Eve. Couldn't you, just once, just fucking *once* . . .'

She closes her eyes. 'I promise you, I . . .'

'So could I come too?'

'Er, yes, I guess.' She feels her eyelids flutter. 'I mean, Lance will be there, but we can still—'

'Lance? Human cockroach *Lance*?'

'You know perfectly well who I mean. It's work, Niko. I have no choice.'

'You do have a choice, Eve.' His voice is almost inaudible. 'You can choose to spend your life chasing shadows, or you can choose to have a real life, here, with me.'

They're staring at each other, beyond words, when the doorbell sounds. Mark precedes his wife. He's wearing strawberry-coloured trousers and a Guernsey sweater and carrying an enormous bottle of wine. A magnum, at least.

'Hi, guys, sorry, got lost crossing the street.' He pushes the bottle at Niko. 'Ritual offering. Think you'll find it's fairly decent.'

Eve recovers first. 'Mark, how lovely. Thank you. And Maeve . . . Maisie . . . I'm terribly sorry, I've forgotten your—'

'Fiona,' she says, with a mirthless flash of teeth, shrugging off the Whistles coat.

As Niko introduces them to the others, Eve feels a sick sense of things left unresolved. Leila raises an eyebrow, detecting that something is amiss, and Eve beckons her into the kitchen and gives her an abridged version of events as she takes the duck breasts out of the marinade and lays them, hissing, in a heated pan.

'I've been ordered to go to Venice,' she says untruthfully. 'It's an important short-notice thing I can't get out of, half-term or no half-term. Niko seems to think that I can just tell my bosses to go to hell, but I can't.'

'Tell me about it,' says Leila, who knows what Eve does, although not in detail. 'I'm constantly pulled in two directions. Justifying my work to Zbig is more stressful than actually doing it.'

'That's *exactly* what I feel,' says Eve, giving the pan an irritable shake.

Mark, they discover when they rejoin the others, is a compliance manager. 'The youngest the bank's ever had,' says Fiona. 'Top of his training cohort.'

'Gosh,' says Leila faintly.

'Yup, the *enfant terrible* of regulatory compliance.' Mark swings round to face her. 'So where do you hail from?'

'Totteridge,' says Leila. 'Although I grew up in Wembley.'

'No, but where do you come *from*?'

'My grandparents were born in Jamaica, if that's what you mean.'

'That's amazing. We went there on holiday two years ago, didn't we, darling?'

'Yes, darling.' Fiona flashes her teeth again.

'A resort called Sandals. Do you know it?'

'No,' says Leila.

Dizzy with the ghastliness of it all, Eve introduces Zbig, more or less forcefully, to Fiona. 'Zbig lectures at King's,' she tells her.

'That's nice. What about?'

'Roman history,' says Zbig. 'Augustus to Nero, basically.'

'Did you see *Gladiator*? We've got the DVD at home. Mark loves the bit where Russell Crowe chops the guy's head off with the two swords.'

'Yes,' says Zbig. 'That certainly is a good bit.'

'So do you get asked on TV programmes and stuff?'

'I get the odd request, yes. If they need someone to compare the US president to Nero, or to talk about Severus.'

'Who?'

'Septimius Severus, the first African Roman emperor. He invaded Scotland, among other good works.'

'You're shitting me.'

'I shit you not. Septimius was the man. But tell me about yourself.'

'PR. Mostly political.'

'Interesting. What sort of people are your clients?'

'Well, I'm basically working full-time with the MP Gareth Wolf.'

'I'm impressed. Quite a challenge.'

'How do you mean?'

Frowning, Niko holds his wine glass up to the window. 'He means in light of Wolf's persistent lying, his rapacious self-interest, his open contempt for those less fortunate than himself, and his all-round moral vacuity.'

'That's very much a glass-half-empty perspective,' Fiona says.

'What about that expenses scandal?' asks Zbig.

'Oh, that was blown out of all proportion.'

'Like Wolf's girlfriend, after the boob-job he claimed as a legitimate parliamentary expense,' says Leila, and Niko laughs.

'He's done amazing things for trade with Saudi Arabia,' Fiona says, dropping her handbag onto the sofa, and pouring herself another glass of wine.

'I bet you're good at your job.' Eve smiles at her.

'I am,' says Fiona. 'Very.'

Eve scans the room. Why do we put ourselves through this torture? she wonders. Dinner parties bring out the worst in everyone. Niko, usually the gentlest of men, is looking positively vengeful, although obviously this has got a lot to do with her going to Venice for half-term week, rather than spending it on the windy Suffolk coast with him. Mark, meanwhile, is explaining at extraordinary length to Leila, whose jaw is set rigid with boredom, exactly what it is that a regulatory compliance manager does.

'You had that break-in, didn't you?' Fiona asks. 'Did they take anything?'

'Nothing, as far as we can find.'

'Did they catch them?'

'It was a her. And no, not yet.'

'Was this woman Caucasian?' asks Mark.

From the corner of her eye, Eve sees Zbig lay a hand on Leila's arm. 'According to Mrs Khan . . . have you met the Khans?'

'The Asian family? No.'

'Well, according to her, it was an athletic young woman with dark blonde hair.'

Mark grins. 'In that case, I'll leave my windows open.'

Feeling a vestige of sympathy for Fiona, Eve is just about to speak to her when she sees Leila pointing urgently. Pushing through the guests and into the kitchen, she grabs the smoking pan containing the duck breasts, and to a crescendo of sizzling, balances it on the sink.

'Is everything OK?' asks Leila.

'The duck's burned to buggery,' says Eve, levering up one of the blackened breasts with a spatula.

'Edible?'

'Barely.'

'Well, don't worry. Zbig and Niko and I already know you can't cook to save your life, and you're never going to see that dreadful couple again. At least I hope you aren't.'

'No, and I honestly have no idea why I asked them tonight. I saw them leaving their house one morning, just after they'd moved in, and felt I should say something friendly. But then my mind went blank, and I panicked, and before I knew it, I heard myself asking them to dinner.'

'Eve, honestly.'

'I know. But right now I need you to help me make this duck look presentable. Charred side down, I guess, and surrounded with vegetables.'

'Is there some gravy?'

'There's this sort of creosote stuff in the pan.'

'No good. Have you got any jam? Marmalade?'

'I'm sure we have.'

'Right. Heat it up and pour it on. The duck'll still be like shoe leather but at least it'll taste of something.'

Moving from the kitchen to the dining table, a loaded plate in each hand, Eve and Leila discover the others arranged as if in a classic film-still. Beyond them, framed by the open patio door, stands the diminutive figure of Thelma. On the sofa, very much aware that the eyes of all present are upon her, Louise is nervously evacuating her bladder into Fiona's handbag.

'Well, that went well,' says Niko a couple of hours later, pouring the last of the Romanian red wine into his glass and downing it in a single swallow.

'I'm sorry,' Eve tells him. 'I'm a terrible wife. And a worse cook.'

'Both true,' says Niko, putting down his glass, placing an arm round her shoulder, and drawing her to him. 'Your hair smells of frazzled duck.'

'Don't remind me.'

86

'I quite like it.' He holds her for a moment. 'Go to Venice next week, if you really have to.'

'I really have to, Niko. I have no choice.'

'I know. And Lance, I'm sure, will prove the ideal travelling companion.'

'Niko, please. Surely you don't think—'

'I don't think anything. But when you get back, it ends.'

'What ends?'

'All of it. The conspiracy theories, the chasing after imaginary assassins, the whole fantasy.'

'It's not a fantasy, Niko, it's real. People are being killed.'

He lets his arm drop. 'If that's true, all the more reason to leave it to those who are trained to deal with that kind of stuff. Which, by your own admission, you're not.'

'They need me. The person we're after, Niko. This woman. The only person who's begun to figure her out is me. It'll take time, but I'll get her.'

'What do you mean, "get her"?'

'Stop her. Take her out.'

'Kill her?'

'If necessary.'

'Eve, do you have any idea what you're saying? You sound completely deranged.'

'I'm sorry, but that's the reality of the situation.'

'The reality of the situation is that there's a loaded handgun in your bag and people from the security forces watching this house. And that's not the life I want for us. I want a life where we do things together, like a normal married couple. Where we talk to each other, and I mean really talk. Where we trust each other. I can't carry on like this.'

'What are you saying?'

'That you go to Venice, and then draw a line under the whole thing. Resign, leave, whatever. And we make a whole new start.'

She looks round the room. At the detritus of the dinner party, the half-empty wine glasses, the remains of the tiramisu. From the sofa, Louise gives an encouraging bleat.

'OK,' she says, and allows her head to fall forward onto Niko's chest. He puts both arms around her and holds her tight.

'You know I love you,' he says.

'Yes,' she says. 'I do.'

4

Villanelle has been studying Linder, and deciding how to kill him, for twenty-four hours now. She's beginning to understand her target, despite the thicket of disinformation with which he has surrounded himself. All the interviews he has given propagate the same fictions. The humble beginnings, the fervent identification with the classical ideals of valour and duty, the self-taught political philosophy, the passionate identification with the 'true' Europe. This mythology has been skilfully fleshed out with invented detail and anecdote. Linder's childhood obsession with Leonidas, the Spartan king who died facing overwhelming odds at Thermopylae. His overcoming of school bullies with his fists. His lifelong persecution for his political beliefs by left-wing intellectuals, and for his sexual orientation by homophobic conservatives and religious bigots. In fact, as a memorandum attached to his file dispassionately notes, Linder comes from a well-off liberal background, and is a failed actor who turned to fascist politics as an outlet for his extreme racist and misogynist tendencies.

'Good luck,' says Anton, holding out his hand. 'And good hunting.'

'Thank you. I'll see you when it's done.'

As always, now that she is in play, Villanelle is serene. There's a sense of things falling into place, as if impelled by gravity. All leading up to the kill, that moment of absolute power. The dark rapture flowing into every vestige of her being, filling and possessing her utterly.

In his office, her requisition list on the desk in front of him, Anton watches as Villanelle waits on the platform deck, a slight figure against the bruise-grey sky. The helicopter materialises, touches down for a moment, and is gone, swinging away on the wind. He stares after it. He can still feel the imprint of her hand in his, and from a desk drawer he takes a small bottle of sanitising gel. God knows where her fingers have been.

It's raining as Eve and Lance cross the Piazza San Marco in Venice. Eve is carrying a plastic Sainsbury's bag with the Van Diest bracelet and packaging inside it. The paving stones shine in the watery light. Pigeons rise and fall in desultory flocks.

'Looks like we've brought the weather with us,' says Lance. 'How was your breakfast?'

'Good. Lots of strong coffee with bread and apricot jam. Yours?'

'Same.'

Eve has never been to Venice before and left the hotel at 7 a.m. to explore. She found it beautiful but melancholy. The vast, rain-washed square, the wind-roughened expanse of the lagoon, the waves slapping at the stone quays.

Flanked by Balenciaga and Missoni, the Van Diest boutique is on the ground floor of a former ducal residence.

It's an elegantly appointed space, with dove-grey carpets, walls faced in ivory silk, and glass-topped jewellery cases picked out by discreet spotlights. Eve has made an effort with her clothes and hair, but feels herself wilting before the expressionless gaze of the assistants. Lance's presence doesn't help. Dressed in a horrible simulacrum of casual wear, and looking more rodent-like than ever, he's staring about him open-mouthed, as if awed by the gold and the gemstones. Never again, Eve tells herself. The man is a total liability. Approaching one of the assistants, she asks to speak to the *direttrice*, and an elegant woman of indeterminate age materialises.

'*Buongiorno, signora*, how can I help?'

'This bracelet,' says Eve, taking it from the bag. 'Is it possible to tell if it was bought at this store?'

'Not without a receipt, signora.' She examines the bracelet with a critical eye. 'Did you want to return it?'

'No, I just need to know when it was bought, and whether anyone can remember making the sale.'

The woman smiles. 'Is this a police matter?'

Lance steps forward, and wordlessly shows her an Interpol identity card.

'*Prego*. One minute.' The manageress examines the bracelet, and touches the screen of the terminal on the desk. A further dance of her fingers and she looks up.

'Yes, signora, a bracelet of this design was bought here last month. I cannot guarantee it is the same one.'

'Do you remember anything about the person who bought it?'

The woman frowns. Peripherally, Eve can see Lance examining a sapphire necklace and drop earrings. The assistants watch him uncertainly, and he winks at one of them. Jesus wept, Eve thinks.

'I do remember her,' the manageress says. 'Perhaps twenty-seven, twenty-eight. Dark hair, very attractive. She paid cash, which is not unusual for Russians.'

'How much did it cost?'

'Six thousand, two hundred and fifty euros, signora.' She frowns. 'And there was something strange. She was very . . . *come si dice, insistente*—'

'Insistent?'

'Yes, she wouldn't touch the bracelet. And when I wrapped it up and put it in a carrier bag, she wanted that bag to be put in a second bag.'

'She was definitely Russian?'

'She was speaking Russian with her companion.'

'You're sure?'

'Yes, signora. I hear it spoken every day.'

'Can you describe the companion?'

'Same age. A little taller. Short blonde hair. Strong physique. She looked like a swimmer or a tennis player.'

'Do you have security-camera footage of these women?'

'I can certainly look for you, and if you give me an email address, I can send you anything we have. But it's a month since the sale, and I'm not sure we keep the footage that long.'

'I see. Well, let's hope.' Eve questions the manageress for a further five minutes, gives her one of the Goodge Street email addresses, and thanks her.

'That bracelet, signora. It could have been chosen for you.'

Eve smiles. 'Goodbye for now.'

'*Arrivederci, signora.*'

As they step outside into a squall of rain, Eve turns to Lance. 'What the fuck were you playing at in there? Jesus. There's me, trying to get some answers out of that woman, and you're acting like Benny Hill, gawping at those women and . . . Fuck's sake, Lance, did you honestly think you were helping?'

He turns up his collar. 'Here's Zucchetti. Let's go in and grab a coffee and some of those pastries.'

The *pasticceria* is an intoxicating place, the air warm with the scent of baking, the counter an array of sugar-dusted pastries, golden rolls and brioches, meringues, macaroons and millefeuilles.

'So,' says Eve, five minutes later, her mood softened by a plate of *galani* and the best cappuccino she's ever drunk.

Lance leans forward over the tiny table. 'When V bought the bracelet, the woman with her was almost certainly her girlfriend. Or at least a girlfriend.'

Eve stares at him. 'How do you know?'

'Because once I'd convinced those shop assistants that I was a gormless idiot who didn't speak a word of Italian, they started to chat to each other. And they all remembered V and her friend. One of them, Bianca, speaks Russian, and usually deals with the Russian customers, but she didn't on this occasion because V also spoke perfect English, so your chum Giovanna looked after her.'

'Go on.'

'According to Bianca, the two women were having a lovers' tiff. V was telling the girlfriend off for eating in the shop, and the girlfriend was pissed off because V was buying a pretty bracelet for the "*angliskaya suka*", and she couldn't understand why.'

'You're sure? For the "English bitch"?'

'That's what Bianca said.'

'So you speak fluent Italian? You might have told me.'

'You didn't ask. But that's not all. The shop assistants all assumed that we were here to investigate some rich Ukrainian guy who's gone missing.'

'We don't know anything about that, do we?'

'First I've heard of it.'

'Do we have a name?'

'No.'

Eve looks out at the rain-blurred expanse of the piazza. 'Just suppose,' she says, licking the last of the sugar-powder from her fingers, 'that V was in Venice at the same time that this unnamed Ukrainian went missing . . .'

'I'm already supposing it.'

'I owe you an apology, Lance. Really, I'm—'

'Forget it. Let's ask the staff here if they remember two Russian women buying pastries a month ago, which they won't, and then let's get out of here. I need a smoke.'

Outside, the air is vaporous and the sky bruise-dark. As they cross the piazza, Eve feels a creeping discontent, which seems to relate to the two women buying the bracelet together. Who was that other woman, the one who called her a bitch, and what was her role in all this? Was she really V's lover?

Eve feels a flush of shame. It couldn't really be *jealousy* she's feeling, could it? She's embarrassed to even ask herself the question. She loves Niko and misses him. He loves her.

To be gazed at while you slept, though.

The bracelet.

The sheer, dazzling effrontery of it.

The *questura*, or central police station, of Venice is in Santa Croce, on the Ponte della Libertà. It has a river entrance, with blue-painted police launches moored at its jetty, and a rather less picturesque street entrance, fortified by steel security barriers and guarded by agents of the Polizia di Stato.

It's 5.30 p.m., and Eve and Lance are sitting in the waiting area, waiting to speak to the *questore*, the local chief of police. To arrange this has taken numerous phone calls, and now that they have an appointment, it turns out that Questore Armando Trevisan is 'in conference'. Hunching forward on the slatted wooden bench, Eve stares through the armoured glass of the entrance doors at the traffic. The rain stopped at midday, but she can still feel the dampness in the air.

A lean figure in a dark suit appears from a corridor, his purposeful air disrupting the somnolent atmosphere of the place. Introducing himself in English as Questore Trevisan, he leads them to his office, a monochrome space dominated by filing cabinets.

'Please, Mrs Polastri and Mr . . .'

'Edmonds,' says Lance. 'Noel Edmonds.'

They seat themselves opposite his desk. Trevisan opens a folder, removes a photocopied head-shot, and hands it to Eve.

'You want to know about our vanished Ukrainian? Well, so do we. His name is Rinat Yevtukh, and last month he was staying at the Danieli Hotel with a young woman named Katerina Goraya and several bodyguards. We were alerted to his presence, and details of his background, by colleagues in AISE, our external security agency.'

'He was known to them, then?' Eve asks.

'Very much so. Based in Odessa, where he was the head of a gang involved in drugs, prostitution, people-smuggling and the usual related activities. Very wealthy, very powerfully connected.'

From the folder Trevisan takes a second document. His movements are economical, and there's an alertness about him that tells Eve that this is a fellow spirit, an ally. A man who will only be satisfied by the truth. 'Here's the timeline of Yevtukh's stay here in Venice. The usual tourist activities, as you can see, and always accompanied by Miss Goraya. A gondola tour, a visit to Murano, shopping in San Marco, etcetera. And then, on this morning here, and without the knowledge of Miss Goraya, he leaves in a *motoscafo*, a motor launch, with a woman whom he had met in the hotel bar the evening before.'

Eve and Lance exchange glances.

'According to the waiter the woman ordered the drinks in Italian but spoke English to Yevtukh. Both fluently. She looked, according to the waiter, like a film star.'

'Any particular film star?'

'I think he meant more in a general way, but he did help us create an e-fit.'

Trevisan slides another photocopy across his desk. Eve forces herself not to grab it, but the image is wholly unrevealing. The heart-shaped face, shoulder-length hair and wide-set eyes have a blank, generic look. The subject could be any age between twenty and forty.

'We made this portrait three days after the waiter served her in the bar. It's the best he could manage. Yevtukh's bodyguards saw her briefly on the morning of his disappearance, but they were even less help. She was wearing large sunglasses, apparently, and they couldn't even agree on the colour of her hair.'

'Witnesses,' says Lance.

'Indeed, Mr Edmonds, witnesses. To continue, this woman meets Yevtukh at the river entrance to the hotel the next morning, and they leave together in the *motoscafo*. When Yevtukh doesn't reappear that night the bodyguards think their boss is enjoying a romantic assignment, and say nothing to Miss Goraya, but the following morning she goes to see the hotel manager and makes a big *furore* and the manager calls us. At that point the bodyguards agree to tell the truth.'

Initially, Trevisan tells them, Yevtukh was considered a low-risk disappearance, and the investigation a formality. And then someone at the *questura* matched the description of a *motoscafo* stolen from a marina in Isola Sant'Elena with the bodyguards' description of the vessel they had seen outside the hotel, and a full-scale search was set in motion. A helicopter overflight of the lagoon revealed the *motoscafo* sunk in the Poveglia Canal, but of Yevtukh, not a trace. And there the enquiry stalled.

'So what do you think happened?' asks Eve.

'Initially, I thought that this was a story of a rich man and his lovers. But the stolen *motoscafo*, and its deliberate sinking, changed my mind. And now, Mrs Polastri, here you are from MI6 in London, confirming that this is indeed no simple disappearance.'

'Signor Trevisan, may I make a suggestion?'

'Please do.'

'I may be able to help you move this investigation forward. In return I would ask that you keep our conversation confidential. That you mention it to no one, from your service or mine.'

'Go on.'

'Yevtukh is dead, I have no doubt of that whatsoever. The woman he met in the bar, and who took him out in the motor launch the next day, is almost certainly a professional assassin. Multilingual, but probably Russian. Name unknown. She was in Venice with another woman, again probably Russian, and possibly her lover. The two of them had been shopping in San Marco two days earlier, and had visited the Van Diest boutique, the Pasticceria Zucchetti and other shops in the area. Both are highly CCTV-aware, and the assassin is extremely skilful at altering her appearance. We think that she's slim, of medium height, with high-cheekboned features and dark blonde hair. Eyes probably grey or grey-green, but we think that she often wears coloured contact lenses. Also hair-pieces and wigs. The other woman has been described as sporty-looking, with short blonde hair.'

'You're sure of this?'

'I'm sure. And the pair of them must have stayed somewhere locally, either together or separately, given that there're two days between the San Marco shopping trip and Yevtukh's disappearance.'

'We can certainly see if we can find any record of them.' Trevisan looks at her intently, and Eve is suddenly conscious of her appearance, and, in particular, of the ugly nylon sockettes showing round the edges of her shoes. For years now she has sought others' approval of her professional competence, giving little or no thought to how they actually see her. But being here in Venice, seeing how Italian women carry themselves, and how they take pleasure in themselves as elegant, sensual beings, makes her want to be appreciated for more than the sharpness of her mind. She would like to walk through San Marco and feel the swirl of a beautifully cut skirt, and the breeze from the lagoon in her hair. Those shop assistants in Van Diest, this morning. They were dressed, it seemed, entirely for their own pleasure and enjoyment. Their clothes whispered secrets that endowed them with confidence and power. In her damp rain-jacket and jeans, Eve doesn't feel confident or powerful at all. She feels lank-haired and clammy beneath the arms.

The conversation winds down. 'Tell me,' Eve asks, as Trevisan ushers them to the entrance. 'Where did you learn your excellent English?'

'In Tunbridge Wells. My mother was English, and we spent every summer there when I was a child. I used to watch *Multi-Coloured Swap Shop* on BBC1 every Saturday, which is why I'm so honoured to meet Noel Edmonds in person.'

Lance winces. 'Ah.'

'Please, I understand professional discretion. Mrs Polastri, I'm glad we were able to help each other. Officially, as you requested, this meeting never took place. But it has been a great pleasure.'

They shake hands, and he's gone.

'For fuck's sakes,' says Eve, as they step out into the moist dusk. 'Noel Edmonds?'

'I know,' says Lance. 'I know.'

On the way back they catch a *vaporetto*, a water-bus. It's crowded, but Eve's feet are sore and it's a relief not to be walking. The *vaporetto* takes them the length of the Grand Canal. Some of the waterside buildings are illuminated, their reflections painting the broken surface of the water with gold, but others are shuttered and unlit, as if guarding ancient secrets. In the half-dark, there is a sinister edge to the city's beauty.

Lance rides the *vaporetto* all the way to San Marco, but Eve gets off at the stop before, and walks up towards the Fenice opera house, and a tiny boutique that she spotted earlier in the day. In the window is a beautiful scarlet and white Laura Fracci crêpe wrap dress, and she can't resist a closer look. The boutique looks terrifyingly expensive, and part of her hopes that the dress doesn't fit, but when she tries it on it's perfect. Barely glancing at the price, she hands over her credit card before she can change her mind.

It occurs to her to look in at the Van Diest store, to find out if they've found any CCTV footage of the two women. They haven't, she learns, as the video was deleted two days ago. Seeing her disappointment, the manageress looks thoughtful.

'There was another thing about the woman who bought the bracelet that I remember,' she says. 'Her scent. I always notice scent, it's my passion. My mother used to work at a perfume shop, and she taught me to recognise the . . . *ingredienti*. The sandalwood, cedar, amber, violet, rose, *bergamotto* . . .'

'So do you remember what scent this woman was wearing?'

100

'I didn't recognise it. It certainly wasn't one of the usual designer brands. Freesia top note, I think. Base notes of amber and white cedar. Very unusual. I asked her about it.'

'And?'

'She told me what it's called, but I can't remember the name. I'm sorry, I'm not being very helpful.'

'You are. Truly. You've been a great help. Perhaps if you remember the name of the scent, or anything else about these two women, you could speak to Questore Armando Trevisan at the police station in Santa Croce, and he will pass it on to me.'

'Certainly. Can I have your name? And perhaps your mobile phone number?'

Eve tells her, gazing wonderingly at the jewellery in the cases. A collar of incandescent sapphires and diamonds. A necklace of emeralds like a cascade of green fire.

The manageress pauses, pen in hand. 'I can see you admire fine jewellery, Signora Polastri.'

'I've never seen pieces like this. Close enough to touch. I see why people want them so much. Why they fall in love with them.'

'May I make a suggestion? I'm going to a reception tonight at the Palazzo Forlani. It's the launch of Umberto Zeni's new jewellery collection. I was going to take my sister, but her daughter's ill. You're welcome to join me if you're free.'

'That's very kind,' Eve says, taken aback. 'Are you sure?'

'Absolutely I'm sure. It would be my pleasure.'

'Well, then . . . Yes. Gosh. How exciting. I've never been to a party in a palace before.'

'Perhaps you could wear your bracelet?'

'I could, couldn't I.'

'In that case, *è deciso*. Palazzo Forlani's on the Dorsoduro. Cross the Accademia Bridge and it's a hundred metres or so on the left. Say you're with Giovanna Bianchi from Van Diest. I'll be there from nine o'clock.'

'Um . . . sure. Why not. Thank you, Giovanna. That would be lovely'

She extends her hand. '*Allora a dopo*, Signora Polastri.'

'It's Eve.'

'*A dopo*, Eve.'

Back at the hotel she sits on her bed with her laptop, encrypting her report on Yevtukh Rinat and the probable involvement in his disappearance of V and her Russian friend, lover, whatever. When she's dispatched it to Billy at Goodge Street, she calls Lance's room. There's no answer, but a couple of minutes later he knocks at her door, and when she opens it he's carrying beer bottles and an enormous pizza.

'The restaurants round here are all tourist rip-off joints,' he tells her. 'So I went for the takeaway option.'

'Perfect. I'm starving.'

For the next half-hour they sit in front of the small balcony drinking cold Nastro Azzurro and eating pizza topped with sliced potatoes, rosemary and Taleggio cheese.

'That was seriously good,' says Eve, when she can manage no more.

'You have to put up with a lot as a spy,' Lance says. 'But I draw the line at crap food.'

'I never knew you cared.'

'Funny old world, isn't it? Mind if I have a smoke on the balcony?'

'Go ahead. I should call my husband.'

When she eventually finds her phone in her bag, she realises it's been turned off all day. To her horror, she sees that Niko has tried to ring six times, and left three messages.

'Fuck. *Fuck* . . .'

It turns out he's had an accident. He's spent most of the day in Accident and Emergency at the Royal Free Hospital, and is now back at home, on crutches.

'Niko, I'm really, really sorry,' Eve says, when she finally gets through to him. 'I've just discovered my phone's been off all day. What happened?'

'School parent dropping her son off. Son steps out in front of a moving car, I run forward and pull him out of the way. Bang.'

'Oh, my love. I'm so sorry. Is it bad?'

'Broken ankle, basically. Fractured tibia and torn ligaments.'

'Painful?'

'Put it this way, you're going to be doing more of the cooking.'

'Oh God, you poor thing. For the accident, I mean, not for my cooking. Although that's not good news, either . . . Sorry, it's been a long day.'

'Indeed it has. How's Venice?'

'Lovely, actually, despite the fact that's it's been raining all day.'

'And Lance? In good health?'

'Niko, please. Lance is fine, work is fine, and I'll be back tomorrow night. Are you going to be OK till then?'

'My ancestors fought the Ottomans at Varna. I'll survive.'

'Is there enough hay for Thelma and Louise?'

'You might pick some up at Duty Free.'

'Niko, stop it. I'm sorry, OK? For leaving my phone off, for being here in Venice, for your accident. I'm sorry for all of it. Did the hospital give you painkillers?'

'Yes. Codeine.'

'Take them. With water, not whisky. And go to bed. I hope that boy's parents are grateful.'

'Parent. Singular. And she was.'

'Well, I'm proud of you, my love. Truly.'

'So what are you doing tonight?'

'I've got to go out later and speak to someone about some CCTV footage.' The lie slips out easily, effortlessly. 'Then to bed with a book.'

'What are you reading?'

'A novel by Elena Ferrante.'

'What's it about?'

'The complicated relationship between two women.'

'Is there an uncomplicated kind?'

'Not in my experience.'

She's still staring at the phone when Lance comes back into the room, trailed by a whirl of cigarette smoke.

'So what's the plan?' she asks him.

'Phoned someone earlier. Bloke I used to work with in Rome who's moved up here. Thought I might have a word with him about our disappeared Ukrainian.'

'When are you meeting him?'

'Half an hour. Bar near that police station we were at earlier. What about you?'

'Going to some sort of reception thing with Giovanna from the jewellery shop. The security footage has been wiped, but I'm sure there's more she can tell us.'

104

'I'm sure there is.'

'What's that supposed to mean?'

'Nothing.'

'You're smirking, Lance.'

'That's not a smirk, it's a facial tic. I'm very sensitive about it.'

'Look, you were good this morning. Really good. And that pizza was seriously delicious. But if you're going to smirk whenever I mention another woman's name this isn't going to work.'

'No, I see that.'

'Fuck off, Lance.'

'Absolutely. Right away.'

Ten minutes later, Eve has changed into the Laura Fracci dress, pinned her hair into a passable French twist, and is stepping out into the dusk with the rose gold bracelet on her wrist. The day's rain has sharpened the air, which smells of dampness and drains. Crossing the piazza she threads her way westwards, past lingering groups of tourists, to the Accademia Bridge. Halfway across the bridge she stops, entranced by the view. The darkening canal, the illuminated waterside buildings, and, at the distant mouth of the lagoon, the dome of Santa Maria della Salute. Almost too much beauty to bear, and all of it dying. As are we all, a voice in her head whispers. There's no tomorrow, there's only today.

Looking out over the glimmering canal, poised between the upstream and the downstream of her life, Eve considers her adversary. All she's seen of her is her eyes, but the eyes are enough. I am death, that gaze seemed to say, and if you're not intimate with death, can you ever feel truly alive?

From such a challenge, Eve now knows, there's no retreating, no walking away. Wherever it leads, she has to follow, and if she has to lie to Niko, then so be it. A seaward breeze flickers up the canal, flattening the soft folds of the dress to her thighs, and her phone vibrates in her bag.

It's Giovanna. She'll be there in ten minutes.

In her narrow room on the first floor of the Gasthof Lili in Innsbruck, Villanelle is sitting cross-legged on her bed in front of a laptop, scrolling through architectural blueprints of the Felsnadel. The hotel, a futuristic slice of glass and steel wrapped around a frozen Tyrolean crag, is Austria's highest. It stands on a ledge, some two and a half thousand metres above sea level, on the eastern flank of the Teufelskamp mountain.

Villanelle has been prowling the building in her imagination for hours now, testing possible entry and exit points, memorising the layout of the guest quarters and the kitchens, noting the whereabouts of storerooms and service areas. For the last thirty minutes she's been examining the fittings and locking mechanisms on the triple-glazed windows. Details like these, Konstantin impressed on her, can mean the difference between success and failure, between life and death. It saddens Villanelle to think that, somewhere along the line, Konstantin himself neglected a detail.

She yawns, baring her teeth like a cat. She always enjoys the preparatory phase of an operation, but there's an overload point. A moment when the plans blur, and the words on the screen start to run together. In addition to researching the mission, she's been teaching herself German, a language she's never previously studied. She will not be required to pass herself off as German at the Hotel Felsnadel; her cover story is that she's French. But she will be required to speak it, and it's an operational necessity that she understands everything that she hears.

These and other preparations are mentally tiring. Villanelle is less susceptible to stress than most people, but when she's faced with long periods of waiting, a familiar need tends to make itself felt. Locking down the laptop so that any attempt to log in will cause total data-erasure, she stands, and stretches. She's wearing a cheap black tracksuit, she hasn't showered for thirty-six hours, and her unwashed hair is raked back into a scrappy ponytail. She looks, and smells, feral.

Herzog-Friedrich-Strasse is pretty in the fading light, its illuminated buildings framing the distant mountains like a stage set. But it's cold, with an insistent wind whistling through the narrow streets, and this cuts straight through Villanelle's skimpy clothing as she hurries towards the Schlossergasse and the golden glow of the Brauhaus Adler. Inside, noise levels are high, and the air warm and beery. Edging round the throng, Villanelle notes a line of men with their backs to the bar, surveying the crowd with an amused, predatory air. At intervals, they exchange comments and knowing smiles.

Villanelle watches for a minute or two, and then, unhurriedly, walks up to the bar. Strolling along the line of men, taking casual repossession of the space they've annexed, she eyeballs them one by one before coming to a halt in front of a fit-looking guy in his early twenties. He's handsome, he knows it, and he meets her stare with a confident grin.

Villanelle doesn't return it. Instead, she takes his stein of beer, drains it, and walks away without looking back. An instant later he follows, pushing through the crowd after her. Wordlessly, she leads him out of the main entrance, then turns into a side street, and again into a narrow alley behind the bar. Halfway along the alley is a shadowed space between two overspilling refuse bins. Above the further of these, an extractor fan vents kitchen exhaust through a dirty grille.

Bracing her back against the brick wall, Villanelle orders the young man to kneel in front of her. When he hesitates she grabs a handful of blond hair and forces him down. Then she drags her tracksuit bottoms to her ankles with her free hand, parts her legs and pulls her knickers open to one side. 'No fingers,' she tells him. 'Just your tongue. Get on with it.'

He glances up at her, his eyes uncertain, and she tightens her hold on his hair until he gasps with pain. 'I said get on with it, *dummkopf*. Lick my pussy.' She shuffles her feet wider apart, the wall cold against her buttocks. 'Harder, it's not a fucking ice cream. And higher. Yes, there.'

Sensation flickers through her, but it's too irregular, and her new acquaintance too inexpert, to take her where she needs to go. Through half-closed eyes she sees a kitchen worker in a soiled apron and skullcap step from a doorway and stop, open-mouthed, at the sight of her. She ignores him, and the blond guy is much too busy searching for her clitoris to sense the presence of a spectator.

The kitchen worker stands there, hand on groin, for the best part of a minute, then a voice recalls him to the kitchen in profanity-laden Turkish. By now Villanelle is pretty sure that if she wants to come, she's going to have to go back to her room and finish the job herself. Her thoughts wander, dissolving into refracted images which, quite suddenly, coalesce into the figure of Eve Polastri. Eve with her *skuchniyy* clothes, and that English decency that Villanelle wants, so badly, to disrupt. Imagine if she were to look down, right now, and see that face between her thighs. Eve's eyes looking up at her. Eve's tongue scouring her.

Villanelle cleaves to this image until, with a brief shuddering of her thighs, she comes. At which point the image of Eve dissolves into that of Anna Leonova. Anna, to whom all the blood-trails lead. Anna who, in another life, showed Oxana Vorontsova what love could be, and then denied it to her for ever. Opening her eyes Villanelle takes in her filthy surroundings. The wind touches her face and she realises that there are tears on her cheeks.

The blond guy is grinning. 'That was good, *ja?*' Standing, he fishes a pubic hair from his mouth with a finger. 'Now you suck my dick, OK?'

Rearranging her underwear, Villanelle pulls up her tracksuit bottoms. 'Please,' she says. 'Just go.'

'Hey, come on now, *schatz* . . .'

'You heard me. Fuck off.'

He meets her stare, and his grin fades. He starts to walk away, and then turns. 'You want to know something?' he says. 'You stink.'

'Good. And a word of advice. Next time you find yourself in a girl's pants, bring a map.'

The Palazzo Forlani is at the eastern end of Dorsoduro. The street entrance, through which Eve arrives, is nondescript. There's a poorly lit cloakroom staffed by dark-suited attendants and supervised by an unsmiling figure who looks as if he might have once earned his living as a boxer. Beyond them, two young women in identical black moiré cocktail dresses sit at an antique desk, checking the names of new arrivals on a printed list.

Eve approaches them. '*Sono con Giovanna Bianchi.*'

They smile. 'OK, no problem,' one of them says. 'But my friend needs to fix your hair.'

Eve raises a hand and encounters a hairclip swinging from an errant tress. 'Oh my goodness, could you really?'

'Come,' says the friend and, beckoning Eve to a chair, swiftly and expertly reworks her coiffure. As she's inserting the final pin Giovanna arrives.

'Eve. You look stunning . . . *Ciao, ragazze.*'

'*Ciao*, Giovanna. Just fixing a little hair emergency here.'

'My French twist came adrift,' Eve explains.

Giovanna smiles. 'That's why you should always go Italian.'

A curtain parts, and they move from the twilit foyer into a warm blaze of illumination. The street entrance to the palazzo, Eve realises, is in fact the back entrance, like a stage door. They're in a wide, stone-floored atrium, thronged with guests, at whose centre is a rectangular space concealed by hanging drapes imprinted with the Umberto Zeni logo. Opposite Eve and Giovanna is the much grander and more ornate canal entrance, dominated by an arched portal through which the gleam of water is visible. As Eve watches, a motor launch draws up, and two guests step out onto a jetty, and are ushered inside by a doorman.

Around her, the crowd ebbs and flows. She can smell scent, face-powder, candle wax, and the faint, muddy tang

110

of the canal. It's an intoxicatingly strange scene, a collision of the antique and the dazzlingly fashionable. Eve feels poised, soignée even, but she can't imagine actually talking to anyone here. There's a nucleus of ageless men in dark suits and heavy silk ties, and women whose lacquered hair and ornate designer gowns are clearly chosen to intimidate rather than to attract. Circling around these figures, like pilot fish around sharks, is a retinue of socialites and hangers-on. Lizard-like designers with implausible tans, gym-toned young men in ripped jeans, willowy models with wide, vacant eyes.

'And that's Umberto,' says Giovanna, swiping two glasses of champagne from a passing waiter's tray, and nodding towards a tiny figure dressed from head to foot in leather fetish-wear. 'An interesting crowd, don't you think?'

'Amazing. And so not my world.'

'So what is your world, Eve? Forgive me for asking, but you come into my shop with this man who shows me identification from Interpol and then pretends to be *un cretino* while he eavesdrops on my assistants' conversations – oh, don't worry, I saw him – and then you ask me about a bracelet that was bought by a woman who came into the shop with her girlfriend, but which you are now wearing? *Per favore*, what is going on?'

Eve takes a deep swallow of her champagne, and turns her wrist so that the diamonds glitter. 'It's a long story.'

'Tell it to me.'

'We want this woman for a series of crimes. She knows I'm after her, and she sent me this bracelet to insult and intimidate me.'

'How so?'

111

'Because this is the kind of luxurious thing I could never afford, and could never imagine myself wearing.'

'Nevertheless, Eve, you are wearing it.'

Their conversation is interrupted by a dimming of the lights. Then, to a deafening burst of industrial metal music, and whoops and applause from the onlookers, the curtains at the centre of the atrium rise, and spotlights illuminate the tableau within. Rising from the floor is a massive concrete column, into which a white Alfa Romeo sports car appears to have crashed at speed. The car, wrapped around the column, is a total wreck. Two passengers, one male, one female, have been thrown through the windscreen, and are sprawled on the car's crumpled bonnet.

At first Eve thinks that these are horribly life-like, or perhaps death-like, dummies. Then she sees that they are breathing, and real. Belatedly, she recognises the famous boy-band singer and his supermodel girlfriend. Shane Rafique, dressed in a white T-shirt and jeans, is lying face down. Jasmin Vane-Partington is on her back, one arm outflung, her breasts exposed by her ripped blouse.

Where there might have been blood and torn flesh, however, there are jewels. Jasmin's forehead is not studded with fragments of windscreen glass, but enclosed in a tiara of diamonds and blood-red garnets. A string of Burmese rubies snakes down her belly like a fatal gash. Tourmalines glitter in Shane's hair and a topaz necklace cascades from his mouth. Vermilion gemstones spatter the car's bodywork.

As cameras flash, the music plays, and the applause rises and falls, Eve stares open-mouthed at this glittering *tableau mort*.

Giovanna smiles. 'So what do you think?'

'It's quite an extreme way of selling jewellery.'

'People want extremes here, they get bored very easily. And the fashion press will adore it. Especially with Jasmin and Shane.'

After ten minutes, when the photo flashes have subsided, and Umberto Zeni has made a short speech of which Eve understands not a single word, the curtain descends on the crashed Alfa Romeo and the celebrity corpses. Unhurriedly, the guests begin to make their way up a worn stone stair-case, past faded tapestries, to the first floor. Eve and Giovanna join them, collecting fresh glasses of champagne en route.

'Having fun?' asks Giovanna.

'So much fun. I don't know how to thank you.'

'Finish your story.'

Eve laughs. 'I will, one day.' For the first time in months, perhaps years, she is having a fabulous time that she won't have to account for. She feels an airy rush of elation, and floats up the staircase, weightless.

The galleries set around the stairwell swiftly fill with noise and people. Everyone seems to know Giovanna and she's soon surrounded by an excitable clique, exchanging observations in rapid-fire Italian. Fluttering her fingers in a vague, see-you-in-a-minute gesture, Eve drifts away. Taking a third glass of champagne, she winds purposefully through the crowd, smile in place, as if she's just caught sight of an acquaintance. She's always felt like an outsider at parties, torn between the desire to be swept along on a tide of conversation and laughter, and to be left alone. The essen-tial thing, she's found, is to keep moving. To stand still, even for a moment, is to present a vulnerable profile. To announce yourself a target for every cruising shark.

Adopting a connoisseurial attitude, she examines the art on the panelled walls. Allegorical scenes from Greek mythology hang next to vast contemporary paintings of skulls; eighteenth-century Venetian aristocrats cast a jaundiced eye over explicit life-size photographs of a couple having sex. Eve supposes she should know the names of the artists in question, but isn't quite interested enough to find out. What strikes her forcibly is the sheer, bludgeoning force of the wealth on display. These art objects are not here because they are beautiful, or even thought-provoking, but because they cost millions of euros. They're currency, pure and simple.

Moving on, she finds herself in front of a gilded porcelain sculpture, again life-size, of the late Michael Jackson fondling a monkey. One push, Eve muses. One good, strong shove. She imagines the crash, the gasps, the shocked silence.

'*La condizione umana*,' says a voice beside her.

She glances at him. Registers dark hair and aquiline features. 'I'm sorry?'

'You're English. You don't look English.'

'Really? In what way?'

'Your clothes, your hair, your *sprezzatura*.'

'My what?'

'Your . . . attitude.'

'I'll take that as a compliment.' Turning to face him she meets amused brown eyes. Notes the broken nose and the sensual, deeply incised mouth. 'You, on the other hand, could be nothing but Italian.'

114

He grins. 'I'll take that as a compliment. My name is Claudio.'

'And I'm Eve. You were saying?'

'I was saying that this sculpture represents the human condition.'

'Seriously?'

'Of course seriously. Look at it. What do you see?'

'A pop singer and a monkey. A giant version of the china ornaments my grandmother used to buy.'

'OK, Eve, now I believe you're English. You want to know what I see?'

'I'm sure you're going to tell me.'

'*Dio mio.* You look at me with those beautiful eyes and you bust my balls.'

'*The same pretty eyes. The same sad smile . . .*'

'I apologise,' he says. 'I've offended you.'

'No, not at all.' She touches his shirt sleeve, feels his arm warm beneath. 'Truly. I just . . . thought of someone.'

'Someone special?'

'In a sense, yes. But go on. Tell me what you see.'

'Well, I see a man so lonely, so detached from his fellow humans, that his only companion is this monkey, Bubbles. And eventually, even Bubbles moves on. He can't live in this fantasy.'

'I see.' Eve lifts her champagne flute to her mouth but it's empty. She realises that she is quite drunk, and that this doesn't matter. Perhaps it's even a good thing.

'This sculpture is Michael Jackson's dream. A golden forever. But it takes us back to the reality of his life, which is grotesque and sad.'

They stand there for a moment in silence.

'Perhaps your grandmother was right, with her china ornaments. Perhaps she understood that the things we really long for, we cannot buy.'

A wave of melancholy sweeps over Eve, she teeters dizzily on her heels, and a single tear runs down her nose. 'Now you've made me cry,' she says. 'Really, you're impossible.'

'And your glass is empty.'

'It should probably stay that way.'

'As you wish. Come and see the view from the balcony.' He takes her hand, which makes Eve's heart lurch, and leads her through the gallery to a marble-floored expanse hung with baroque mirrors. A projection screen is mounted on one wall, showing, on repeat, a video prequel to the Umberto Zeni installation, in which Shane Rafique and Jasmin Vane-Partington are shown running from a bank vault, laden with stolen jewellery, leaping into the white Alfa Romeo, and roaring away.

Like Giovanna, Claudio seems to know everyone, so their progress is stately, with much waving and greeting and air-kissing. An animated group is gathered round Umberto Zeni, who is explaining, in English this time, that dying in an automobile crash is the contemporary equivalent of Catholic martyrdom. As if to illustrate his point, a waiter is offering round a tray of petits fours shaped like sacramental objects. There are frosted pink sacred hearts, spun-sugar crowns of thorns, candied angelica crucifixion nails. Most exquisite of all are the tiny marzipan hands with red jelly stigmata.

'Divine, no?' says Umberto.

'Totally,' says Eve, biting off a mouthful of marzipan fingers.

Finally they reach the balcony, which is grand and spacious, and fronted by a carved balustrade, against which several guests are already leaning, smoking. Normally Eve hates cigarette smoke but at this moment, with the night darkening the Grand Canal and Claudio's arm around her shoulder – how did that get there? – she couldn't care less.

'I'm married,' she says.

'I would be very surprised if you weren't. Look upwards.'

She turns, and leans back against the balustrade. Above them, weathered by age and affixed to the building's facade, is a crest carved from stone.

'The coat of arms of the Forlani family. Six stars on a shield, surmounted by a doge's crown. The palace dates from 1770.'

'That's amazing. Do the family still live here?'

'Yes,' he says, turning back to face the canal. 'We do.'

She stares at him. 'You? You . . . own this?'

'My father does.'

She shakes her head. 'That must be . . . extraordinary.'

Half turning to her, he runs a finger down her cheek. 'It is what it is.'

She looks back at him. The sculpted features, their perfection at once marred and confirmed by the broken nose. The crisp whiteness of the linen shirt against his skin, with the cuffs rolled just so high up his tanned forearms. The elegant musculature displayed by jeans that look ordinary enough, but undoubtedly cost many hundreds of euros. The nonchalant absence of socks, and the black velvet loafers embroidered with what, on inspection, turns out to be the Forlani family crest.

She smiles. 'You're just that tiny bit too good to be true, aren't you? And you're not quite as young as you'd have me believe, either.' She mirrors his gesture, running a finger across his cheekbone. 'How many other women have you brought out here? Quite a few, I'm sure.'

'You're a scary woman, Eve. I haven't even kissed you yet.'

Desire ripples through her with unexpected force. 'That sounds lovely, but it's not going to happen.'

'Seriously?'

She shakes her head.

'That's a pity, Eve. For you and for me.'

'I expect we'll both survive, one way and another. And now I have to find my friend.'

Looking into the interior, she sees Giovanna moving towards them. 'And here she is. Claudio, this is—'

'I know who it is. *Buona sera*, Giovanna.'

'*Buona sera*, Claudio.' There's a moment's silence.

'I should go,' Claudio says. He bows, with just detectable irony, to both of them. '*Arrivederci*.'

'Well,' says Giovanna, watching him disappear into the crowd. 'You don't waste any time. And as it happens, neither do I. I have some news for you.'

'Tell me.'

'I was talking to the Contessa di Faenza, a big customer of mine. And I realised that the woman standing next to her was wearing the scent I told you about. The one the Russian who bought your bracelet . . .'

'Oh my God. Go on.'

'Well, the contessa is talking to me about some prêt-à-porter show she's been to in Milan, and I see the other woman walk away. Obviously I can't just follow her, but I watch her, and remember what she's wearing, and five minutes later, when the contessa finally lets me go, I set off in search of her.'

'And?'

'I can't find her. I look everywhere, on both floors, but she's disappeared. And then I go into the Ladies', and there she is, standing in front of the mirror, actually putting on the scent. So I walk behind her, and check that it's the one I remembered, and it is.'

'You're sure?'

'Absolutely sure. Freesia, amber, white cedar . . . So I tell her how much I like it, we get talking – her name's Signora Valli, it turns out – and I ask her what her scent is called.' She hands Eve a folded slip of paper. 'I wrote the name down this time, to make sure.'

Eve opens the paper and stares at the single word written there. There's a moment of ferocious clarity, as if ice-water is racing through her veins. 'Thank you, Giovanna,' she whispers. 'Thank you so, so much.'

Oxana is lying on a steel bunk in a Russian *stolypin* prison train surrounded by grey, indistinct figures. There are no windows; she has no idea of the terrain through which the train is moving, nor does she know how long she has been on the train. Days, certainly, perhaps weeks. The steel-panelled *stolypin* compartment is her whole world. It smells of shit and piss and rancid bodies, but the cold is worse. The cold is like death, and its icy hand is closed around her heart.

A figure stirs on the bunk opposite her. 'You're wearing my bracelet, Villanelle.'

She tries to explain, to show Eve her bare, shackle-bruised wrists. 'My name is Oxana Vorontsova,' she says.

'Where's Villanelle?'

'Dead. Like the others.'

Jolting awake, her heart pounding, Villanelle gradually identifies the outlines of her room at the Gasthof Lili. It's just gone 3 a.m. The room is cold, she's naked, and the duvet has slipped from the narrow bed onto the floor. 'Fuck you, Polastri,' she mutters, pulling on her tracksuit and wrapping herself in the duvet. 'Get out of my head.'

Four hundred miles away, Eve is also awake, sitting on the side of her hotel bed in her bunny-print pyjamas. Her feet are on the terrazzo-tiled floor and her head is in her hands. She's pretty sure she's going to be sick. She closes her eyes. Immediately, her equilibrium goes into free-fall, and she staggers towards the window, bile rising in her throat. A desperate fumble with the shutters, a glimpse of the canal rocking dark and greasy below, and she's clutching the rail of the balcony, and vomiting, far from silently, into a moored gondola.

5

It's late afternoon, and an animated buzz and the clink of glassware rises from the departure lounge at Flugrettungs-zentrum, Innsbruck's heliport, as Max Linder's invited guests talk, laugh and sip Pol Roger champagne. Those present are not the entire contingent of guests; some were flown up to the Felsnadel earlier in the day, others will follow tomorrow, and the atmosphere is one of high anticipation. In far-right circles Linder is known as a witty, generous and imaginative host. To be invited to one of his mountain retreats is not only to be identified as one of the elite, it is to be guaranteed a spectacularly good time. Max, everyone agrees, is *fun*.

No one pays much attention to the slight figure with the scrappy ponytail standing by the plate-glass exit door. Her passive demeanour and her cheap clothes and luggage clearly identify her as a person of no consequence, and she speaks to no one. When she arrived at the heliport an hour ago she identified herself to the Felsnadel Hotel representa-tive as Violette Duroc, a temporary room attendant sent by a local personnel agency. The hotel representative glanced at a clipboard, crossed her name off a list, and made it clear to her that although she was to be flown up to the Felsnadel with the hotel guests, fraternising with them was strictly *verboten*.

If Villanelle is invisible to her fellow travellers, they are not invisible to her. Over the course of the last fortnight, she has researched most of them in considerable depth. The highest-status person in the room is probably Magali Le Meur. As the recently elected leader of France's Nouvelle Droite party, and an advocate of pan-European nationalism, Le Meur is regarded as the future of the country's far-right tendency. In the flesh, her broad, raw-boned features look older than on the posters slapped en bloc onto every derelict wall and motorway bridge in France. She probably wouldn't wear that thousand-euro Moncler coat to address her party's rank and file, Villanelle reflects. Or that Cartier diamond watch. Would she be amusing in bed? Unlikely. Nice eyes, but that thin, intolerant mouth told another story.

Le Meur touches her glass to that of Todd Stanton, formerly a CIA psy-ops officer, more recently an expert in the harvesting and manipulation of online personal data. Often described as the dark cardinal of the American far right, Stanton is widely believed to be the architect of the Republican Party's recent electoral victories. Today, he's wearing a wolfskin coat, which does little to flatter his corpulent frame or to distract from his florid complexion.

Beyond them, by the bar, three men and a woman circle each other warily. Leonardo Venturi, a tiny, wild-haired figure sporting a monocle, is an Italian political theorist and the founder of Lapsit Exillis, described on its website as 'an initiatory guild for aristocrats of the spirit'. Venturi is explaining the guild's mission in exhaustive detail to Inka

122

Järvi, the statuesque leader of Finland's Daughters of Odin. Adjacent to them, not quite part of their conversation, are two Britons. Richard Baggot, a paunchy figure with a crocodile grin, is the leader of the UK Patriots Party, while pencil-thin Silas Orr-Hadow is an upper-caste Tory whose family have furnished England with several generations of fascist sympathisers.

The other three figures Villanelle doesn't recognise. They weren't on her list of probable Felsnadel guests or she would certainly have remembered them. There's an imperious, pantherine woman with a severe bob of dark hair, who flicks a briefly curious glance at Villanelle, and two sharply handsome men. All are probably in their late twenties, and are outfitted in black uniforms with a distinctly military edge.

'Are you Violette?' a voice asks at her side.

'Yes.'

'Hi, I'm Johanna. I'm from the agency too.' She has close-set eyes, freckles and a substantial bust zipped into a pink quilted jacket. She looks like Khriusha the Pig, a puppet character from a TV series Villanelle watched as a child in Perm. 'Have you ever worked at the hotel before?'

'No,' says Villanelle. 'What's it like?'

'Amazing place, but the money's shit, as you've probably found out. And the manageress, Birgit, is a real *arschfotze*. You have to work like a slave or she's on your tits the whole time.'

'What about the guests?'

'Really fun. And some quite . . .' She giggles. 'I worked here last year when Max's party came. There was a fancy dress party on the last night and it was like, crazy.'

'So how long are you going to be working up there this time?'

'Just a couple of weeks. I'm temporarily replacing an African girl. Obviously they couldn't have an immigrant up there with these guests, so they laid her off.'

'Without pay?'

'*Natürlich*. Why would they pay her if she isn't working?'

'Right.'

'See, Violette, the thing about Max Linder's guests is that they like traditionally minded staff. Girls they can relate to. Some of the men can get quite frisky.' She glances downwards at her chest with a complacent smile. 'But maybe they'll leave you alone.'

'So who are those three? They look younger than most of the people here.'

'The band, Panzerdämmerung. They played up there last year. Weird music, super-dark, super-loud, not really my thing. But the two brothers, Klaus and Peter Lorenz. *Total geil*.'

'And the woman in the leather coat and the boots?'

'Is the singer, Petra Voss. Apparently . . .' – Johanna lowers her voice to a whisper – 'she's a lesbian.'

'Never!'

Departure is announced, and the guests make their way through the glass doors to the helipad where the Airbus helicopter is waiting. Villanelle and Johanna leave last, and then have to edge past the other passengers to reach their seats at the back of the aircraft.

'Don't I remember you from last year?' Richard Baggot asks Johanna as she passes, and when she smiles and nods,

124

reaches across and pats her bottom. 'Looks like I'll be needing room service, then.' He turns to Villanelle. 'Sorry, love. Prefer a little more flesh on the bone, if you get my drift.'

Todd Stanton grins, Silas Orr-Hadow looks appalled, and the others ignore Baggot altogether. As she buckles herself into her seat, Villanelle entertains a brief fantasy of leaning forward and garrotting the Englishman with his golf club tie. One day, she promises herself, and glances at Johanna, on whose pink features a dimpled smirk has appeared.

The helicopter takes off with a roar and a shudder. Beyond the Plexiglas window the sky is steel grey. Soon they are above the snowline, and climbing. Gazing out at the face of the Teufelkamp, at the precipitous crags and blue-white icefields, Villanelle feels a prickling anticipation. To those present she is a menial, not worth a second glance, barely even fuckable. But inside herself she can feel the demon of her fury coil and uncoil. With the tip of her tongue, she touches the pale knot of scar tissue on her upper lip, feels its throb echoed in her chest, the pit of her stomach and her groin.

The helicopter swings upwards and rounds a vertical spur. And there, like a crystal set into the black rock face, is the hotel, and in front of it, a horizontal shelf marked out with lights as a landing area. The passengers applaud, gasp and crane towards the windows.

'What do you think?' asks Johanna. 'Amazing, no?'

'Yes.'

They touch down, the door opens, and frozen air blasts into the interior of the Airbus. Climbing out after Johanna, Villanelle steps into a flurry of wind-blown snow, and follows the other guests into the hotel, pulling her cabin bag behind her.

The entrance hall is spectacular, its plate-glass walls affording a breathtaking view of the darkening *massif*. A hundred feet below, clouds stream past, carried on the racing wind. Above are silhouetted peaks, and the glitter of the stars.

'Johanna, come with me. And you must be Violette. Quickly now, both of you.'

The speaker is a severely dressed woman in her forties. Without introducing herself she leads them at a fast clip through a side door and into a service corridor leading to the staff quarters at the back of the hotel. She deals with Villanelle first, briskly pushing open a numbered door into a small, low-ceilinged room containing twin beds. A pale young woman in a tracksuit and woollen beanie is lying on one of these, asleep.

'Get up, Maria.'

Blinking, the young woman jumps nervously to her feet, pulling off the beanie.

'Violette, you're in here with Maria. You're both on duty for dinner tonight; Maria will tell you the house rules, and where to find your uniform. She'll also explain your room-service duties for tomorrow. Understood, Maria?'

'Yes, Birgit.'

'Violette?'

'Yes.'

'Yes, *Birgit*.' She regards Villanelle intently. 'You're not going to be trouble, are you? Because I swear, try anything on with me – *anything* – and you'll regret it. Won't she, Maria?'

126

'Yes, Birgit,' Maria says. 'She will.'

'Good. I'll see you both in an hour.' She starts to leave and then switches back. 'Violette, show me your fingernails.'

Villanelle holds out her hands. Birgit examines them frowningly.

'Teeth.'

Villanelle complies.

'How did you get that scar?'

'A dog bit me. Birgit.'

Birgit stares at her suspiciously. 'Wash your face before you appear in the restaurant.' She leans towards Villanelle, her nose wrinkling. 'And your hair. It smells.'

'Yes, Birgit.' Villanelle and Maria watch as the manager-ess leaves the room, followed by the still-smirking Johanna.

'Welcome to the insane asylum.' Maria smiles wearily.

'Is she always like that?'

'Sometimes worse. I'm not kidding.'

'Fuck.'

'*Tak*. And you're stuck here now. That's your bed. And the bottom two drawers are yours.'

Maria is Polish, she tells Villanelle. There are men and women from at least a dozen countries employed at the Felsnagel, and although spoken German is a requirement, the staff usually speak English among themselves.

'Watch out for Johanna. She pretends to be really friendly, and on your side, but anything you tell her goes straight back to Birgit. She's a spy.'

'OK, I'll remember. So what are these house rules?'

Maria recites a litany of fetishistically precise regulations. 'Hair always to be worn braided, with plain steel pins,' she says in conclusion. 'No make-up, ever. Max Linder hates make-up on women, so no foundation, lipstick, anything. And no perfume. The only thing you're allowed to smell of is disinfectant soap, and you have to use that regularly. Birgit checks.'

'She's employed by the hotel?'

'God, no. She's employed by Linder, to make sure that everything runs the way he likes it. She's a fucking Nazi, basically, like him.'

'So what happens if you break the rules?'

'First time, she cuts your pay. After that, I don't know, and I don't want to find out. There are stories that she whipped a girl once for wearing mascara.'

'Wow. That's quite sexy.'

Maria stares at her. 'Are you serious?'

'I'm joking. Where's the bathroom?'

'End of the corridor. There's usually not much hot water, especially by this time. Your soap's in the top drawer. I'll fill you in about tonight when you get back. And Violette . . .'

'What?'

'Don't make trouble. Please.'

It's just after 6 p.m., London time, when Eve and Lance walk into the Goodge Street office, carrying their overnight bags. They've taken the Underground from Heathrow, which was slow, but not as slow as battling through the rush-hour traffic in a taxi.

Billy swivels his chair to face them. On the floor beside him is a small tower of foil takeaway cartons. He stretches lethargically and yawns, like an inadequately exercised cat. 'Good flight?'

'Had worse.' Lance drops his bags and noses the air. 'Did something die in here while we were away?'

'How are you, Billy?' Eve asks.

'Not bad. Tea?'

'God, yes please.'

'Lance?'

'Yeah, go on.'

Eve resists the urge to open the streaming window and let a little air into the curried fug of the office. She's anxious for Billy to do two things. To find out everything possible about Rinat Yevtukh, the Ukrainian who went missing in Venice, and to launch a worldwide search of recent internet traffic for the name, or codename, Villanelle. Both undertakings are likely to be complex, and experience has taught Eve that to get the best out of Billy, you don't rush him.

'How's it been?' she asks him.

'Same,' Billy says, moving unhurriedly towards the sink and flipping a tea bag into each of the mugs on the draining board.

'What the lady means is, did you miss us?' says Lance.

'Didn't really notice you weren't here, to be honest.'

Lance unzips his overnight bag and pulls out a package, which he throws to Billy.

'What's this?'

'Souvenir of Venice, mate. Just to show we were thinking about you slaving away while we were living the dream.'

'Nice one.'

It's a gondolier's red and white striped T-shirt. Eve darts a grateful look at Lance; never once did it occur to her to pick up anything for Billy.

'So where are we?' she asks Billy, when the tea has been circulated.

'I've been chasing Tony Kent.'

'Anything new?'

'Bits and pieces.'

'Spill.'

Billy swivels back towards his screens. 'OK, background. Kent is an associate, friend, whatever, of Dennis Cradle, now dead. The money that the Twelve used to pay Cradle was routed via Kent, and the original source for this information is a document provided to Eve in Shanghai by Jin Qiang of the MSS, the Chinese Ministry of State Security. Agree so far?'

Eve nods.

'Open source intelligence on Kent is hard to find. Basically, his online presence has been scrubbed. Not a whisper on social media, and highly selective bio-data. Enough detail not to look deliberately redacted, but nothing that leads anywhere.'

In her pocket, Eve's phone vibrates. Without looking she knows it's Niko. Billy glances at her, wondering if she's going to take the call, but she ignores it.

'Even so, I've been able to join up one or two of the dots. Kent is fifty-one years old. No kids, two divorces.'

'Are the ex-wives contactable?'

'Yes, one now lives in Marbella, in Spain, and the other runs a Staffordshire bull-terrier rescue centre in Stellenbosch, South Africa. I rang them both, saying I was trying to get in touch with Tony. The first one, Letitia, was so drunk she could hardly speak, even though it was only eleven o'clock in the morning. She said she hadn't seen Kent in years, had no idea how to contact him, and if I saw him to tell him to go and – I quote – "fucking throttle himself". Ring a bell, Lance?'

'Loud and clear. Last time I saw my ex she said much the same thing.'

'Lol. Anyway, the South Africa one, Kyla, was perfectly friendly but said that she was bound by law from discussing her ex-husband with anyone, which I took to mean that she'd signed a non-disclosure agreement as a condition of her divorce settlement. So not much help there. Anyway, back to Kent. He grew up in Lymington, Hampshire, and was educated at Eton College. As, it turns out, was Dennis Cradle.'

'They weren't there together, were they?' Eve asks.

'Yes, Kent was Cradle's fag. Which means, apparently, that he was like his personal servant, and had to clean his shoes and make him tea and warm his toilet seat in the winter.'

'Seriously?'

'Totally.'

'Bloody hell. I knew those places were weird, but . . .' She blinks. 'How did you find all this out?'

'I asked Richard to run both names through the Security Services vetting records, and both were on file.'

'Cradle, obviously. But why Kent?'

'After Eton, Cradle goes to Oxford, takes the Civil Service exam, and is headhunted by MI5. Four years later Kent goes to Durham, and after graduating, tries to join Cradle at Thames House, but fails selection.'

'Any idea why?' Eve asks.

'Put it like this: one of the assessors ended his evaluation with the words "Sly, manipulative, untrustworthy".'

'Sounds like the ideal candidate,' says Lance.

'The MI5 selection panel don't think so. They bin him, and the following year he goes to Sandhurst, and is commissioned as a second lieutenant in the Royal Logistics Corps. Serves two tours of duty in Iraq, leaves the army in his late twenties, and from that point onwards things get hazy. I found only two very brief press references to his activities over the next decade. One describes him as a London-based venture capitalist, one as an international security consultant.'

'Which can mean pretty much anything,' Eve says.

'Yeah, well. Turns out that Kent owns no residential or commercial property in London, and a search at Companies House reveals that he holds no directorships, executive or non-exec, of UK-registered companies. So given the Twelve connection, I start looking for Russian interests. I don't speak Russian fluently, but a lot of the international registries are in English, including the database of the Federal State Service for Statistics. Anyway, I discover that Kent's a partner in a private security company named Sverdlovsk-Futura Group or SFG, based in Moscow. He's also a partner in an offshoot of the company, SF12, which is registered in the British Virgin Islands.'

'And do we know what these companies do?'

'Well, this is the point at which my lack of Russian becomes a problem. I'm learning the language via the MI6 online course, but I'm nowhere near fluent. So Richard puts me in touch with a Russian-speaking investigator from the City of London Economic Crime department, a guy called Sim Henderson. And what Sim tells me is that private security companies, known as *Chastnye Voennie Companiy*, or ChVKs, have become the go-to option for Russian military activities abroad. Official and deniable. Under the Russian constitution, any deployment of ChVK personnel must be approved by the upper house of parliament. But here's where it gets interesting. If the company's registered abroad, Russia and its parliament are not legally responsible.'

'And you say that the offshoot company, whatever it's called, is registered in the BVI?' Eve says.

'Exactly.'

'So on the one hand you've got the official company, with a turnover of . . .'

'A hundred and seventy million dollars, give or take. SFG handle everything from security for hospitals, airports and gas pipelines to military adviser contracts.'

'All transparent and above board?'

'Basically, yeah. I mean, this is Russia we're talking about, so they're almost certainly paying a hefty percentage to the Kremlin for the privilege of staying in business, but . . . yeah.'

'And meanwhile the not-so-official, foreign-registered arm—'

'SF12.'

'SF12, yes, is going its own merry way, doing whatever . . .'

'Exactly. Whatever weird dark-side shit it feels like.'

Max Linder has specified that, for the duration of his private gathering, the female catering staff of the Felsnadel should wear the uniform of the Bund Deutscher Mädel, the female equivalent of the Hitler Youth. Accordingly, Villanelle is wearing a blue skirt, a short-sleeved white blouse, and a black neckerchief secured by a leather woven knot. Her hair, still damp from her tepid shower, is in a short pigtail. She's holding a circular tray of cocktails.

There are perhaps twenty guests in the dining hall, which is set with a single long table. Apart from those she arrived with, Villanelle recognises a number of prominent far-right figures from Scandinavia, Serbia, Slovenia and Russia. Most have entered into the spirit of the occasion. There are polished boots, cross-straps and daggers hanging from stable-belts. Magali Le Meur has a forage cap pinned to her blonde up-do, while Silas Orr-Hadow is sporting leder-hosen and white knee socks.

'So what have we here, *fräulein*?'

Her smile tightens. It's Roger Baggot, in a loud tweed suit.

'Cocktails, sir. This is a Zionist, this is a Snowflake, and this is an Angry Feminist.'

'What's in this one?'

'Mostly Crème de Menthe and Fernet Branca.'

'So why's it called an Angry Feminist?'

'Probably because it's difficult to get it to go down, sir.'

He roars with laughter. 'Well, you're a sharp little piece of work, aren't you? What's your name?'

'Violette, sir.'

'I take it you're not a feminist, Violette?'

'No, sir.'

'Glad to hear it. Now please point me to where I can get some decent beer. We're in fucking Germany, after all.'

'Over there, sir. And for the record, sir, until the estab-lishment of the Fourth Reich, we're in fucking Austria.'

134

Baggot retreats, grinning bemusedly, and at that moment, to loud whoops and applause, Max Linder enters the dining hall. It's Villanelle's first sight of the man she has come to kill, and she takes a long hard look. Elegant in a high-buttoning Bavarian *trachten* jacket, his platinum-blond quiff shining in the spotlight, Linder looks less like a politician than a member of a fascistically inclined boy band. His smile reveals orthodontically perfect teeth, but there's something avid about it too. A twist to the lips that suggests a hunger for the extreme.

They sit down to dinner, Linder taking the head of the table. As the courses come and go – lobster thermidor, roasted boar with juniper, crêpes Suzette flambés, Dachsteiner and Bergkäse cheese – Villanelle and the other serving women pour the accompanying wines and spirits. As she does so, Villanelle catches fragments of the diners' conversations. Max Linder is sitting next to Inka Järvi, but spends much of the meal talking across her to Todd Stanton.

'Can you guarantee the result?' Linder asks Stanton.

The American, his face flushed, drains his etched crystal glass of Schloss Gobelsburg Riesling, and indicates to Villanelle that he wants it refilled. 'Look, Max, the population of Austria is eight and three-quarter million. Four and three-quarters of those use the same social media platform. Mine that data, and you'll know more about those dumb motherfuckers than they know about themselves.'

'And the cost?' Inka Järvi interjects, as Villanelle pours Stanton's wine.

'Well now . . .' Stanton begins, but at that moment Villanelle sees Birgit beckoning to her from the other end of the room.

Birgit tells Villanelle that she is to take part in a ceremony in front of the hotel at the meal's conclusion.

'So what does it involve?'

'Whom are you addressing, Violette?'

'I'm sorry. What does it involve, *Birgit*?'

'You'll see. Wait in the entrance hall after the meal.'

'No problem, Birgit. Where's the staff toilet, by the way? I need to—'

'You should have gone earlier. Right now, you need to return to the guests.'

'Birgit, I've been standing up for an hour and a half.'

'I'm not interested. Exercise some self-control.'

Villanelle stares at her, then slowly turns and walks back to her place. Stanton, his face by now flushed a livid mauve, is still talking across Inka Järvi to Linder. 'I said, dude, think about it. *The Protocols of the Elders of Zion* as a musical. Give me one motherfucking reason why not.'

On the bus going home, squashed into her seat by an obese man who smells of damp hair and beer, Eve attempts to organise her thoughts. Beyond the rain-streaked windows, Warren Street tube station and the Euston Road intersection pass in an illuminated blur, so familiar that she only half sees them. She's left Billy with instructions to find out all he can about Rinat Yevtukh, and to search the darkest reaches of cyberspace for any mention of Villanelle. She feels a rush of exhilaration. It's good to be back. Venice is already a dream, and now she's going home to Niko. And the goats.

It comes as a shock to see him on crutches, with one foot in an orthopaedic boot. She'd forgotten that he's broken his ankle. Forgotten about the boy stepping into the road, the accident, the entire phone conversation. The realisation freezes her to the spot, and when she lunges forward to give Niko a hug she almost pushes him off balance. 'I'm sorry,' she says, wrapping her arms around his chest. 'I'm so, so sorry.'

'For what?'

'I don't know. Being a shit wife. Not being here. Everything.'

'You're here now. Hungry?'

He's made a stew. Ham hock, Polish sausage, porcini mushrooms and juniper berries. Two cold bottles of Baltika beer stand next to the casserole dish. It's a lot better than anything she had in Venice. 'I spent half a day in the main police station, and it only occurred to me afterwards that that's where I should have asked where to go to eat. Cops always know.'

'How was it with Lance?'

'How was it? You mean working with him?'

'Working with him, hanging out with him . . .'

'Better than I expected. Street-smart but socially dysfunctional, like a lot of older field agents.' She tells him the Noel Edmonds story.

'Smooth.'

'Yeah, I just wanted to . . .' She shakes her head. 'Tell me about your foot.'

'Ankle.'

'I mean ankle. What did they say at the hospital?'

He shrugs. 'That it's fractured.'

'That's all?'

He smiles faintly. 'They did suggest some exercises I could do to make the bone mend faster.'

'So have you been doing them?'

'No, they involve you.'

'Ah, those exercises.' She touches his face. 'Perhaps we could pencil something in for tomorrow night?'

'We could make a start now.'

'I'm pretty wiped out. And you look tired too. Why don't we watch TV in bed? You choose something. I'll clear up.'

'I suppose I could settle for that. Will you put the girls to bed?'

Thelma and Louise bleat and snicker as Eve orders them off the sofa and dispatches them to their quarters. Hearing the clump of Niko's orthopaedic boot in the bedroom, she remembers Claudio's neat, tanned feet in the velvet loafers embroidered with the Forlani crest. Claudio, she reflects, would not see the point of the goats at all.

Taking her phone from her bag, she runs a search for 'Villanelle, scent' and is directed to the website of Maison Joliot, in the rue du Faubourg St Honoré in Paris. The perfumery has been owned by the same family for many generations, and its most expensive range is named Poésies. It comprises four fragrances: Kyrielle, Rondine, Triolet and Villanelle. All come in identical vials, the first three with a white ribbon at the neck. The fourth, Villanelle, has a scarlet ribbon.

Gazing at the screen, Eve is possessed with a sudden and unexpected longing. She's always thought of herself as a fundamentally cerebral person, contemptuous of extravagance. But gazing at the tiny image on the screen, she feels her certainties shifting. Recent events have taught her that she is not as immune to luxury and the purely sensual things of life as she once thought. Venice at nightfall, the weightless caress of the Laura Fracci dress, the touch of a six-thousand-euro bracelet on her wrist. All so seductive, and all in some essential sense so corrupt, so cruel. Villanelle, she reads, was the favourite scent of the Comtesse du Barry. The perfume house added the red ribbon after she was guillotined in 1793.

'Niko, sweetie,' Eve calls out. 'You know you say you love me.'

'I may at some point have mentioned something to that effect, yes.'

'Because there's something I'd really, really like. Some scent.'

At the Felsnadel Hotel, the meal is in its terminal stages, with bottles of Cognac, Sambuca, Jägermeister and other spirits circulating. Leonardo Venturi, his tiny hands cradling a balloon glass of Bisquit Interlude Reserve brandy, is explaining his personal philosophy to Magali Le Meur. 'We are the descendants of the grail knights,' he says, glaring at her breasts through his monocle. 'New men, beyond good and evil.'

'And new women, perhaps?'

'When I say men, I mean women too, naturally.'

'Naturally.'

In the entrance hall, Birgit issues Villanelle and the other serving women with floor-length black cloaks and long-handled combustible torches. Villanelle has asked once again to be allowed to go to the toilet, and has once again been refused. Sympathetic glances from her fellow staff members suggest that they've been victims of the same obsessively controlling behaviour. Ordering them outside onto the snow-covered plateau in front of the hotel, Birgit positions the serving women in lines of six on either side of the helicopter landing pad. This has now been swept of snow and converted into a music stage, with speaker-towers to left and right. At the front of the stage is a microphone stand, at the rear a drum-kit bearing the Panzerdämmerung logo.

When the twelve women are in place, Birgit walks to each of them in turn and lights the wicks of their torches with an electronic gas lighter. 'When the guests come out, lift the torches up in front of you, as high as you can,' she orders them. 'And on pain of dismissal, do not move.'

It's piercingly cold, and Villanelle pulls her cloak around her. The burning oil in the torches sputters faintly in the frozen air. Ice particles swirl on the wind. Finally the guests saunter out of the hotel, warmly wrapped in coats and furs, and Villanelle raises her flaming torch in front of her. The guests arrange themselves on either side of the stage and then Linder appears, picked out by a spotlight, and marches to the microphone.

'Friends,' he begins, raising his hands to silence the applause. 'Welcome to Felsnadel. I can't tell you how inspiring it is to see you all here. In a minute the band are going to start playing, but before they do, I just want to say this. As a movement, we're gathering speed. The dark European soul is awakening. We're creating a new reality. And that's in great part due to all of you. We're winning supporters every day, and why? *Because we're fucking sexy.*'

Pausing, Linder acknowledges the cheers of his guests.

'What woman, and what sensible man, doesn't fancy a bad-boy nationalist? Everyone wants to be us, but most people just don't dare. And to all those sad liberal snow-flakes out there, I say this. *Watch out, bitches.* If you're not at the high table with us, tasting the glory, you're on the menu.'

This time the whoops and cheers are deafening. As they finally die away Linder steps to one side of the stage and the three members of Panzerdämmerung enter from the other. As Klaus Lorenz slips his arm through the strap of a bass guitar, and Peter Lorenz takes his place behind the drums, Petra Voss walks to the microphone. She's dressed in a white blouse, calf-length skirt and boots, and carrying a blood-red Fender Stratocaster guitar slung like an assault rifle.

She starts to sing, her fingers picking softly at the strings. The song is about loss, about forgotten rituals, extinguished flames and the death of tradition. Her voice hardens and her guitar-playing, underlined now by Klaus Lorenz's bass, takes on a steely resonance. She doesn't move or sway but just stands there, motionless except for the dance of her fingers. For a long moment she stares straight at Villanelle, expressionless.

Villanelle stares back, and then turns her attention to the guests, who stand rapt in the flickering torchlight. Max Linder is watching them too. His gaze scans the group dispassionately, noting their reactions to the spectacle that he has created for them.

On the drums, Peter Lorenz has been maintaining a tick-ing backbeat, but now he ramps up the pace. A recorded track of a political speech, ranting and incoherent, coun-terpoints Petra Voss's edgy, insinuating guitar. The drums continue to build until all other sound is annihilated. It's the sound of battalions marching through the night, of lands laid waste, and as it reaches a climax and stops dead, a starburst of spotlights pierces the darkness, illuminating the surrounding mountain peaks. It's an awesome sight, ghostly and desolate in the ringing silence. The guests break into applause, and Villanelle, taking advantage of the diversion, lengthily and copiously pisses herself.

Eve and Niko doze through most of the TV show they're watching in bed. Opening her eyes to discover the end-titles rolling, Eve reaches for the remote control. For several minutes she lies there in near-darkness, her thoughts vague, as Niko shifts beside her. Every time he moves he's twitched into wakefulness by his fractured ankle, but eventually fatigue and codeine prevail, and he sleeps.

Claudio. Suppose she'd let him kiss her. How would it have gone from there?

The kiss itself would have been brief and efficient. A formal statement of his intention and of her acquiescence. He would have taken her somewhere in the palazzo, into some suggestively appointed chamber for which he always carried the key. There would be few words and no wasted time. He would be a serial womaniser with a well-worn routine, refined by scores or perhaps hundreds of such encounters. The choreography would be fluent and the narrative arc conventional, proceeding to a showy money-shot for which she would be expected to display gasping and incredulous gratitude. He would be back in his clothes within minutes, his handmade loafers barely cooler than when he kicked them off. She would be left with a crumpled dress, the musky taint of his cologne, and sticky breasts.

Nevertheless, as Niko's breathing slows to an even rise and fall, her hand steals down her belly, and she finds herself shockingly ready. But it's not Claudio, or indeed Niko, who's waiting behind her closed eyes, but a much more imprecise figure, all contradictions. Soft skin over coiled muscle, a killer's fingers, a rasping tongue, eyes of twilit grey.

I climbed in one night to watch you sleep.

Eve rolls onto her hand, her fingers wet. Fear and desire fold into each other in successive waves until her shoulders and neck rise, her forehead presses the sheet, and the breath leaves her body in a long, ebbing sigh.

After a while she turns onto her side. Niko is watching her, his gaze unblinking.

6

Eve slips from the bed before Niko wakes. When she emerges from Goodge Street Underground station the pavement is still shining from the night's rain, but the sky is washed with a thin sunlight. The office door, to her surprise, is unlocked; she enters hesitantly.

'Billy, hi. It's not even eight yet. How long have you been here?'

'Er, all night.'

'Shit, Billy. That's way beyond the call of duty.'

He blinks and runs a hand through his black-dyed hair. 'Yeah, well. Kicked off the search into that guy Yevtukh, and one thing led to another.'

'Anything we can use?'

'Yeah, I'd say so.'

'Good. Hold that thought. I'm going down to the café.'

'We've got instant. And tea bags.'

'That kettle's gross. What do you want?'

'Well, if you're buying, an almond croissant and a latte. And perhaps a shortbread finger.'

She's back five minutes later. It's clear that Billy's fading. His eyes gleam with exhaustion. Even his lip-ring looks dull. 'Eat,' she says, placing his order in front of him.

Billy takes a large bite of the croissant, showering his keyboard with crumbs, then washes it down with a gulp of coffee. 'OK, Yevtukh. Basically the guy's your typical Sov-bloc gang boss. Or was. Headed up an outfit called the Golden Brotherhood, based in Odessa. Usual stuff. Sex trafficking, people-smuggling and drugs. The Ukrainian police also have him down for at least a dozen murders, but have never been able to get anyone to testify against him.'

'We know all this.'

'OK, but you probably don't know what happened earlier this year. According to a file sent to the Europol database, there was a major shoot-out at a luxury property Yevtukh owned in a place called Fontanka, about fifteen kilometres outside Odessa. By the time the local cops got there the house was pretty much wrecked, and half a dozen people were dead. It was obviously gang-related, so at that point the investigation was handed over to the Ukrainian Criminal Police, who handle serious and violent crime.'

'Was Yevtukh implicated?'

'Not directly. He was in Kiev at the time, seeing his family, but it was his foot-soldiers who died at Fontanka.'

'So do we know who carried out the attack?'

'This is where it gets weird. One of the people found dead at the house was nothing to do with Yevtukh. He was somebody his men had been holding prisoner. He'd been badly beaten up and then shot, and the police couldn't immediately identify him. So a photograph, fingerprints and a DNA sample were sent to the interior security service in Kiev, and they knew who he was straight away. His name was Konstantin Orlov, and he was an ex-head of operations at Directorate S in Moscow.'

'That's more than weird. You know what Directorate S is?'

'I do now. It's the espionage and agent-running wing of the SVR.'

'Exactly. And its Operations Department is like our E Squadron. A special forces team responsible for executing deniable and deep-cover operations overseas.'

'Assassinations, for example.'

'For example.'

Billy stares into the middle distance, almond filling oozing from his croissant.

'Anything else in that Europol report?'

Billy shakes his head. ''Fraid not. No one seems to be able to work out what an ex-Russian spymaster was doing locked in a Ukrainian gangster's house in Odessa. It doesn't make any sense. Or none that I can see. We should ask Richard. Bet he knew this Orlov bloke.'

The door opens and they both look round. It's Lance, an unlit roll-up between his lips.

'Morning, Eve, Billy. Looking a bit rough round the edges, squire, if you don't mind my saying so.'

Taking a deep swig of coffee, Billy makes an up-your-arse gesture with the shortbread finger.

'He's been up all night,' Eve says. 'And he's discovered something a bit bloody brilliant. Listen to this.' Briefly, she puts Lance in the picture.

'So if Orlov was SVR, why would a scumbag like Yevtukh want to go anywhere near him, let alone lock him up and torture him? I'd have thought the last thing someone like that would want to do is to make enemies of the Russian secret service.'

'Orlov was ex-SVR,' Billy says. 'He'd been out for a decade.'

'Doing what, do we know?' asks Lance.

'Stop,' says Eve. 'Both of you. Sorry, but I think we're coming at this from the wrong end.'

'As the actress, etcetera . . .'

'Lance, shut the fuck up. Billy, my coffee. Both of you just . . . shush a minute.' She stands there, motionless. 'OK. Let's ignore for a moment what Orlov was doing, or not doing, in Yevtukh's house in Odessa. Let's think about our assassin, and quite possibly her girlfriend, making Yevtukh disappear in Venice. Why is she, or why are they, doing that?'

'Contract hit?' Lance suggests.

'Almost certainly. But why? What's the motive?'

Lance and Billy shake their heads.

'Suppose it was revenge.'

'Revenge for what?' Billy asks.

'For the killing of Orlov.'

Silence for a heartbeat. 'Bloody hell,' Lance murmurs. 'I see where you're going with this.'

'You're going to have to take it slowly,' says Billy, rubbing his eyes. 'Because I don't.'

'Let's take it from the top,' says Eve. 'Orlov heads up the Operations Department of Directorate S, a bureau whose existence is denied by the authorities, but which is, nevertheless, a reality. He runs a worldwide network of operatives, drawn from secret units in the Russian military and trained as deep-cover spies and assassins. Imagine what kind of man Orlov must have been, to have reached a position like that. Imagine what kind of experience he must have had. And then imagine what happens when he leaves the SVR, as he did ten years ago, armed with all that knowledge and experience.'

'He goes into the private sector,' says Lance.

'That would be my guess. He's recruited by an organisation that needs his particular, perhaps unique, skillset.'

'The Twelve, for instance?'

Eve shrugs. 'It explains the link between him and our female assassin.'

'You're sure we're not making false connections?' Lance says. 'Joining imaginary dots to convince ourselves we're moving forward?'

'I don't think so,' Eve says. 'But I need to talk to Richard. If anyone can shine any light on a figure like Orlov, he can. And one thing's becoming increasingly clear: everything points to Russia. Sooner or later we're actually going to have to go there.'

Lance grins. 'Now you're talking. Proper old-school intelligence work.'

'Cold at this time of year, though,' Billy says. 'Snow makes my asthma flare up.'

'You'd love Moscow, mate. Fit right in.'

'What d'you mean?'

'It's wall-to-wall geeks and metalheads.'

'I've never actually been abroad. Mum doesn't like it.'

'Never?' Eve asks.

'Well, I was going to go to prison in America at one point, but that fell through.'

'What actually happened with all that?' Eve asks. 'I've read the file, but . . .'

In answer Billy pulls up his T-shirt sleeve. There's a tattoo on his doughy upper arm. Five black dots arranged in a grid.

'Fuck's that?' Lance asks.

'Glider pattern from the Game of Life.'

Eve peers at it. 'I literally have no idea what you're talking about.'

'It's a hacker emblem. When I was seventeen, I was in this collective. We never met face to face, but we'd communicate online. We had some pretty advanced tools and basically we'd hack anything we could, especially US corporate and government sites. We didn't do it because we were like, anarchists or anything, but just for the arse of it. Anyway, there was a sort of unofficial leader of the group, called La-Z-boi, who used to direct us to sites, especially foreign government sites. And I will honestly never know how we didn't figure this one out, it's so obvious, but La-Z-boi worked for the FBI, and took us down. Everyone went to prison except me.'

'How come you didn't?' Lance asks.

'Under age.'

'So what happened?'

'Released on bail. Had to live at home with my mum, which is where I lived anyway, but under curfew, and with no access to the internet.'

'And that's when MI6 came knocking?' Eve asks.

'Basically, yeah.'

She nods. 'Get onto Richard. Set up a secure meeting. We need to know more about Orlov.'

Even if it's only a means to an end, Villanelle takes little pleasure in her work at the hotel. She and the other room attendants are required to rise at six thirty, eat a hurried breakfast of cheese, bread and coffee in the kitchen, and then start vacuuming the public spaces of the hotel. When this is complete the morning room-cleaning shift begins.

There are twenty-four guest bedrooms at Felsnadel, and Villanelle is responsible for eight of them. She is expected to start cleaning each room at the end furthest from the door, so that no detail is missed. Every surface – dressing tables, desks, televisions, headboards, wardrobe doors – is to be dusted or wiped down. Wastepaper baskets are emptied, and anything on the desks or bedside table tidied. Beds are then stripped and neatly remade with fresh sheets and pillowcases. In the bathrooms, where room staff are required to wear rubber gloves at all times, cleaning is carried out from top to bottom, starting with mirrors. Baths, shower-stalls and toilets are cleaned and sanitised, towels and toiletries replaced. The suite and its carpets are then vacuumed.

Some rooms require more work than others, and all are revealing of their occupants. Magali Le Meur's room is chaotic, with towels, bedclothes and used underwear strewn over every surface. Her dressing table holds a carton of menthol cigarettes and a half-empty bottle of Peach Amore Schnapps. The bathroom floor is sodden, the toilet unflushed.

Silas Orr-Hadow's room, by contrast, looks barely touched. He's made his own bed, folded and put away all his clothes, and left the bathroom exactly as he has found it. On the desk, every book, paper and pencil is aligned and squared off. On his bedside table is a photograph of an anxious-looking bespectacled boy, recognisably Orr-Hadow himself, holding the hand of a uniformed nanny. Beside it are two well-thumbed hardback books: *Winnie the Pooh* and *Mein Kampf.*

By the time Villanelle reaches Roger Baggot's room, her eighth and last, she's in a vengeful mood. The place reeks of cologne, and when Villanelle strips the bed she discovers a woman's crumpled thong, which she guesses to be Johanna's, and a used and knotted condom. When the room is finally presentable, Villanelle allows herself to sink into one of the calfskin-upholstered chairs. If the work is unpleasant, and at times revolting, Villanelle is conscious that her room-attendant duties afford her some badly needed privacy. Maria is a friendly enough room-mate, but her depressive character irritates Villanelle, as does her snoring.

The morning briefing with Birgit has also yielded a single, salient fact: the whereabouts of Linder's room. He's on the first floor, in a spacious suite overlooking the front of the hotel. None of the rooms that Villanelle services is on the first floor. Killing her target is going to require careful timing.

For Linder's guests, the pace of life at Felsnadel is leisurely. There is an extended breakfast offered in the dining room until eleven o'clock. Following this drinks are available outside on the terrace, where reclining chairs, warmed by infrared heaters, are placed to take advantage of the view of the High Tyrol. The sky is a hard, pure blue, against which the snowy ridge-line of the Granatspitze massif shimmers like a blade.

Inside, a series of informal talks is under way. As Villanelle enters the reception area to report to Birgit that her rooms have all been cleaned, the tiny Italian fascist Leonardo Venturi is holding forth to half a dozen admirers.

'Then, finally, the old order will fall,' he declaims. 'And a new golden age will come into being. But this will not be painless. For the new Imperium to be born, the roots of the old must be cut away without pity.'

'Without what, old chap?' asks Orr-Hadow.

'Without *pity*. Without mercy.'

'Sorry, thought for a moment you said without PT.'

'What is PT?'

'Physical training. At my prep school we had it every day. The instructor was an ex-military policeman, and if you didn't do your press-ups properly you had to report for a cold shower. And he'd jolly well watch to make sure you stood there for a full five minutes, too. Marvellous old boy. Sorry, you were saying?'

But Venturi has lost his train of thought, and in the brief hiatus Villanelle makes her way across the reception area to the desk.

Birgit looks up, her expression frosty. 'Room Seven. A complaint. You need to go straight away and deal with it.'

'Yes, Birgit.'

Room Seven is Petra Voss's. When Villanelle knocks on the door and opens it with her pass key, Petra is lying on the bed, smoking. She's wearing jeans and an ironed white shirt.

'Come over here, Violette. That is your name, isn't it?'

'Yes.'

Petra stares at her. 'You're quite a piece of work in that uniform, aren't you? Quite the Aryan cutie-pie.'

'If you say so.'

'I do say so. Bring me something I can use as an ashtray.'

In response, Villanelle reaches forward, and takes the cigarette from Petra's mouth. She walks over to the window, opens it, admitting a blast of cold air, and throws the cigarette out into the snow.

'So. You don't approve of me.'

'You're a guest. Obey the rules.'

Petra smiles. 'Actually, I'm not a fucking guest. I'm paid to be here. A lot.'

'Whatever.'

'Such attitude from the maid.' Languidly, Petra swings her legs from the bed, and stands so that she is eye to eye with Villanelle. Very slowly and deliberately, she draws Villanelle's black neckerchief through its woven leather knot. 'But then I'm your type, aren't I?'

Villanelle considers. According to the hotel schedule the afternoon's guest entertainment is an hour-long helicopter flight through the high peaks of the Tyrol and Carinthia, hosted by Linder. It's due to depart from the landing strip at 2 p.m. She's got, perhaps, an hour.

'You might be,' she says.

'Konstantin Orlov,' says Richard. 'How strange to hear his name after all these years.'

He and Eve are sitting at a window table in a department store café. The café is on the fourth floor, overlooking Oxford Street. Eve is drinking tea, and Richard is staring without enthusiasm at a plate of reheated shepherd's pie.

Eve smiles. 'You're wishing you hadn't ordered that now, aren't you?'

'I panicked. *Embarras du choix*. Orlov's dead, you say.'

'Apparently, yes. Killed in unexplained circumstances, near Odessa.'

'Sadly appropriate. His life was a series of unexplained circumstances.' He looks out over the rooftops for a moment, then takes up his fork and determinedly addresses his meal. 'So what's his death got to do with our enquiry?'

'He was killed in the house of a Ukrainian gangster called Rinat Yevtukh. A nasty piece of work.'

'As they so often are. Go on.'

'Last month Yevtukh vanished off the face of the earth while on holiday in Venice, after taking off in a motor launch with an unknown, and reportedly glamorous, young woman. Now we know that our female assassin was in Venice at that time, and I'm wondering if she killed Yevtukh as some kind of punishment for Orlov's death.'

'That presupposes a connection between her and Orlov. Is there any reason to think that such a connection exists?'

Eve sips her tea and lowers her cup to its saucer. 'Not yet. But bear with me. We know that our female assassin – who we're calling Villanelle, by the way, for reasons that I'll explain – was in Venice. We know that she's employed by the Twelve, the organisation that Cradle told us about.'

'Whoever they might be.'

'Yes. Now suppose, for argument's sake, that Orlov worked for them too.'

'Yes, I can see that if you suppose that, you can construct a revenge motive. But just because this woman and Orlov both had a connection to, um . . .'

'Yevtukh.'

'Exactly, to Yevtukh, it doesn't mean to say that they knew each other. Equally, just because she's in Venice at the same time as Yevtukh, it doesn't mean she . . .'

They fall silent as an elderly woman pushes a shopping trolley very slowly past their table. 'I had the cauliflower cheese,' she confides to Eve. 'It tasted of nothing at all.'

'Oh dear. My friend's enjoying his shepherd's pie.'

'That's nice.' The woman peers at Richard. 'Bit simple, is he?'

They watch her go. Eve swallows the last of her tea, and leans forward. 'Of course she killed him, Richard. He went off with her and never came back. The whole affair has her name written all over it.'

'So what is her name again?'

'I'm pretty sure that the name she uses professionally, or as a codename, is Villanelle.'

'How did you arrive at that?'

She explains.

He puts down his fork. 'You're doing it again.'

'What?'

'This woman leaves you a card, sprayed with her scent and signed V. You discover that she uses a scent called Villanelle, so you conclude that she calls herself the same thing. That's guesswork, not a logical consequence of the known facts. And the same is true of the connection between the woman—'

'Villanelle.'

'All right then, if you insist, between Villanelle and Orlov. You want it to be so, so you deduce that it is so. My personal opinion is that we should pursue the Sverdlovsk-Futura line of enquiry that you outlined in your report. Follow the money, in other words.'

'Of course. We should do that. But with respect, I need you to trust me on this, because I'm getting to understand our assassin and how she operates. She gives an impression of recklessness, giving me that bracelet, for example, but actually she takes very calculated risks. She guessed that I'd follow her to Venice, sooner or later, and that I'd figure out that she killed Yevtukh. That's all part of her plan. Because knowing I'm there, just a couple of steps behind, gives the game its edge. She's a psychopath, remember. Emotionally and empathetically, her life is a flatlining blank. What she wants, above all, is to *feel*. Killing gives her a rush, but only a temporary one. She's good at it, it's easy, and the thrill diminishes each time. She needs to jack up the excitement. To know that her wit and her artistry and the sheer horror of what she's doing are appreciated. That's why she's drawing me in. That's why she told me her name, using the perfume. She likes setting me these perverse little puzzles. It's intimate and sensual and hyper-aggressive, all at the same time.'

'Assuming that this is true, why you?'

'Because I'm the one who's after her. I'm the source of the greatest danger to her, and that excites her. Hence the provocations. All that erotic bait-and-switch.'

'Well, it's clearly working.'

'By which you mean what, exactly?'

'I mean that she's calling all the shots.'

'I acknowledge that. I admit that she's been fucking with my head. What I'm suggesting is that we get ahead of the game. Let me go to Russia. I agree that it's possible that

Villanelle and Orlov have no connection, that their lives don't intersect at all, but let's just look and see what we find. Please. Trust me on this.'

Richard is expressionless. For perhaps half a minute he stares out of the window at the busy street below. 'We share a birthday. Shared, I should say.'

'You and Konstantin Orlov?'

'Yes.'

'Were you the same age?'

'No, he was a couple of years older. He fought as a conscript in the Soviet-Afghan War. Served under Vostrotin and was wounded, quite badly, at Khost. Won a medal, a good one, which must have brought him to the attention of someone with a bit of pull, because a couple of years later he turned up at the Andropov Academy. That's the finishing school for spies outside Moscow. It used to be run by the KGB, but by the time Orlov left they'd become the SVR.'

'So this was all . . . when?'

'Khost was in 1988, and Orlov graduated from the Academy in, I'd guess, 1992. One of Yevgeny Primakov's brightest and best, by all accounts. There was a posting in Karachi and then another in Kabul, which is where I met him. Very clever, very charming, and I'd guess completely ruthless.'

'He was declared?'

'Yes, diplomatic cover. So he was on the circuit. But he had fast-track SVR written all over him. And he knew exactly who I was too.'

A staff member, name-tagged 'Agniezka', appears at their table. 'I take?' she asks, nodding at Richard's abandoned shepherd's pie.

'Thank you, yes.'

'Don't like?'

'No. Yes. Just . . . Not hungry.'

'You want feedback form?'

'No, thank you.'

'I give you anyway. You're welcome.'

'Why, in a free world, would you choose to have a tongue piercing?' Richard asks when Agniezka has gone.

'I have no idea.'

'Is it a sex thing?'

'Truly, I don't know. I'll ask Billy. Go on about Orlov.'

'I'll tell you a story about him. We met at a reception at the Russian embassy – this was in Kabul – and after directing me to the best vodka, he introduced me to a colleague of his whom he described as a secretary although we both knew she was no such thing. Anyway she was attractive, and obviously clever, and laughed at my jokes despite my far-from-brilliant Russian, and when she went it was with a backwards glance that lasted just that moment longer than it needed to. It was all done with a very light touch, and when I told Konstantin that I'd love to see her again but just couldn't face the paperwork, he laughed and gave me another glass of Admiralskaya.

'Anyway, I reported the encounter in the usual way and the next day I got a couriered message from Konstantin. He remembered that I'd said I liked bird-watching, and wondered if I'd like to go on a short drive with him outside the city. So I logged the approach, and a couple of days later I met Konstantin in Dar-al-Aman Road outside his embassy, where two vehicles turned up with Afghan drivers and half a dozen wild-looking locals armed with AKs.

We drove out of the city on the Bagram road, past the airport, and half an hour later we turned off in the middle of nowhere, drove round a low hill, and there were all these parked vehicles, and tents, and the smoke from fires. There were thirty or forty people there. Arabs, Afghans, tribespeople and a team of heavily armed bodyguards. So I asked Konstantin, rather nervously, what the hell was this place? And he said, don't worry, it's all fine, look closer.

'And that's when I saw these lines of perches, and on them, these superb birds of prey. Sakers, lanners, peregrines. It was a falconry camp. I followed Konstantin into one of the tents, and there, hooded and ready to fly, were half a dozen gyrfalcons, the most beautiful and expensive hunting birds in the world. There was also a white-bearded guy there, extremely fierce-looking, who Konstantin said was a local tribal chieftain. He introduced us, someone brought us lunch, Coca-Cola and some kind of meat on skewers, and then we drove further into the desert and the falconers flew their birds at bustard and sand-grouse. It was truly spectacular.'

'I would never have had you down as a bird-watcher.'

'I wasn't one until I joined the Service. Then I found out that several of the top Russia hands were birders, and that it wasn't enough to know your Pushkin and Akhmatova, you had to know your waxwings from your wagtails too. So I took it up, and caught the bug.'

'So you had a good day with Orlov?'

'It was an extraordinary day, and I honestly didn't care that I was probably spending it with arms traders, opium dealers and the high command of the Taliban. I wouldn't even have been surprised to have come face to face with Osama bin Laden, who I later learned owned several gyrfalcons.'

'And Orlov didn't make any kind of approach?'

'Lord, no. He was much too smart for that. We talked very little except about the birds and the wildness and strangeness of the occasion. And while he obviously had his professional reasons for cultivating me, I sensed that he took a real pleasure in my enjoyment of the day. I liked him very much, and I meant to return the invitation in some way. I felt that it was important not to be in his debt. But I never got the chance. He was recalled to Moscow shortly afterwards, and we later learned that he'd been appointed chief of Directorate S.'

'Did you ever see him again?'

'Once, very briefly. It was in Moscow at a party for Yuri Modin, who fifty years earlier had been the KGB controller for Philby, Burgess, Maclean and Blunt, the Cambridge spies. Modin, by then pretty old, had just written a book about it all, and Konstantin was something of a disciple of Modin's. They met, I'm guessing, at the Andropov Academy, where Modin was a guest lecturer. He taught a course named "Active Measures", which included subversion, disinformation and assassination, and from the way that Konstantin ran the directorate, it was clear that he had taken Modin's philosophy very much to heart.'

'Then in 2008 Konstantin leaves the SVR altogether. Jumped or pushed?'

'Put it like this: when you're running an SVR directorate it's up or out. And he wasn't promoted.'

'So he might be resentful of his old bosses?'

'From the little I knew of him, that wouldn't have been his way. Konstantin was an old-school Russian fatalist. He'd have taken it philosophically, packed his bags, and moved on.'

'To what, do we know?'

'No. From then to now, when he turns up dead in Odessa, we have absolutely no knowledge of his whereabouts or activities. He vanishes.'

'You don't think that's strange?'

'I do, and it is. But it doesn't tie him to our killer.'

'So what do you think he was doing for the last decade?'

'Gardening at his dacha? Running a nightclub? Salmon fishing in Kamchatka? Who knows?'

'How about placing a lifetime's experience of covert operations at the disposal of the Twelve?'

'Eve, there is no logical reason in the world to believe that that's the case. None.'

'Richard, you didn't hire me for my logical skills. You hired me because I was capable of making the imaginative leaps that this investigation demands. Villanelle might play with the idea of leading us on, of leading *me* on, but when it really matters she covers her tracks like a professional. Like a professional who's been trained by the best. By a man like Konstantin Orlov.'

He frowns, steeples his fingers, and opens his mouth to speak.

'Seriously, Richard, we've got nothing else to go on. I agree with you about the money-trail and the Tony Kent connection, but how long's that going to take us to untangle? Months? Years? The three of us at Goodge Street certainly don't have the resources. Or the experience.'

'Eve—'

'No, listen to me. I know there's a chance that Orlov and the Twelve aren't connected. But if there's a chance they are, even a small one, then surely we have to follow it up. Surely?'

'Eve, it's a no. You can investigate the hell out of Orlov from here, but I'm not sending you to Russia.'

'Richard, please.'

'Look, either you're wrong, and there's no connection, in which case it's a waste of your time and my resources. Or you're right, in which case I'd be encouraging you, in the most irresponsible fashion imaginable, to place yourself in harm's way. You turn up in Russia and start asking questions about political assassinations and the careers of men like Orlov . . . I don't even want to think about the consequences. Or, for that matter, about what I'd tell your husband if anything happened to you. We're talking about a country so traumatised, so abused by its leaders, so systematically ransacked by its business class that it can barely function. You start making enemies in Moscow, and a teenager will shoot you in the face for the price of an iPhone. There are no rules any more. There's no pity. It's just havoc.'

'It may be all those things – and I'm going to pretend I didn't hear what you said about my husband – but it's also where the answers are.'

'Possibly. But you've said it yourself. Who do we trust? If we're to believe Cradle, and in the light of events we've got no choice but to believe him, the Twelve are buying up precisely the kind of people we'd need to help us.'

162

'That's what I want to ask you. There must be someone you know over there who's clean. Some man or woman of principle who can't be bought.'

'You don't give up, do you?'

'No, I don't. If I was a man you'd send me, and you know it.'

He nods. 'Eve, please. We can talk further if you want, but there's a couple over there staring at us, and I think they want this table. Also, I need to get back to the office.'

Petra Voss yawns and stretches. 'Well, that was nice. I'm glad I rang for you.'

'Happy to be of service.' Villanelle extricates her naked thigh from between Petra's. 'Just don't forget who's really in charge around here.'

'Remind me.'

'Again?'

'I've got a terrible memory.' Taking Villanelle's hand, Petra pulls it between her legs.

'Tell me about Max Linder,' Villanelle says.

'Are you serious?'

'I'm curious.'

Petra bucks against Villanelle's hand. 'He's weird.'

'In what way?'

'He's got this . . .' She gasps, and pushes Villanelle's fingers deeper.

'He's got this what?'

'This thing for . . . Mmm, yes. There.'

'This thing for?'

'Eva Braun, apparently. Please, don't stop.'

'Eva Braun?' Villanelle raises herself on one elbow. 'You mean, Hitler's—'

'No, I mean the cat's mother. *Scheisse!*'

'What kind of thing?'

'Like he's her reincarnation. Are you going to fuck me again or not?'

'I'd love to,' says Villanelle, withdrawing her hand. 'But I should get back to work.'

'Seriously?'

'Yes. I'm just going to borrow your shower.'

'So you've got time for a shower, then?'

'If I don't have one, I'll end up in the shit with Birgit. And that I don't need.'

'Who's Birgit?'

'Max's crazy bitch manageress. She sniffs us to make sure we're clean. If I walk into her smelling of pussy she'll fire me.'

'Well, we don't want that, do we? I might join you in the shower.'

'Be my guest.'

'I already am.'

Back in the staff quarters, the temperature is, as usual, several degrees lower than elsewhere in the hotel. In the room they share Villanelle finds Maria sitting on her bed, wrapped in a blanket, reading a Polish paperback.

'You missed lunch,' Maria says. 'Where were you?'

Villanelle takes her rucksack from the chest of drawers and, turning her back on Maria so as to block her view, reaches inside it and takes out a ring of keys. 'A guest wanted me to make up her room again.'

'Shit. Which one?'

'That singer. Petra Voss.'

'That's not fair, not in your lunchbreak. I saved you some food from the kitchen.'

She hands Villanelle an apple, a wedge of Emmental cheese, and a slice of Sachertorte on a saucer. 'We're not supposed to have the cake, I took it out of the room-service fridge.'

'Thanks, Maria. That's nice of you.'

'People don't know how hard it is, all the shit we have to do.'

'No,' mumbles Villanelle, her mouth full of Sachertorte. 'They really don't.'

'So we're not going to Moscow after all,' says Lance. 'That's a shame. I really fancied some of that.'

'Richard thought it was too dangerous to send me. Being a woman and everything.'

'To be fair, you're not field-trained. And you do have a tendency to go a bit off-piste.'

'Really?'

'That last night in Venice, for example. You should have let me know where that jewellery designer's party was.'

'How do you know the party was for a jewellery designer?'

'Because I was there too.'

'You're kidding. I didn't see you.'

'Well, you wouldn't have.'

She stares at him. 'You followed me? You seriously fucking *followed* me?'

He shrugs. 'Yeah.'

'I'm . . . I don't know what to say.'

'I was doing my job. Making sure you were OK.'

'I don't need babysitting, Lance. I'm an adult woman. Which appears to be a problem round here.'

'You have no field training, Eve. That's the issue, and that's why I'm here.' He glances at her. 'Look, you're good, OK? Smart. None of us would be here if you weren't. But when it comes to tradecraft and procedure, you're . . . well, you've got to trust me. No flying solo. We watch each other's backs.'

After pulling on a pair of rubber cleaning gloves, Villanelle uses her pass-key to let herself into Linder's room, which Maria has serviced earlier. She works fast. The bathroom cupboards reveal little of interest, beyond a predilection for rejuvenating face creams. The clothes in the wardrobe are good quality, but not so showy and expensive as to alienate his working-class supporters, or to give the lie to his supposedly spartan lifestyle.

In the base of the wardrobe there's an aluminium-bodied briefcase fitted with a lock. Villanelle's keyring holds several conventional door keys – enough to give a normal profile on an airport scanner – but also locksmith's jigglers and a bump key. A delicate twist of one of the smaller jigglers, and the lock springs open. Inside are an Apple laptop computer, several unmarked DVDs in plain boxes, a plaited leather bullwhip, an Audemars Piguet Royal Oak watch, a boxed pair of cougar-head cufflinks by Carrera y Carrera, a Waffen SS ceremonial dagger, a death's-head ring, a display case holding a heavy steel dildo ('The Obergruppenführer'), and several thousand euros in unused banknotes.

Leaving the case open, Villanelle conducts a quick tour of the rest of the room. On the bedside table is a miniature projector, an iPad tablet, a hardback copy of Julius Evola's *Ride the Tiger*, and a Mont Blanc fountain pen. Beneath these, on the floor, is a cabin-size valise secured by a five-digit combination lock. Glancing at her watch, Villanelle decides not to attempt to open the valise; instead, she tentatively lifts and shakes it. Whatever's inside is light; a faint swish suggests clothes. She replaces the valise, then unzips the large tan leather suitcase that has been placed against the wall. It's empty.

Sitting on the bed, Villanelle closes her eyes. A half-dozen heartbeats, and she smiles. She knows exactly how she is going to kill Max Linder.

Turning round in his chair, Billy takes off his headphones. 'Video file coming in from Armando Trevisan. Subject: attention Noel Edmonds. Is someone taking the piss?'

Eve looks up from the Sverdlovsk-Futura Group's website. 'No, get it up. Best quality you can.'

'Give us a sec.'

A clip of a crowded pavement, shot from about a metre above head-height. A dozen or so pedestrians enter and exit the frame, a couple of them lingering in front of a clothes shop window. The footage is low-resolution grey on grey. It runs for seven and a half seconds and cuts out.

'Is there a message?' Lance asks.

Billy shakes his head. 'Just the vid.'

'That's the Van Diest boutique in Venice,' Eve says. 'Run it again at half-speed. Keep going until I say.'

Billy runs the clip twice before Eve stops him. 'OK, slow it down even more. Watch the women in the hats.'

As they enter the frame the women seem to be together. The nearer of the two is wearing an elegant print dress, and her face is concealed by a broad-brimmed hat. The further figure is taller and broader; she's wearing jeans, a T-shirt and what looks like a straw cowboy hat. A large man steps between them and the camera.

'Out of the way, fatso,' Lance murmurs.

The man's there for a full five seconds, then he turns towards the camera to look behind him, and as he does so the cowboy hat appears to slip back on the second woman's head, momentarily exposing her face.

'The Russian girlfriend?' Lance asks.

'Could be, if the timing fits with when they visited the shop. Which I'm guessing is why Trevisan sent this. Let's see it frame by frame, and see if we can get a look at her.'

The moment replays, infinitely slowly. 'Best I can do,' says Billy finally, moving backwards and forwards between frames. 'You've either got the full profile blurred, or the part-profile with her hand in the way.'

'Print both,' Eve tells him. 'And the frames bracketing them.'

'OK . . . Hang on, there's another email from Venice.'

'Read it out.'

'Dear Ms Polastri, I hope this CCTV footage from Calle Vallaresso is of use. It corresponds to the time of the two women's visit to the Van Diest shop as described by yourself and confirmed to me by the manager Giovanna Bianchi. In this connection two Russian-speaking females, registered as Yulia and Alyona Pinchuk, stayed at the Hotel Excelsior

168

on the Lido for one night, two days after the date on the CCTV footage. Hotel staff have confirmed that the Pinchuks, described as sisters, might have been those shown in the footage. With compliments – Armando Trevisan.'

'Run a check on those names, Billy. Yulia and whatever the other one was Pinchuk.' She grabs the first of the print-outs, as the printer wheezily disgorges it. 'That's got to be Villanelle in the dress. Look how she angles the hat so that it completely hides her face from the CCTV camera.'

'Might be just coincidence.'

'I don't think so. She's totally surveillance aware. And I'll bet that's the girlfriend, too. Remember what Giovanna at the jewellery shop said. The same age but a little taller. Short blonde hair. The physique of a swimmer or a tennis player.'

Lance nods. 'She does fit that description. Broad shoulders, definitely. Can't tell if she's blonde, but the hair's definitely very short. Just wish the face wasn't so blurred.'

Eve stares at the printout of the two women. The features of the woman with the cropped blonde hair are pixilated and indistinct, but the essence of her is there. 'I'll know you when I see you, Cowgirl,' she murmurs savagely. 'You can count on that.'

'OK. Yulia and Alyona Pinchuk,' says Billy. 'Seems they're the co-proprietors of an online dating and escort agency called MySugarBaby.com, based in Kiev, Ukraine. The contact address is a post office box in the Oblonskiy district of the city.'

'Can you dig a bit deeper? See if you can find pictures or any biographical stuff? I'm sure they're just cover identities, but let's make sure.'

Billy nods. He looks dazed with exhaustion, and Eve feels a stab of guilt. 'Do it tomorrow,' she tells him. 'Go home now.'

'Sure?' he asks.

'Absolutely sure. You've done more than enough for one day. Lance, what's your plan for the evening?'

'I'm meeting someone. The bloke from the Hampshire Road Policing Unit whose bike was nicked by your, um . . .'

'She's not my anything, Lance. Call her Villanelle.'

'OK. By Villanelle.'

'He's coming to London, this bloke?'

'No, I'm taking a train from Waterloo out to Whitchurch, which is where his unit is based. Apparently they serve a nice pint at the Bell.'

'Will you be able to get back OK?'

'Yeah, no problem. Last train's around eleven.'

Eve frowns. 'Thank you both. Seriously.'

An hour before the dinner shift, Villanelle knocks at Johanna's door. Unlike the other temporary staff members, Johanna has a room to herself. She is also, alone of the twelve of them, not required to serve at dinner. Kissing Birgit's ass has its rewards.

The door opens slowly. Johanna is wearing tracksuit pants and a crumpled sweater. She looks half-awake. '*Ja*. What do you want?'

'I want you to take my place at dinner tonight.'

Johanna blinks and rubs her eyes. 'I'm sorry, I don't work the evening shift, except for turndown service on the upper corridor. Ask Birgit.'

Villanelle holds up a clear plastic bag containing the grubby thong retrieved from Roger Baggot's bed. 'Listen, *schatz*. If you don't take that dinner shift for me I'm going to have to tell Birgit where I found this. I don't think she'll be pleased to find out you've been fucking the guests.'

'I'll deny it. You can't prove that's mine.'

'OK, let's go and speak to Birgit right now. We'll see who she believes.'

For a moment Villanelle thinks her bluff is going to be called. Then, slowly, Johanna nods.

'OK. I'll do it,' she says. 'Why's it so important to you, anyway?'

Villanelle shrugs. 'I've had enough of Linder's guests. I can't stand another evening of their stupid conversation.'

'So what do I say to Birgit? She's going to think it's strange that I'm doing a shift I don't have to.'

'Tell her what you like. Say I'm in my room, throwing up. Say I've got the shits. Whatever.'

She nods sulkily. 'So can I have my *tanga* back?'

'Later.'

'*Scheisse*, Violette. I thought you were a nice person. But you're a bitch. A real fucking bitch.'

'My pleasure. Just be there at dinner, OK?'

When Villanelle gets back to her room, she can hear the weak splash of the shower. When Maria steps back into the room, shivering in an undersized towel, Villanelle tells her that she's feeling ill, and that Johanna will be covering her at dinner. If Maria is surprised at this turn of events, she says nothing.

After locking herself in the bathroom, Villanelle applies a thin layer of pale cake make-up, and dusts it with cornstarch. A faint smudge of shadow beneath each eye, and she's the picture of unhealth. Retching into her hand as she passes Maria, she goes in search of Birgit.

She finds her in the kitchen, bullying one of the sous-chefs. Haltingly, Villanelle tells Birgit about her stomach upset and her arrangement with Johanna. Birgit is furious to hear that Villanelle is not going to be serving in the restaurant, and tells her that she's thoroughly unreliable and disrespectful and that she will be docking her pay.

By the time she gets back to the room, Maria is in her serving uniform, and on the point of setting off for the restaurant. 'You really don't look well,' she tells Villanelle. 'Make sure you wrap up warmly. Take the blanket from my bed if you want.'

After she's gone, Villanelle waits for a further ten minutes. By now, everyone should be congregating in the main building for pre-dinner drinks. Opening the door onto the staff corridor she peers cautiously out, but can hear nothing. She's alone.

She retreats back inside, takes her phone and a steel-bodied ballpoint pen from the bedroom chest of drawers, and locks herself in the bathroom. Kneeling on the tiled floor, she removes the back from the phone and, lifting out the battery, extracts a tiny foil envelope containing a copper-bodied micro detonator. Then, taking a small violet-scented oval of soap from her wash-bag, she strikes it with controlled force against the porcelain base of the sink, so that the outer shell of the soap cracks open. Inside it is a 25g plastic-wrapped disc of Fox-7 explosive, which Villanelle returns to the washbag.

It's joined there by the micro detonator, the ballpoint pen, and the clippers, cuticle-pushers and scissors from her manicure set.

She dislikes Anton but she has to admit he's provided everything she's asked for. The detonator and the Fox-7 explosive are state-of-the-art, the manicure items are engineered steel, capable of doubling as professional DIY tools, and the pen, with very little adjustment, turns into a miniature 110V soldering iron.

Now, there's just one more thing she needs.

Goodge Street tube station is crowded. It's always this way during the after-work rush hour, which is one of the reasons that Eve likes to take the bus. She's not claustrophobic precisely, but there's something about being hemmed in by bodies while hurtling through an underground tunnel, with the possibility that the lights may flicker and go out at any second, or the train unaccountably stop, as if its functions have suddenly and catastrophically failed, that makes her profoundly anxious. There are just too many parallels with death.

The first train that arrives, a Northern Line train via Edgware, is already full to capacity, and as the ranks of commuters on the platform press forward, trying to force their way aboard, Eve retreats to a bench.

'Crazy, no?' says an expressionless voice next to her.

He's in his late thirties, forty at a push. Skin that hasn't seen the sun in months. She looks frostily ahead.

'I have something for you.' He passes her a brown office envelope. 'Read please.'

It's a handwritten note.

You win. This is Oleg. Do everything he says. R.

Frowning hard to disguise her elation, Eve puts the envelope and note in her bag. 'OK, Oleg. Tell me.'

'OK. Tomorrow morning, very important, you meet me here on station platform, eight o'clock, and give me passport. Tomorrow evening six o'clock meet me here again, and I give back. Wednesday you flying Heathrow to Moscow Sheremetyevo, and staying at Cosmos Hotel. You speak Russian, I think? Little bit?'

'Not much. I learned it at school. A-levels.'

'A-levels Russian. *Eto khorosho*. Have you been before?'

'Once. About ten years ago.'

'OK, no problem.' He opens a briefcase, and takes out two flimsy sheets printed with the tiny, smudgy script common to visa application forms the world over. 'Sign, please. Don't worry, I fill in the rest.'

She hands the forms back to him.

'Also, Moscow very cold now. Raining ice. Take strong coat and hat. Boots.'

'Am I going alone?'

'No, also your *kollega*, Lens.'

It takes her a moment to realise that he means Lance.

'Thanks, Oleg, *do zavtra*.'

'*Do zavtra*.'

It's only at this point that she starts to wonder what the hell she's going to tell Niko.

It takes Villanelle fifty-five minutes, working calmly and steadily, to prepare the explosive device with which she intends to kill Linder. When it's ready she changes into her

Bund Deutscher Mädel uniform, pockets the device and her pass-key, and leaves the room. Arriving at the guest wing she pauses. The corridor is silent; the guests are still at dinner. Walking unhurriedly to Roger Baggot's room, she knocks quietly on the door, gets no response, and lets herself in. Having pulled on her rubber cleaning gloves, Villanelle takes an envelope from her pocket. In it is a pair of nail scissors and the plastic film in which the Fox-7 explosive was wrapped. In the bathroom she finds Baggot's washbag, makes a small cut in the lining with the nail scissors, and pushes the plastic film inside. The envelope goes in the small pedal waste-bin beside the sink. The scissors go in the bathroom cabinet.

She leaves Baggot's room and ascends to the first floor, and Linder's room. Once again she knocks quietly on the door, but there's no sound from within. She lets herself in, her breathing steady, and carefully plants the device that she's prepared. For a moment she stands in the middle of the room, calculating blast and shockwave vectors. Then her body registers alarm, and she realises that she can hear a faint, muffled tread climbing the stairs. It might not be Linder, but it might.

Villanelle considers calmly walking out of the room as if she's just finished turning down the bed linen. But the linen isn't turned down, and there's no time now to do so. Besides, others might see her leaving, and remember. So, exactly as she's rehearsed in her mind, she moves at speed to the tan suitcase, and pulls open the twin zips. Stepping inside, she kneels, contracts, angles her shoulders, and tucks in her head. Then reaching upwards, she draws the zips together, leaving a four-inch space to breathe and look through. It's a brutally tight fit, impossible for anyone who didn't exercise and stretch regularly, but Villanelle ignores the straining tendons in her back and legs and concentrates on regularising her breathing. The case smells of musty pigskin. She can feel the steady beat of her heart.

The door to the room opens, and Max Linder walks in. He hangs the Do Not Disturb sign over the outside handle, and bolts the door from the inside. Rounding the bed, he stoops to pick up the valise, which he places on the bed and unlocks, using a combination code. From inside this, he takes a ginger-coloured garment of some kind, and drapes it from the bed.

He crosses the room. Villanelle can't see the wardrobe because the bed is in the way, but she hears the creak of its double doors, and then the springing click of the lock as Linder opens the briefcase. Pressing one eye to the narrow aperture between the zips, she feels cold sweat crawling from her armpits to her ribs. A moment later Linder walks back into view carrying the laptop computer and a CD, which he places next to the miniature projector on the bedside table. There's a pause as he connects them, and then a dim, projected image appears on the wall of the room, runs for a couple of seconds, and stops. Villanelle can only see the image at an acute angle, but it appears to be the countdown timer of an old black and white film.

Touching a wall-switch Linder turns off the overhead light, so that the only remaining illumination is provided by the lamp on the bedside table, and the beam of the projector. Then, unhurriedly, he strips naked, and taking the garment from the bed steps into it. It's a dirndl, a traditional Alpine dress with a laced-up bodice, a white blouse with puff sleeves, and a frilled apron. White knee socks complete the costume. Villanelle can't see Linder clearly, but she can see enough to know that the look doesn't suit him. Bending down, he takes a female wig from the valise, and teases it into place on his head. The wig is neatly coiffed and waved, in a stern, mid-twentieth-century style.

Her back and calf muscles screaming now, Villanelle stares through her tiny viewing slit, and remembers what Petra Voss told her.

He's turning himself into Eva fucking Braun.

Returning to the briefcase in the wardrobe, Linder takes out the rectangular box that houses the Obergruppenführer dildo. Given that less than an hour ago Villanelle has fitted the Obergruppenführer with a military-grade detonator and a lethal payload of Fox-7 explosive, this is not good news. Briefly she considers bursting out of the suitcase, killing Linder with her bare hands, and then pitching him out of the window into the snowy darkness outside, but quickly dismisses the idea. Discovery would not be immediate, but it would be inevitable. And weirdly, illogically, she feels safe folded into the suitcase. She likes it in there.

Linder switches on the projector, and as black and white images begin to flicker on the wall, he inserts a pair of in-ear headphones and lies down on the bed. Despite the distorted angle, Villanelle can see that the film is of Hitler, delivering a ranting, histrionic speech to a vast crowd, perhaps at Nuremberg. All she can hear of the speech is a faint whisper from the headphones, but the lace apron of the dirndl is soon twitching like a tent in a high wind. '*Oh mein sexy Wolf*,' Linder mutters, clutching himself. 'Oh *mein Führer.* Fuck me with that big wolf's *schwanz.* I need *anschluss.*'

Villanelle closes her eyes, presses her forehead to her knees, covers her ears with her hands and opens her mouth. Her neck and shoulder muscles are quivering now, and her heart pounding.

'Invade me, *mein Führer*!'

The air ruptures, tearing like fabric, and a roar of sound slams from wall to wall, wrapping around Villanelle so tightly that she can't breathe, lifting and upending her. For an extended moment she's weightless, then there's a hard impact and the suitcase bursts open. Lungs heaving, faint with shock, she rolls into a frozen, singing silence. The room's half dark, and there's no plate-glass window any more, just an empty black space. The air is filled with feathers, whirling like snowflakes on the inrushing mountain air. Some, flecked with red, drift to the floor. One settles softly against Villanelle's cheek.

Effortfully, she raises herself on one elbow. Max Linder is all over the place. His head and torso, still wearing the laced-up bodice of the dirndl, have been thrown back against the headboard. His legs, all but severed, hang loosely over the bed's end. In between, on the exploded duvet, is a glinting mess of blood, viscera and broken glass from the blown-out overhead light. Above Villanelle's head, something detaches from the ceiling and splatters into her hair. She brushes it away absently; it feels like liver. The ceiling and walls are glazed with blood-spray, and flecked with faecal and intestinal matter. Linder's severed right hand lies, palm down, in the courtesy fruit-bowl.

Slowly, Villanelle gets to her feet and takes a few shaky steps. Vaguely conscious that she's hungry, she reaches for a banana, but its skin is sticky with blood and she lets it fall onto the carpet. Her eyes ache with fatigue, and she's desperately, mortally cold. So she lies down again, curling up like a child at the foot of the bed, as the body fluids of the man that she has killed drip and congeal around her. She doesn't hear the splintering of the door, or the shouts and the screaming that follow. She dreams that she's lying with her head in Anna Leonova's lap. That she's safe, and at peace, and Anna is stroking her hair.

7

Sleet is spattering against the window of the Airbus as it taxis to the runway. A stewardess with over-bleached hair is giving a listless safety demonstration. Canned music rises and falls in volume.

'I know the hotel,' Lance says. 'It's on Prospekt Mira, and absolutely bloody enormous. Probably the biggest in Russia.'

'Are they serving drinks on this flight, do you think?'

'Eve, this is Aeroflot. Relax.'

'Sorry, Lance, it's been a really shit couple of days. I think Niko may even have left me.'

'That bad, eh?'

'That bad. Venice was tricky enough; this time I can't even tell him where I'm going. He'd totally freak if he knew. And even though he knows that you and I are absolutely, you know . . .'

'Not having sex?'

'Yeah, even though he knows that, I'm still going to wherever it is that I'm going with some other guy.'

'You told him I was coming?'

'I know I shouldn't have. But better than not saying anything, or lying, and him then finding out.'

Lance glances at the passenger on his left, a bullet-headed figure wearing a bulky jacket in the black and red colours of FC Spartak Moscow, and shrugs. 'There's no answer. My ex-wife hated that I never talked to her about my work, but what can you do? She liked a gossip with her pals, and with a couple of drinks inside her she got very chatty indeed. There are couples who cope better than others, but that's as far as it goes.'

Eve nods, and wishes she hadn't. She feels hung over, sleep-deprived and emotionally fragile. She and Niko were up until almost 3 a.m., drinking wine that neither of them felt like drinking, and saying things that could not be unsaid. Eventually she announced that she intended to go to bed, and Niko insisted with wounded determination on sleeping on the sofa.

'Don't be surprised if I'm not here when you get back from wherever the fuck it is you're going,' he said, leaning balefully on his crutches.

'Where will you go?'

'Why? What difference does that make?'

'I'm just asking.'

'Don't. If I don't have the right to know your movements, you don't have the right to know mine, OK?'

'OK.'

She fetched him blankets. Sitting on the sofa with his head bowed and his crutches at his side he looked lost, a displaced person in his own home. It distressed Eve to see him like this, so steeped in hurt, but some cold and clear-thinking part of her knew that this battle had to be fought and won. That she might back down was an alternative she never considered.

'How long's this flight?' she asks Lance.

'About three and a half hours.'

'Vodka's good for a hangover, isn't it?'

'Tried and tested.'

'As soon as we're airborne, catch that stewardess's eye.'

The hotel, as Lance has described, is vast. The lobby is the size of a railway station, its pillared expanse and functional grandeur redolent of high Sovietism. Their twenty-second-floor rooms are drab, with worn furnishings, but the views are spectacular. Opposite Eve's window, on the far side of Prospekt Mira, is the complex of ornate pavilions, walk-ways, gardens and fountains comprising the former All-Russia Exhibition Centre. At a distance it still has a fading glamour, especially beneath the enamel-blue October sky.

'So what's the plan?' Lance asks, as they drink a second cup of coffee in the hotel's Kalinka restaurant.

Eve reflects. She feels renewed by the night's sleep, and unexpectedly optimistic. The fight with Niko, and the issues surrounding it, have receded to a background murmur, a distant shimmer. She's ready for whatever the day and the city might bring. 'I'd like to go for a walk,' she says. 'Get some Russian air in my lungs. We could go to that park opposite; I'd love to take a closer look at that sculpture of the rocket.'

'Oleg said we'd be contacted at the hotel at eleven o'clock.'

'Then we've got two and a half hours. I don't mind going by myself.'

'If you go, I come with you.'

'You seriously think that I'm at risk? Or that we are?'

'This is Moscow. We're here under our own names, and we can count on those names being on some list of foreign intelligence operatives. Our arrival won't have gone unnoticed, trust me. And obviously our contact knows we're here.'

'Who is this person? Any idea?'

'No names. Just that it's someone Richard knows from his time here. An FSB officer would be my guess. Probably someone quite high-up.'

'Richard was head of station here, right?'

'Yeah.'

'So does that happen a lot? Senior officers keeping lines of communication open with the other side?'

'Not a lot. But he always had a way of getting on with people, even when things got frosty at the diplomatic level.'

'I remember Jin Qiang saying much the same in Shanghai.'

'I think Richard saw those relationships as a kind of fail-safe. So that if one of their leaders, or ours, were to go completely off the rails . . .'

'Wiser heads might prevail?'

'That sort of thing.'

Fifteen minutes later they're standing at the foot of the Monument to the Conquerors of Space. This is a hundred-metre-high representation, in shining titanium, of a rocket rising on its exhaust plume. Beside them, a kebab vendor is setting up his stand.

'I always felt so sorry for Laika, that dog they sent up,' Eve says, pushing her hands deep into the pockets of her parka jacket. 'I read about her when I was a child, and I used to dream of her alone in the capsule, far away in space, not knowing that she would never return to earth. I know there were humans who died in the space programme, but it was Laika that I found so heartbreaking. Don't you think?'

'I always wanted a dog. My Uncle Dave managed a waste depot outside Redditch, and every so often he'd invite us kids round and we'd send his terriers in after the rats. They'd kill maybe a hundred in a session. Complete bloody mayhem, and the smell was diabolical.'

'What a lovely childhood memory.'

'Yeah, well. My dad always said Dave made a fortune out of that place. Most of it from turning a blind eye when blokes turned up at night with lumpy shapes rolled up in carpeting.'

'Seriously?'

'Put it like this. He retired aged forty, moved to Cyprus, and hasn't lifted a finger since, except to play golf.' He hunches into his coat. 'We should keep moving.'

'Any particular reason?'

'If anyone's got surveillance on us, and that's somewhere between possible and probable, we're not going to know if we stay still.'

'OK. Let's walk.'

The park, built in the mid-twentieth century to celebrate the economic achievements of the Soviet state, is vast and melancholy. Triumphal arches, their columns flaking and weather-streaked, frame empty air. Neo-classical pavilions stand padlocked and deserted. Visitors huddle on benches, staring into the middle distance as if defeated by the attempt to make sense of their nation's recent history. And above it all, that almost artificially blue sky, and the scudding white clouds.

184

'So Lance, when you were here before . . .'

'Go on.'

'What were you actually doing?'

He shrugs. A solitary roller skater whirrs past them. 'Bread-and-butter stuff, mostly. Keeping an eye on people who needed an eye kept on them. Seeing who came and went.'

'Agent-handling?'

'I was more of a talent-spotter. If I felt one of their people had potential, and wasn't being fed to us, I'd pass it on and an approach would be made. With walk-ins, I helped filter out the obvious nutters.'

They're rounding an ornamental lake, its surface furrowed by the wind. 'Don't look now,' Lance says. 'Hundred metres behind us. Single gent in a grey overcoat, pork-pie hat, looking at a map.'

'Following us?'

'Certainly keeping eyes on us.'

'How long have you known?'

'He picked us up when we left the rocket statue.'

'What do you suggest?'

'That we do what we're going to do anyway. Go and have a look at the metro station, like good tourists, and make our way back to the hotel. If possible resisting the temptation to turn round and stare at our FSB chum.'

'Lance, I'm not that naive.'

'I know. Just saying.'

Entry to the metro station is via a circular pillared atrium. Inside it's bustling but spacious, and after buying a ticket each they descend by escalator to the palatial underground concourse. At the sight of it Eve stops dead, causing a woman to ram her behind the knees with a shopping trolley before pushing brusquely past. Eve, however, is captivated. The central hall is vast, and lit with ornate chandeliers. The walls and vaulted ceiling are white marble; archways faced in green mosaic lead to the railway platforms. Passengers hurry to and from the trains in swirling cross-currents, a young man is playing a song Eve vaguely recognises on a battered guitar, a beggar displaying military service medals kneels with head lowered and hands outstretched.

Lance and Eve allow themselves to be drawn along the concourse by the crowd. 'What's that song?' she asks. 'I'm sure I know it.'

'Everyone thinks they know it. It's the most annoying song ever written. It's called *"Posledniy Raz"*. The Russian equivalent of the "Macarena".'

'The things you know, Lance, honestly . . .' She stops. 'Oh my goodness gracious. Look.'

An elderly man is sitting on a stone bench. At his feet is a cardboard box full of new-born kittens. He grins toothlessly at Eve. His eyes are a pale, watery blue.

As Eve falls to one knee, intending to touch a finger to the impossibly soft head of one of the kittens, a fluttering wind touches her hair, followed by a smacking sound. The face of the man on the bench seems to fold inwards, grin still in place, as his skull bloodily voids itself against the marble wall.

Eve freezes, wide-eyed. She hears the tiny mewing of the kittens, and as if from a distance, screaming. Then she's dragged to her feet, and Lance is strong-arming her towards the exit. Everyone else has the same idea and as the crowd presses around them, shoulders barging and elbows shoving, Eve is lifted from her feet. She feels herself losing a shoe and tries to duck down for it, but is swept forward, the press of bodies against her ribcage so unyielding that she gasps for breath. The clamp tightens, points of light burst before her eyes, a voice yells in her ear – '*Seryozha, Seryozha*' – and the last thing she knows before her legs give way and the darkness rises to meet her is that from somewhere, somehow, she can still hear that maddening, insinuating song.

Catching her, hoisting her up so that her head lolls on his shoulder, Lance carries her onto the escalator. This too is packed tight with passengers but finally they reach the atrium, and he lowers her into a seated position against a pillar. Opening her eyes she blinks, gulps air, feels the waves of dizziness rise and fall.

'Can you walk?' Lance scans the area urgently. 'Because we really, really need to get away from here.'

Her lungs heaving, Eve kicks off the remaining shoe as Lance pulls her to a standing position. She sways for a moment, the floor cold beneath her bare feet, and attempts to order her thoughts. Someone has just tried to shoot her in the back of the head. The old man with the kittens has had his brains blown out. The shooter might at any moment catch up with them.

Eve knows that she should act decisively, but she feels so light-headed and nauseous that she can't bring herself to move. Shock, a small voice tells her. But knowing that she's in shock doesn't dispel the meaty smack of the bullet, the infolding face, the brains tumbling from the skull like summer pudding. *Posledniy Raz*. The kittens, she thinks vaguely. Who will look after the kittens? Then she leans forward and vomits noisily onto her bare feet.

Immediately outside the metro station, four solidly built men are waiting. Behind them, a black van bearing the insignia of the FSB is drawn up on the tarmac. A fifth man, wearing a pork-pie hat, stands a short distance from the others, making no attempt to disguise the fact that he's watching the outpouring passengers closely.

Eve's retching, and the evasive action taken by those passing her, attracts the men's attention. By the time she straightens up, wet-eyed and shaking, they're moving determinedly towards her.

'Come,' says one of them, in English, placing a hand on her elbow. He's wearing a leather flat cap and a padded winter jacket, and looks neither friendly nor unfriendly. Like his three colleagues, he has a large handgun holstered on his belt.

'*Kogo-to zastrelili*,' Lance tells him, pointing into the metro. 'Someone's been shot.'

The man in the leather cap ignores his words. 'Please,' he says, gesturing towards the black van. 'Go in.'

Eve stares at him wretchedly. Her feet are freezing.

'I don't think we've got much choice,' Lance says, as passengers continue to stream past them. 'Probably safer there than anywhere else.'

The drive is conducted in silence and at high speed, the van swerving aggressively from lane to lane. As they race southwards down Prospekt Mira, Eve attempts to focus her thoughts, but the swaying van and the overpowering smell of petrol, body odour, cologne and her own vomit make

188

her nauseous, and it's all she can do not to throw up again. Staring through the windscreen at the road in front of them, she runs a hand through her hair. Her forehead is clammy.

'How are you feeling?' Lance asks.

'Shit,' she answers, not turning round.

'Don't worry.'

'Don't *worry*?' Her voice is a rasp. 'Lance, someone just tried to fucking shoot me. I've got bits of sick between my toes. And we've been abducted.'

'I know, not ideal. But I think we're safer with these guys than on the street.'

'I hope so. I fucking hope so.'

They swing into a wide square, dominated by a vast and cheerless edifice in ochre brick. 'The Lubyanka,' Lance says. 'Used to be the headquarters of the KGB.'

'Great.'

'Now occupied by the FSB, who are basically the KGB with better dentistry.'

The driver takes a road to the side of the building, makes a turn, and parks. The rear of the Lubyanka is a wasteland of building works and litter. Wire grilles cover windows impenetrable with grime. The man in the leather cap steps down from the front passenger seat, and slides open the van door.

'Come,' he says to Eve.

She turns to Lance, wide-eyed with apprehension. He tries to get up but is pressed firmly back into his seat.

'She come, you stay.'

She feels herself boosted towards the van door. Leather-cap waits outside, blank-faced.

'This could be what we came for,' says Lance. 'Good luck.'

Eve feels empty, even of fear. 'Thanks,' she whispers, and steps down onto a cold scattering of builders' grit. She's hurried past an entrance covered by corrugated iron to a low doorway surmounted by a hammer and sickle in carved stone. Leather-cap presses a button, and the door gives a faint, expiring click. He pushes it open. Inside, Eve can see nothing but darkness.

Oxana Vorontsova is walking at the side of a road in a city that both is and isn't Perm. It's evening, and snow is falling. The road is bordered by tall, flat-fronted buildings, and between these the dark expanse of a river is visible, and ice-floes painted with snow. As Oxana walks, the landscape takes shape ahead of her, as if she's in a 1990s computer game. Walls rise up, the road unrolls. Everything is made up of graduated flecks of black, white and grey, like the wing-scales of a moth.

The knowledge that she is living in a simulation reassures Oxana: it means, as she's always suspected, that nothing is real, that her actions will have no consequences and she can do what she likes. But it doesn't answer all her questions. Why is she driven to this constant search, this endless walking of this twilit road? What lies behind the surfaces of the buildings that rise up to either side of her like stage scenery? Why is it that nothing seems to have depth or sound? Why does she feel this terrible, crushing sadness?

Far ahead of her, an indistinct figure waits. Oxana walks towards her, her step determined. The woman is looking forward, into a snow-blurred infinity. She doesn't seem to be aware of Oxana's approach, but at the last moment she turns, her gaze a spear of ice.

Villanelle snaps awake, wide-eyed, heart pounding. Everything is sunlit white. She's lying in a single bed, with her head supported by pillows. Wound dressings and compression bandages cover much of her face. In the direction that she's facing she can see light streaming through net curtains, a cast-iron radiator, a chair and a bedside table holding a bottle of mineral water and a box of Voltarol tablets. When she first woke up here forty-eight hours ago, she felt utterly wretched. Her ears ached excruciatingly, bile rose in her throat whenever she swallowed, and the slightest movement sent pain jolting through her neck and shoulders. Now, apart from a faint, residual ringing in her ears, she just feels drained.

Anton walks into her field of vision. Apart from a mostly silent young man who has brought Villanelle her meals, he's the first person she's seen since arriving here. He's wearing a down-filled jacket, and carrying a zip-up cabin bag.

'So, Villanelle. How are you?'

'Tired.'

He nods. 'You've had primary blast wave concussion and whiplash. You've been on strong sedatives.'

'Where are we?'

'A private clinic in Reichenau, outside Innsbruck.' He steps to the window, pulls back the net curtains, and peers out. 'Do you remember what happened to you?'

'Some of it.'

'Max Linder? The Felsnadel Hotel?'

'Yes. I remember.'

'So tell me. What the fuck went down? How did you get caught in the explosion?'

She frowns. 'I . . . I went to Linder's room and prepared the device. Then he came in. I suppose I hid. I can't remember what happened next.'

'Nothing at all?'

'No.'

'Tell me about the device.'

'I'd worked through a lot of ideas. Phone, digital alarm clock, laptop . . .'

'Speak up. You're slurring your words.'

'I thought about different methods. I wasn't happy with any of them. Then I found Linder's vibrator.'

'And you rigged it with the micro-det and the Fox-7?'

'Yes, after planting forensic evidence on one of the other guests.'

'Which guest? What evidence?'

'The Englishman, Baggot. I hid the plastic wrapping from the explosive in the lining of his washbag.'

'Good. He's a moron. Go on.'

Villanelle hesitates. 'How did I get out?' she asks him. 'After the explosion, I mean?'

'Maria messaged me. Said Linder was dead and you'd been found unconscious at the scene and needed a rapid exfil.'

'Maria?' Villanelle raises her head from the pillow. 'Maria works for you? Why the fuck didn't you—'

'Because you didn't need to know. As it happened, there was a high-altitude blizzard that night, and no emergency helicopters could get up there. So the guests were forced to spend the night of the explosion in the hotel, which apparently caused a certain amount of panic and distress. At least Linder's body was properly refrigerated. After you blew out the plate-glass window, the temperature in that room must have dropped to minus 20 degrees.'

'And me?'

'Maria kept an eye on you overnight. At first light I chartered a helicopter, and had you picked up before the police got there.'

'No one thought this was weird?'

'The guests were asleep. The hotel staff assumed it was official, and given the state you were in, were probably glad to see you go. The last thing they needed was a second corpse on their hands.'

'I don't remember any of this.'

'You wouldn't.'

'So what happens now?'

'At the Felsnadel? You don't need to worry about that. Your part is done.'

'No, what happens to me? Are the police going to turn up?'

'No. I drove you here and checked you in myself. As far as everyone at the clinic is concerned, you're a French tourist convalescing after a driving accident. They're very discreet here, as they should be, given the price. Apparently they get a lot of post-operative cosmetic surgery patients. There's some sort of treatment where they pack your face in snow.'

Villanelle touches the dressings on her face. The scabbing cuts are starting to itch. 'Linder's dead, as you requested. I'm worth everything you pay me and more.'

Seating himself on the bedside chair, Anton leans forward. 'He's dead, as you say, and we appreciate that. But right now it's time to get your shit together, and fast. Because thanks to your antics in Venice with Lara Farmanyants, and your *Hello!* magazine approach to assassination, we have a major fucking problem. Namely that Eve Polastri is currently in Moscow, discussing Konstantin Orlov with the FSB.'

'I see.'

'You see? Is that the best you can come up with? For fuck's sake, Villanelle. When you're good, you're brilliant, so why do you have to act up in this childish, narcissistic fashion? It's almost as if you want Polastri to catch and kill you.'

'Right.' She reaches for the Voltarol tablets, and he snatches them away.

'That's enough of those. If you're in pain, I want you to remember that it's wholly self-inflicted. All this drama you create. Speedboats, made-up aristocratic titles, exploding dildos ... You're not living in a fucking TV series, Villanelle.'

'Really? I thought I was.'

He throws the cabin bag onto the bed. 'New clothes, passport, documents. I want you in London and ready to work by the end of the week.'

'And what will I be doing there?'

'Terminating this shitstorm once and for all.'

'By which you mean?'

'Killing Eve.'

Escorted by the men who were in the FSB van, Eve walks into the building. The interior is not quite dark, as it appeared from outside. To one side is a battered steel desk behind which a uniformed officer is seated, eating a meat-ball sandwich by the light of a desk lamp. As they enter he looks up, and puts down his sandwich.

'*Angliskiy spion*,' says the man in the leather cap, slapping a crumpled document onto the desk.

The officer looks at Eve, reaches unhurriedly for a rubber stamp, inks it from a violet pad in a tin, and applies it to the document. '*Tak*,' he says. '*Dobro pozhalovat' na Lubyanku.*'

'He says "Welcome to Lubyanka,"' Leather-cap informs her.

'Tell him I've always wanted to visit.'

Neither man smiles. The officer lifts the receiver of an ancient desk telephone, and dials a three-figure number. A minute later two heavily built men in combat trousers and T-shirts arrive, look Eve up and down, and beckon her to follow them.

'I have no shoes,' she tells Leather-cap, pointing at her dirty bare feet, and he shrugs. The desk officer has already returned to his sandwich. She accompanies the two men down a long, sour-smelling corridor, through a pair of double doors, and into a courtyard littered with cigarette ends. High buildings, some of yellowish brick, some faced with weather-stained cement, rise on all sides. Uniformed and plain-clothes personnel lean against the walls, smoking, and stare expressionlessly at Eve as she passes. The two men lead her to a low door.

Inside is a tiled hall and a trestle table behind which two male officers are lounging, their crested caps tilted at jaunty angles on their shaved heads. One looks up briefly as they enter, then returns to his perusal of a body-building magazine. The other unhurriedly rises and, advancing on Eve, gestures that she should empty her possessions into a plastic tray on the table. She does so, divesting herself of her watch, phone, passport, hotel room keys and wallet. She's then made to remove her parka, and subjected to a body-scan with a hand-held metal detector. She asks for the jacket back, but is refused, leaving her shivering in a thin sweater, vest and jeans.

From the reception hall she's led to a flight of stairs giving on to a small landing. From here a dim-lit, concrete-walled corridor leads into the building's interior. The men walk fast, purposefully, and in silence. Their necks are thick and the back of their heads bristled. Pig-men, Eve thinks. An increasingly painful stabbing in her right heel tells her that she's trodden on something sharp. The pig-men cannot fail to see her limping but they don't slow down.

'*Pozhalusta*,' she says. 'Please.'

They ignore her, and Eve's hope that the situation is stage-managed, and designed to deliver her to Richard's contact, begins to ebb. The corridor turns at right-angles several times, each change of direction delivering an identical vista of bare bulbs and concrete walls. Finally they reach an atrium, and a large service elevator. The air smells of garbage and decay; the stench catches in Eve's throat. All this sends a very bad message. Is she under arrest? Do they really think she's a *spion*, a spy?

You are a spy, an inner voice whispers. It's what you always wanted. You're here because you chose to be here. Because, in the face of wiser counsel, you insisted on it. *You wanted this*.

'Please,' she says again in halting, pleading Russian. 'Where are we going?'

196

Once again the pig-men ignore her. Her heel hurts badly now, the pain driving upwards like a blade. But the pain is nothing compared with the fear. One of the men presses the elevator's call button, and there's a distant mechanical clanking. Eve's shaking now. The possibility of imposing herself on the situation has evaporated. She feels utterly, mutely helpless.

The service elevator doors open with a metallic shriek, and Eve is led inside. The doors close and the elevator begins a slow, grinding descent, the pig-men leaning against the dented walls with folded arms and blank faces. From somewhere in the building Eve senses a mechanical pulse. Faint at first, but growing louder as the elevator moves downwards. The noise becomes a roar, making the elevator shudder. She digs her fingernails into her hand. This is the twenty-first century, she tells herself. I'm an Englishwoman with a husband, a Debenhams store card, and a kilo of fresh tagliatelle in the freezer. Everything will be all right.

No, the voice whispers. It fucking well won't. You're a pathetically amateurish spy, hopelessly out of your depth, and now you're paying the price of your fantasies. This nightmare is real. This is really happening.

Finally, the doors open. They're in an atrium identical to the one they left just minutes ago. The light is a sulphurous mustard colour, and the noise, relentless and terrifying, is all around them. The pig-men march Eve into yet another corridor, and she follows them as best she can. If the journey is grim, she's certain that the arrival will be worse.

Ten minutes later, she's utterly disoriented. She senses that they're underground, but that's all. The mechanical roar is quieter now, although still audible, and the place seems to have other occupants. She can hear doors rattling and creaking, and a faint sound that could be shouting. They turn a corner. A tiled floor underfoot, the peeling walls suffused in that horrible mustard-coloured light. At the head of the corridor a door is open, and her guards pause long enough for Eve to look inside. At first glance the interior resembles a shower room, with a sloping concrete floor, a drain, and a coiled hose. But three of the walls are padded, and the fourth is made of splintered logs.

Before Eve has time to guess at the implications of this room, she's moved into a row of cells, with reinforced doors and observation hatches. The pig-men stop outside the first of these, and pull it open. Inside there's a stoneware basin, a bucket and a low bench against one wall. On the bench is a soiled palliasse. Light is provided by a low-wattage bulb protected by a wire grille. Open-mouthed and disbelieving, Eve allows herself to be manhandled inside. Behind her, the door slams shut.

Locking and bolting the door of her Paris apartment behind her, Villanelle drops her bag and curls, catlike, into a grey leather and chrome armchair. With her eyes half closed she looks around her. She's grown very attached to its restful sea-green walls, anonymous paintings and worn, once-expensive furniture. Beyond the plate-glass window, framed by heavy silk curtains, is the city, silent in the twilight. She gazes for a moment at the faint shimmer of the illuminations on the Eiffel Tower, and then dips into her bag for her phone. The SMS message is still there, of course. The one-time burn code dispatched with a single keystroke.

They were in bed together in Venice when Lara showed Villanelle her phone. 'If you ever get this text, I've been taken and it's all over.'

'That won't happen,' Villanelle replied.

But it has happened, and here is the text. 'I love you.'

Lara did love her, Villanelle knows. She still does, if she's alive. And for a moment, Villanelle envies her that capacity. To share another's happiness, to suffer another's pain, to fly on the wings of real feeling rather than to be forever acting. But how dangerous, how uncontrollable, and ultimately how ordinary. Better, by far, to occupy the pure, arctic citadel of the self.

It's bad that Lara's been taken, though. Very bad. Rising from the grey leather chair, Villanelle walks to the kitchen, and takes a bottle of pink Mercier champagne and a cold tulip glass from the fridge. In thirty-six hours she flies to London. There are plans to be made, and they are complex.

In Eve's cell, the light flickers and goes out. She has no idea what time it is, or even if it's night. No guards have returned with food, and although she's painfully hungry, she's also desperate to avoid the shame of having to empty her bowels into the bucket. Thirst has forced her to take sips from the tap in the basin. The water is brownish and tastes of rust, but Eve is beyond caring.

She seems to have been lying on the hard bench for hours, her mind alternately racing off at frantic tangents and sinking into a sick fog of despair. At intervals, she's overtaken by shaking fits, caused not by the cold, although it is cold, and her sweater painfully thin, but by the endlessly reshuffling memory of events in the metro. Nothing in her life has prepared her for the flutter of a bullet parting her hair. For the sight of an infolding face, and outpouring brains. Who was he, the old man with the pale eyes, whose last living act was to smile at a stranger? Who was the man she killed? Because I did kill him, Eve tells herself. I killed him with my stupid, misplaced self-belief, as surely as if I shot him myself.

She stands up in the dark, endures another bout of the shakes, and limps around the cell, trying not to think about the probable infection in her heel. She can't sleep. Her stomach is twisting with hunger, the bench is hard, and the palliasse smells of vomit and shit. She makes her way to the door. The random shouting that once seemed distant sounds closer now. A phrase, not quite intelligible, is repeated over and over again in a male voice. Others respond angrily. There's a low groaning, suddenly interrupted.

Warily, Eve lifts the small wooden panel in the door — wide enough to slip a food bowl through — and looks out. From the end of the corridor, in the direction from which she was led earlier, come dim, flickering lights. The shouting starts again, the same unintelligible phrase delivered in a furious, desperate rasp. It's met with the same responses, and the same sharply curtailed groaning. It occurs to Eve that she's listening to a recording, some kind of looped tape. But if so, why? What would be the point? To intimidate her? That was hardly necessary.

Then, as she crouches by the hatch, looking out, a figure moves into her peripheral vision, and starts walking up the corridor towards her. At the sight of him, Eve once again starts to shake. A man of about forty, with thinning brown hair, wearing a boiler suit, a long leather apron and rubber boots.

As he passes her door, Eve closes the hatch to a crack. She can't stop watching, and she can't stop shaking. Moving with the unhurried air of a doctor on a hospital round, the man goes into the room with the hose and the drain and the sloping floor. Perhaps a minute passes, then the two pig-men arrive at the opposite end of the corridor and unlock a cell door. Marching inside, they come out supporting a thin, blankly staring figure in a suit and shirt, and walk him past Eve's door and into the same room.

Moments later they leave without him, and Eve sinks to the floor of her cell, her eyes as tightly shut as she can force them, and her hands clamped over her ears. But she still hears the shots. Two of them, seconds apart. And she's so terrified she can no longer think, or breathe, or control any part of herself, and she just lies there in the darkness, shaking.

Somehow, probably from sheer exhaustion, she sleeps, and is woken by a hammering at the cell door. The lights are on again and there's a faint smell of cooked meat. At that moment the only thing that she's sure of is her hunger. She limps to the communication hatch, her mouth dry and her guts twisting with longing.

'*Da?*'

'*Zavtrak!*' a voice growls. 'Breakfast.'

With that, the hatch opens and a red box is pushed through by a large, hairy hand. It's a McDonald's Happy Meal, and it seems to be still hot. It's followed by a canned energy drink called Russian Power. Eve stares disbelievingly at these luxuries before ripping open the McDonald's box, and with trembling fingers devouring the contents. In the box with the hamburger and french fries there's a cello-phane-wrapped toy. A tiny plastic teapot with a Hello Kitty face on it.

Eve wipes her greasy, salty fingers on her jeans then rips the tab from the Russian Power can and gulps down as much as she can before sinking back, gasping, onto the bench. Nothing makes sense any more. Pulling the bucket to the door so that she can't be seen through the hatch, she pees in it, pours the urine down the sink, and washes her hands and the bucket with the trickling brown tap water. Her bowels give a warning grumble, but shitting in the bucket is an indignity she's not yet ready for, although she's resigned to the fact that that time will come. Turning the french fries packet inside out, she licks up the last of the salt, and takes a measured sip of Russian Power. Was this a last meal before being dragged to the room with the concrete floor, the hose and the drain? I'm sorry, Niko my love. I'm so, so sorry.

The door swings abruptly open. It's the two pig-men. They beckon to her, and she limps towards them, her hand closed tightly around the little teapot in her pocket. When they lead her past the killing room, her heart is pounding so hard that it hurts. Then, instead of continuing along the corridor, they open a cell door, beyond which is an elevator. Not the filthy service cage that she came down in, but a hotel-style guest elevator with a brushed steel interior. This ascends smoothly and silently to a half-landing, and a short flight of stairs leading to the tiled atrium, where the same two officers in the over-large caps are sitting behind the trestle table. Waiting on the table are her parka jacket and the tray holding her possessions.

Glancing nervously at the officers, who barely acknowledge her presence, she pulls on the parka, glad of its warmth and of the chance to cover up her dirty sweater. Hurriedly, she loads the pockets with her passport, watch, phone, keys and money.

'*Obuv*,' says one of the pig-men, gesturing with his foot to a pair of short winter boots trimmed with rabbit fur.

Gratefully, Eve pulls them on. They fit perfectly.

'OK,' says the other pig-man, moving back towards the stairs to the elevator. 'You come.'

They rise several storeys, and step out onto parquet flooring and a worn carpet the colour of raw liver. At the end of the corridor, a dark wood door stands ajar. Inside, the office is all shadows. Nondescript curtains frame tall windows. Behind a mahogany desk a broad-shouldered, silver-haired figure is hunched over a laptop computer.

'Can you believe Kim Kardashian?' he says, waving a hand to dismiss the pig-men. 'Surely no one's really that shape?'

Eve peers at him. He's probably in his mid-fifties, with buzz-cut hair and a wry, urbane smile. His suit looks handmade.

He snaps the laptop shut. 'Take a seat, Mrs Polastri. I'm Vadim Tikhomirov. Let me order you some coffee.'

Eve sinks into the proffered chair, murmuring bewildered thanks.

'Latte? Americano?'

'Yes, whatever.'

He presses an intercom button on his telephone. '*Masha, dva kofe s molokom* . . . Do you like roses, Mrs Polastri?' Rising, he crosses the room to a side table bearing a bowl of crimson roses, selects one, and hands it to her. 'They're called *Ussurochka*. They grow them in Vladivostok. Do you have cut flowers in your Goodge Street office?'

Eve inhales the rose's rich, oily fragrance. 'Perhaps we should. I'll suggest it.'

'You should insist on it. I'm sure Richard Edwards would approve the budget. But let me ask you: how did you find last night?'

'How did I . . . *find it*?'

'It's an immersive on-site project I'm developing. The Lubyanka Experience. Spend a night as a condemned political prisoner during the Stalinist Purge.' Noting her speechless gaze, he spreads his hands. 'Perhaps someone should have explained the concept to you beforehand, but I saw it as an opportunity for some valuable feedback, so . . . what did you think?'

'It was, quite simply, the most terrifying night of my life.'

'You mean in a bad way?'

'I mean in the way that I thought I was losing my mind. Or that I was about to be shot.'

'Yes, you had the full NKVD Execution package. So you think it needs fine-tuning? Too spooky?'

'Perhaps a little.'

He nods. 'It's tricky, because while this is very much a working secret police environment, we do also have these amazing historical assets. All those underground torture cells and execution chambers, we'd be crazy not to exploit them. And we've certainly got the actors. This organisation's never been short of people who like dressing up in uniforms and scaring people.'

'So I believe.'

'At least you got to wake up in the morning.' He chuckles. 'In the old days your ashes would have been used as fertiliser.'

Eve twiddles the rose-stem. 'Well, I was genuinely terrified, especially since someone actually did try to kill me yesterday, as I'm sure you're aware.'

He nods. 'I am aware of that, and I'm going to get to it in a minute. Tell me, how is Richard?'

'He's well. And he sends compliments.'

'Excellent. I hope we're keeping him busy at the Russia desk.'

'Busy enough. Did he explain to you why I wanted to come here?'

'He did. You want to ask me, among other questions, about Konstantin Orlov.'

'Yes. Specifically his later career.'

'Well, I'll do my best.' Tikhomirov rises, and walks to the window. He stands with his back to her, silhouetted against the pale, slanting light. There's a knock at the door and a young man wearing combat trousers and a muscle T-shirt enters, carrying a tray, which he places on a side table.

'*Spasiba, Dima*,' says Tikhomirov.

The coffee is ferociously strong, and as it races through Eve's system, she feels a faint shiver of optimism. A lifting of the fog of helplessness and shame which, for the last twenty-four hours, has enveloped her.

'Tell me,' she says.

He nods, responsive to the shift in her mood. He's back behind the desk now, his posture languid but his gaze attentive. 'You've heard of *Dvenadtsat*. The Twelve.'

'I've heard of them, yes. Not much more.'

'We think that they started life as one of the secret societies that came into being under Leonid Brezhnev in the late Soviet era. A cabal of behind-the-scenes operators who foresaw the end of communism and wanted to build a new Russia, free of the old, corrupt ideologies. As they saw them.'

'Sounds reasonable.'

Tikhomirov shrugs. 'Perhaps. But history, as so often, has other ideas. Boris Yeltsin's policies in the early 1990s enriched a handful of oligarchs, but diminished and impoverished the country. At which point, it seems, the Twelve went underground, and began to transform into a new kind of organisation altogether. One that made its own rules, dispensed its own justice, and pursued its own agenda.'

'Which was?'

'Do you know anything about organisation theory?'

Eve shakes her head.

'There's a school of thought that holds that sooner or later, whatever its founding ethos, the most pressing concern of any organisation is to ensure its own survival. To this end, it adopts an aggressive, expansionist posture which ultimately comes to define it.'

Eve smiles. 'Like . . .'

'Yes, if you will, like Russia itself. Like any corporation or nation state that perceives itself surrounded by enemies. And this was the point, I think, at which Konstantin Orlov was recruited by the Twelve. Which was entirely logical, because by then the Twelve had their own Directorate S, or its equivalent, and they needed a man with Orlov's highly specialised skill-set to run it.'

'So you're saying that the Twelve is a kind of shadow Russian state?'

'Not quite. I believe that it's a new kind of borderless crypto-state, with its own economy, strategy and politique.'

'And what's its purpose?'

Tikhomirov shrugs. 'To protect and advance its own interests.'

'So how do you join? How do you become a part of it?'

'You buy in, with whatever you've got to offer. Cash, influence, position . . .'

'That's such a weird idea.'

'These are weird times, Mrs Polastri. As was confirmed to me when I saw Orlov earlier this year.'

'You saw him? Where?'

'In Fontanka, near Odessa. The SVR, our domestic intelligence agency, ran the operation against him which ended, regrettably, with his death.'

'In the house of Rinat Yevtukh?'

'Exactly so. The FSB contributed intelligence and manpower to that operation, and in return, I was invited to question Orlov. He told me nothing, of course, and I didn't expect him to. He was old-school. He'd have died before betraying his employers, or the assassins he'd trained for them. The irony, of course, being that they killed him.'

'You're sure of that?'

'Sure enough. The Twelve would have worked out pretty quickly that Orlov hadn't been abducted just so that the local gangsters could collect a ransom payment. They'd have seen the fingerprints of the SVR all over the case. And they'd have liquidated Orlov in case he'd talked.'

'So why might Yevtukh have been killed?'

'If he was, it might have been because he collaborated, willingly or otherwise, with the SVR.'

'So do you have an interest in the Yevtukh case? In knowing exactly who murdered him?'

'We're following developments, certainly.'

'Did Richard mention to you that we have an idea who was responsible?'

'No, he didn't tell me that.' He looks thoughtful. 'Let me ask you something, Mrs Polastri. Are you familiar with the expression "a canary in a coal mine"?'

'Vaguely.'

'In the old days, here in Russia, coal miners used to take a canary in a cage with them when they went down to dig a new seam. Canaries are highly sensitive to methane gas and carbon monoxide, so the miners knew that as long as they could hear the canary singing, they were safe. But if the canary fell silent, they knew they had to evacuate the mine.'

'That's fascinating, Mr Tikhomirov, but why exactly are you telling me this?'

'Have you ever asked yourself, Mrs Polastri, why you were appointed by MI6 to investigate a major international conspiracy? You'll forgive me, but you are hardly experienced in this area.'

'I was asked to investigate a particular assassin. A woman. And I have a number of lines of enquiry that could lead to her identification. I've got closer to her than anyone else has.'

'Hence the attempt on your life yesterday.'

'Perhaps.'

'There's no "perhaps" about it, Mrs Polastri. Fortunately, we had people watching you.'

208

'Yes, I saw them.'

'You saw the ones we intended you to see. But there were others, and they intercepted and arrested the woman who attempted to kill you.'

'You're telling me you've caught her?'

'Yes, we have her in custody.'

'Here? In the Lubyanka?'

'No, in Butyrka, a couple of miles away.'

'My God. Can I see her? Can I question her?'

'I'm afraid that's impossible. I doubt she's even been processed.' He lifts a silver paper-knife in the shape of a dagger, and turns it in his fingers. 'Also, the fact that she's been arrested doesn't mean you're out of danger. Which is why I made sure you were brought here, yesterday, to spend the night as our guest.'

'Do you have a name for this woman?'

He opens a folder on the desk in front of him. 'Her name is Larissa Farmanyants. She's what we call a torpedo, a professional shooter. New photographs will have been taken during her induction at Butyrka, but they haven't sent them over yet, so I've printed out an old press shot for you.'

Three young women standing on a ceremonial dais, in an outdoor sports stadium. They're wearing tracksuits zipped up to their chins, they're holding posies of flowers, and they have medals and ribbons around their necks. The Tass news agency caption identifies them as medallists in the pistol-shooting event at the University Games, six years earlier. Larissa Farmanyants, representing Kazan Military Academy, has won bronze. Blonde-haired, with broad, high-cheekboned features, she stares blankly into the middle distance.

Eve stares back at her, dazed. This person, a young woman she has never met, tried to kill her. To put a bullet through the back of her skull.

'Why?' she murmurs. 'Why here? Why now? Why *me*?'

Tikhomirov looks at her, his gaze level. 'You've crossed the line. You've done what nobody thought you could, or would. You've got too close to the Twelve.'

Eve picks up the Tass printout. 'This Lara woman could be one of the pair who killed Yevtukh in Venice. There's a CCTV clip.'

In response Tikhomirov takes a second sheet of paper from the folder, and hands it to her. It's an identical screen-grab to the one that Billy printed out at Goodge Street. 'We've seen that footage,' he says. 'And we agree.'

'And the other woman?'

'We don't know, although we'd very much like to.'

'I wish I could help you.'

'Mrs Polastri, you've helped us far more than you know. And we're grateful.'

'So what happens now?'

'In the first instance, we will put you on a flight home, under another name, as we did your colleague, yesterday.' He hands her the folder. 'This is for you. Read it on the flight. Give it to the steward before you leave the aircraft.'

She picks up the Tass agency printout and is about to slide it into the folder when something stays her hand. For almost a quarter of a minute she stares disbelievingly at the image of the medal-winners.

'The one who won gold,' she says, glancing at the caption. 'The Perm University student, Oxana Vorontsova. What do you know about her?'

210

Tikhomirov frowns, and flips open his laptop. His fingers stab the keyboard. 'She's dead,' he says.

'Are you sure about that?' Eve asks, suddenly short of breath. 'Are you absolutely one hundred per cent certain?'

Tikhomirov is as good as his word. He gives Eve lunch in the Lubyanka canteen, and then shows her into a Mercedes with darkened windows which is waiting at the entrance to the FSB complex on Furkasovsky Lane. On the rear seat is her suitcase, which has been collected from the hotel. Within the hour she is at Ostafyevo airport, being fast-tracked through the customs and security procedures by the car's driver, a young man in a business suit to whom the airport staff are immediately deferential. He ushers Eve to a first-class waiting room, and sits with her, unobtrusive but vigilant, until her flight is called. As she leaves, with a dozen-strong group of Gazprom executives, he hands her an envelope. 'From Mr Tikhomirov,' he says.

The interior of the Dassault Falcon jet is shockingly luxurious, and Eve sinks pleasurably into her seat. Take-off is delayed, and dusk has fallen by the time the aircraft finally lifts off, banks to port over the glittering sprawl of Moscow, and sets its course for London. Exhausted, Eve sleeps for an hour before waking with a start to find a steward at her side, tendering frosted shot-glasses of Black Sable vodka.

She takes a long swallow, feels the spirit's icy progress through her veins, and inclines her head towards the window, and the darkness beyond. Just forty-eight hours ago, she reflects, I was flying the other way. I was a different person then. Someone who hadn't heard the passing whisper of a silenced bullet. Someone who hadn't seen a man's face infold.

211

I can't do this any more. I need my life back. I need my husband back. I need a routine, familiar things and places, a hand to hold on icy pavements, a warm body next to mine at night. I'll make it up to you, Niko. I promise. All those evenings I spent whispering into my phone and staring at my laptop screen. All the secrets I kept, all the lies I told, all the love I withheld.

Reaching into her bag she searches for her phone, determined to draft a text to Niko, but her fingers find the envelope from Vadim Tikhomirov, which she has forgotten to open. Inside is a single sheet of paper. No message, just a black and white line illustration of a canary in a cage.

What does Tikhomirov mean? What is he not telling her, and why? Who, or what, is the canary?

And that woman in the photograph. Not Larissa Farmanyants, but Oxana Vorontsova, the Perm University gold medallist. Now dead, according to FSB records, but the doppelgänger of the woman she saw in Shanghai on the night Simon Mortimer was killed. Or is she imagining that, and making connections that simply aren't there? She only saw the woman momentarily, after all. Eve winces with frustration. None of it quite fits together. From having too little information to work with, she's now got too much.

Just as well then, that it no longer matters. Just as well that on Monday morning she is going to schedule a meeting with Richard Edwards, at which she is going to admit to him what she has finally admitted to herself, that she is out of her depth. That she's decided to walk away from Goodge Street, MI6, and this whole toxic, terrifying mess, and reclaim her life.

At London City airport, she sends Richard an encrypted text to say that she's back, and takes the tube home. Her phone battery's dying, she's starving and she desperately needs Niko to be at home, preferably cooking and with a bottle of wine open. At Finchley Road station she drags her case up the steps to the exit. Outside, the pavements are shining with rain, and she puts her head down and half walks, half runs through the illuminated darkness. Turning into her street, the wheels of her suitcase whirring and skidding behind her, she sees the unmarked van parked a few cars down from her building, and, for the first time, feels truly grateful for the watchers' presence. Then, seeing that the lights in the flat are unlit, her step slows.

Inside, the air is still and cold, as if long undisturbed. On the kitchen table there's a note, secured in place by a vase of dying white roses whose fallen petals obscure the words.

Hope your trip went well, though don't expect to hear the details. Have taken car and goats, and gone to stay with Zbig and Leila. Not sure how long I'll be gone. Hopefully long enough for you to decide whether you want us to go on being married.

Eve, I can't continue like this. We both know the issues. Either you choose to live in my world, where people do normal jobs, and married couples sleep together and eat together and see their friends together and yes, perhaps it is a bit boring at times, but at least no one's getting their throat cut. Or you choose to continue as you are, telling me nothing and working day and night in the pursuit of whatever and whoever, in which case sorry, but I'm out. I'm afraid it's that simple. Your call. N.

Eve stares briefly at the note, then goes back and double-locks the door to the flat. A quick scavenge through the kitchen produces a tin of tomato soup, three limp samosas in an oily bag, and a date-expired blueberry yoghurt. She wolfs down the samosas and the yoghurt while the soup is heating on the stove. As if in reproach of her habitual untidiness, Niko has left the flat in scrupulous order. In the bedroom the bed is made and the blinds are lowered. Eve considers running a bath but gives it a miss; she's too tired to think, let alone dry herself. After attaching her phone to the charger she takes the Glock automatic from her bedside drawer, and slips it under her pillow. Then she pulls off her clothes, and, leaving them in a pile on the floor, climbs into bed and is instantly asleep.

She's woken around nine thirty by the chattering of the fax machine that Richard has insisted she install, on the basis that it's supposedly more secure than encoded email. It's a hastily scrawled invitation to a private view at an art gallery in Chiswick, west London, where, from midday onwards, Richard's wife Amanda is exhibiting her paintings and drawings. 'Come if you're free, and we can chat,' Richard signs off.

Chiswick is at least an hour away, and Eve doesn't much feel like making the journey, but it will be a chance to tell Richard her decision in a neutral setting. 'See you then,' she faxes in response, then crawls back to bed, burying herself under the sheets for another hour. Fear, she's discovering, is not a constant. It comes and goes, kicking in at odd moments with paralysing suddenness, and then receding, tide-like, to the point where she's barely conscious of it. In bed, it takes the form of a fluttery nervousness just insistent enough to keep her awake.

The desire for breakfast eventually gets the better of her, and she pulls on a tracksuit, drops the Glock in her bag, and makes for the Café Torino in Finchley Road. Richard's watchers know their stuff, surely? And if they don't, and she's beaten to the draw by a torpedo, it's going to be with a large cappuccino and a *cornetto alla Nutella* inside her.

Appetite assuaged, she dials Niko's number. When there's no answer, she's simultaneously frustrated and relieved. She wants to tell him that everything's all right between them, but she can't quite face the intensity of the conversation that will ensue. From the café she walks unhurriedly to the tube station. It's perfect Saturday weather, clear and cold, and she imagines her invisible watchers falling into step behind her. In the half-empty tube train she picks through an abandoned copy of the *Guardian*, reading reviews of books she will never buy.

The gallery in Chiswick is difficult to find, identified only by a small silver plaque on the door. Occupying the ground floor of a Georgian house, it has a sunlit brick frontage and a wide bow window overlooking the Thames. As soon as she steps inside Eve feels out of place. Richard's friends have that casually privileged look that quietly but unmistakably fends off outsiders. For quite a few minutes, no one talks to her, so she affects a frowningly intense interest in the art on display. The watercolours and drawings are accomplished and inoffensive. Landscape views of the Cotswolds, boats at anchor in Aldeburgh, a girl in a straw hat on holiday in France. There's a portrait drawing, quite a good one, of

Richard. Eve is admiring this when a fine-boned woman with eyes as pale as sea-glass appears at her side.

'So what do you think?' she asks.

'It's very like him,' says Eve. 'Benign, but hard to read. You must be Amanda?'

'Yes. And I'm guessing you're Eve. Concerning whom there can be no discussion.'

'I'm sorry?'

'Richard often mentions you. I don't think he's aware quite how often. And obviously, official secrets and so on, I don't ask him about you. But I've always rather wondered.'

'Trust me, I'm not the mysterious type.'

Amanda gives her a pale smile. 'Let me get you something to drink.' She beckons to Richard, who's circulating with a bottle of prosecco wrapped in a napkin. Disconcertingly, given his church-mouse work look, he's wearing a jauntily unbuttoned pink linen shirt and chinos.

'Ah,' he says. 'You two have met. Excellent. I'll just get Eve a glass.'

Richard walks away, and Amanda makes as if to straighten a picture frame. She barely touches it, but the movement draws Eve's attention to the platinum wedding band and glittering baguette diamond ring.

'I'm not sleeping with your husband,' Eve says. 'In case you're wondering.'

Amanda raises an eyebrow. 'I'm glad to hear it. You're not remotely his type, but you know how lazy men are. Whatever's to hand.'

Eve smiles. 'The paintings seem to be selling well,' she says. 'Lots of red stickers.'

'That's mostly the drawings, which are cheaper. I'm counting on Richard to keep pouring wine down people's throats. See if that helps shift some of the paintings.'

'Won't you miss them? All those memories.'

'Paintings are like children. It's nice to have them around the house, but not necessarily for ever.'

Richard returns with a newly washed glass, which he fills and hands to Eve. 'Can I have a brief word? In five minutes?'

Eve nods. She half turns, but Amanda's already drifting away.

'Let me introduce you to our daughter,' Richard says.

Chloe Edwards has long-lashed eyes and her mother's bones. 'You work with Dad, don't you?' she says, when Richard has moved on. 'That's so cool. Mum and I never get to meet his fellow spies so you'll have to forgive me if I get a bit fan-girly. Bet you've got a gun in your bag.'

'Of course.' Eve smiles.

'Actually, come to think, I did meet one once. Another spook, I mean.'

'Anyone I know?'

'Lucky you if you do. We were at our house in Saint-Rémy-de-Provence, Mum was out sketching or shopping or something, and he came over for lunch. Older guy, Russian, devastatingly ravaged-looking. God, I fancied him.'

'How old were you?'

'Oh, fifteen, probably. I don't remember his name. Which was probably fake anyway, right?'

'Not necessarily. Is that you in the painting? In the straw hat?'

''Fraid so. I wish someone would buy it and take it away.'

'Truly?'

'It's so, you know, white girl on holiday.'

'But it must be lovely having a house in Provence.'

'I suppose. The heat and the smell of the lavender fields. All that. But I'm not so much for the rich Parisian boys in their Vilebrequin swim-shorts.'

'Prefer a ravaged Russian?'

'God yes, every time.'

'You should follow your dad into the Service. You'll meet plenty.'

'He says I'm too glam to be a spy. That you've got to be, like, really ordinary-looking. The sort of person you'd walk straight past in the street.'

Eve smiles. 'Like me?'

'No, no, no. *No*. I don't mean—'

'Don't worry, I'm just teasing you. But your dad's right. You're amazing-looking, and you should enjoy it.'

Chloe grins. 'You're nice. Can we stay in touch? Dad's always going on about meeting the right people.' She hands Eve a card. It has her name on it, a phone number and an embossed skull and crossbones.

'Well, I'm not so sure I'm one of the right people, but thanks. Are you at university?'

'I want to go to drama school. I've got auditions in the New Year.'

'Well, good luck.'

Richard winds through the guests towards them, and pats his daughter on the bottom. 'Vamoose, darling, I need to borrow Eve for a few minutes.'

Chloe rolls her eyes, and Eve follows him outside.

Whitlock and Jones, purveyors of pharmaceutical and medical supplies, is one of the longer established businesses in Welbeck Street, in central London. Its sales staff wear white coats, and are known for the tact with which they cater to their customers' often intimate requirements. For sales assistant Colin Dye it's been a slow day. The store caters to many of the private specialists whose well-appointed clinics line nearby Harley Street and Wimpole Street, and in the two years that he's been working here, Dye has come to recognise many of the nurses who drop in when their employers' surgical supplies need replenishing. With half a dozen of these he's on solid bantering terms. His own surname is always a good ice-breaker.

So if he doesn't know the young woman who's approaching the counter, her gaze lingering on the fibreglass mannequins fitted with trusses and lumbar supports, he knows the type. Conservative make-up, sensible shoes, not hazardously pretty, and a generally brisk and capable air.

'So, what can I do you for?' he enquires, and in answer she places a written list in front of him. A blood collection kit, hemostatic forceps, a sharps disposal bag and a packet of large condoms.

'Having a party?'

'Excuse me?' She peers at him. She's slightly cross-eyed, and the clunky glasses don't help, but that apart, Dye concedes, not a total car-crash.

'Well, you know what they say.' He points to his name-tag. 'Live and let . . . *Dye*.'

'Have you got everything on that list?'

'Give me a couple of minutes.'

When he returns, she hasn't moved.

'I'm afraid the condoms only come in standard size. Is that going to be a problem?'

'Do they stretch?'

He grins. 'In my experience, yes.'

She fixes him with one eye, the other looking disconcertingly over his shoulder, and pays for the goods in cash.

He drops the receipt into the Whitlock and Jones bag. 'See you again, perhaps? You know what they say . . . *Dye* another day?'

'Actually no one says that. Asshole.'

Eve follows Richard out of the gallery, across the riverside walkway, and down a slipway to a floating jetty, to which dinghies and other small craft are moored. It's low tide, and the jetty rocks gently beneath their feet. There's a faint smell of ooze and seaweed, and the slow rasp of mooring chains shifting with the river's rise and fall. It's cold, but Richard doesn't seem to notice.

'She's quite a girl, your daughter.'

'Isn't she? I'm glad you liked her.'

'I did.' A breeze shivers the river's thin glitter. 'A professional shooter tried to take me out in the Moscow metro. If it wasn't for the FSB, I might be dead.'

'Lance told me. Said that they took you to the Lubyanka.'

'That's right.'

'I'm sorry, the whole thing must have been bloody frightening.'

'It was. Although clearly it was my fault for insisting on going to Moscow in the first place.'

Richard looks away. 'That's not important now. Just tell me exactly what happened.'

She tells him. The metro, the Lubyanka, the conversation with Tikhomirov. All of it.

When she's finished he says nothing. For almost a minute he seems to be watching a narrowboat edge past the jetty. 'So they've got this Farmanyants woman in custody,' he says finally.

'Yes, in Butyrka. Which I gather is not a soft billet.'

'No. It's bloody medieval.'

'I'm pretty sure she's one of the women who killed Yevtukh in Venice. Tikhomirov thinks so too.'

'Does he now?'

'Richard, you recruited me to find out who killed Viktor Kedrin. I believe that it was a young woman named Oxana Vorontsova, codename Villanelle. A former linguistics student and prize-winning pistol shot from Perm, who was convicted of triple murder at the age of twenty-three. She was recruited and trained by Konstantin Orlov, the former head of the SVR's Directorate S, as an assassin for the Twelve. He lifted her from prison, faked her death, and created a series of new identities for her, before he was killed himself, quite possibly by Villanelle. I'll fax you my report in full over the next forty-eight hours, if I live that long.'

'You really think—'

'Look at it from Villanelle's point of view. She's danger-ously compromised by what I've discovered about her, and her girlfriend's in Butyrka, mostly because of me. So who do you think she's coming for next?'

'The people I've got watching you are the best, Eve. I promise you. You won't see them, but they're there.'

'I hope so, Richard, I really bloody hope so, because she's a killing machine. I'm trying to sound calm, and I'm more or less in control, most of the time. But I'm also scared to death. I mean, really fucking terrified. So terrified I can't even think about the danger I'm in, or take the necessary precautions, because I'm afraid that if I face it straight on, or start thinking about it in any detail, I'm just going to fall to pieces. So there you go.'

He regards her with silent, clinical concern.

'I'm not going back to Goodge Street,' she adds. 'Ever.'

'All right.'

'I'm out, Richard. I mean it.'

'I hear you. But can I ask you one question?'

'As many as you like.'

'Where do you want to be in ten years' time?'

'I'll settle for alive. If I'm still married that would be a bonus.'

'Eve, there are no guarantees in this life, but you are in every sense more secure inside the citadel than outside. Let us take the strain. You were born for the secret life. You live and breathe intelligence work. The rewards could be . . . very great.'

'I simply can't do it, Richard. I can't carry on. And now I'm going to go.'

He nods. 'I understand.'

'I don't think you do, Richard. But either way.' She holds out her hand. 'Thanks for asking me today, and my compliments to Amanda.'

He frowns as he watches her go.

With the medical goods from Whitlock and Jones stowed in her rucksack, Villanelle meets Anton at the ticket barrier at Finchley Road tube station. He looks tense and short-tempered, and they've barely exchanged a few words before

222

he turns away and leads her to the small Italian café outside the station.

Ordering coffee for both of them, he directs her to a corner table. 'Ideally, I want it done tonight,' he tells her. 'The husband's away, staying with friends, and I've just had confirmation he's still there. The weapon, ammunition and documents you requested are in the bag under the table. You also asked for a vehicle, presumably for getting rid of the body?'

'Yup.'

'You'll find a white Citroën panel van parked directly outside Polastri's house. Key's in the bag with the gun. Signal me in the usual way when the job's done, and I'll see you in Paris.'

'OK. *Nyet problem.*'

He looks at her irritably. 'Speak English. And why are you wearing those ridiculous glasses? You look mental.'

'I am mental. Have you seen the Hare psychopathy checklist? I'm off the scale.'

'Just don't screw up, OK?'

'As if.'

'Villanelle, take me seriously. The reason I still need you to do this job is that Farmanyants fucked up in Moscow.'

Villanelle remains expressionless. 'What went wrong?'

'It doesn't matter. What matters is that this one goes right.'

8

On the tube, going home, Eve looks surreptitiously around her. Which of the other passengers are her watchers? There would probably be two of them, both armed. The Goth couple with the Staffordshire bull terrier? The earnest-looking guys in the Arsenal shirts? The young women endlessly whispering into their phones?

She could ask to go to a safe house, but that would just be postponing the problem. The unspoken truth, as she and Richard both know, is that she must make any would-be killer break cover, and this will most easily be achieved by continuing to live in her own flat. The building and the surrounding streets, meanwhile, will be invisibly cordoned off by the protection team. If Villanelle comes anywhere near, the team will move in for a hard arrest, and if she resists, disable or kill her out of hand. One way and another, Eve knows, she's probably safer than at any time since she started working for Richard.

Dragging her keys from her bag, she unlocks the front door, and steps into the small communal hallway. Opening the door to the ground-floor flat she stands there for a moment, listening to the silence, and the faint buzz of the prosecco in her ears. Then, taking out the Glock, and ignoring the thumping of her heart, she closes the door behind her and subjects the place to a brisk and professional search.

Nothing. Collapsing onto the sofa, she flicks on the TV, which Niko has left tuned to the History Channel. A documentary about the Cold War is playing, and a commentator is describing the execution of thirteen poets in Moscow in 1952. Eve starts watching, but she can't keep her eyes open, and the documentary becomes a flickering montage of grainy black and white film and semi-comprehensible Russian. Minutes later, although it could have been an hour, the titles are rolling, accompanied by a scratchy old recording of the Soviet national anthem. Sleepily, Eve hums along:

Soyuz nerushimy respublik svobodnykh:
Splotila naveki velikaya Rus'!

Dreadful lyrics, all that crapola about an unbreakable union of republics, but a stirring tune.

'*Da zdravstvuyet sozdanny voley narodov*'

The will of the people. Yeah, right . . . Yawning, Eve reaches for the remote and flicks the TV off.

'*Yediny, moguchy Sovetsky Soyuz!*'

She freezes mid-yawn. What the fuck? Is that voice in her head? Or is it right here in the flat?

'*Slav'sya, Otechestvo nashe svobodnoye . . .*'

Terror stops Eve's breath. It's real. It's here. It's her.

The singing continues, clear and untroubled, and Eve tries to stand but discovers that her joints are gluey with fear, and her co-ordination all wrong, and she falls back

225

onto the sofa. Somehow, the Glock is in her hand. The singing stops.

'Eve, can you come here?'

She's in the bathroom, with its faint but unmistakable echo, and suddenly Eve is devoured by a curiosity that momentarily mutes her terror. Propelling herself through the living room into the rear of the flat, gun in hand, she pulls open the door and is met by a warm, scented gust of steam. Villanelle is lying in the bath, naked except for a pair of latex gloves. Her eyes are half closed, her hair is a spiky wet tangle, and her skin is pink in the hot, soapy water. Above her feet, lying between the taps, is a Sig Sauer pistol.

'Will you help me do my hair? I can't really manage it in these gloves.'

Eve stares at her open-mouthed, her knees shaking. Registers the catlike features and the flat grey eyes, the half-healed facial cuts, the strange little twist to the mouth. 'Villanelle,' she whispers.

'Eve.'

'What . . . why are you here?'

'I wanted to see you. It's been weeks.'

Eve doesn't move. She just stands there, the Glock heavy in her hands.

'Please.' Villanelle reaches for a bottle of Eve's gardenia shampoo. 'Calm down. Put your gun down there with mine.'

'Why are you wearing those gloves?'

'Forensics.'

'So you've come here to kill me?'

'Do you want me to?'

'No, Villanelle. Please . . .'

226

'Well, then.' She looks up at Eve. 'You haven't got plans for the evening, have you?'

'No, I . . . My husband is . . .' Eve stares around her wildly. At the steamed-up window, the sink, the gun in her hands. She knows that she should take control of the situation but there's something paralysing about Villanelle's physical presence. The wet hair, the livid cuts and bruises, the pale body in the steaming water, the flaking toenail varnish. It's all too intense.

'I read Niko's note,' Villanelle shakes her head. 'It's so crazy that you keep goats.'

'They're just small ones. I . . . I can't believe that you're here. In my flat.'

'You were asleep in front of the TV when I came in. Snoring, in fact. I didn't want to wake you.'

'There's an eight-bar security lock on that front door.'

'I noticed. Quite a good one. I love your place, though. It's so . . . you. Everything's just how I imagined.'

'You broke in. You brought a gun. So I'm guessing that you are, in fact, meaning to kill me.'

'Eve, please, don't spoil everything.' Villanelle tilts her head flirtatiously against the edge of the bath. 'Am I how you imagined me?'

Eve turns away. 'I didn't imagine you. I couldn't begin to imagine anyone who's done the things you've done.'

'Really?'

'Do you even know how many people you've killed? Oxana?'

She laughs. 'Hey, Polastri. You really have been doing your research, haven't you? Top of the class. But let's not talk about me. Let's talk about you.'

227

'Just answer me this one simple question. Did you come here to kill me?'

'Sweetie, you keep on about this. And you're the one holding the gun.'

'I'd like to know.'

'OK. If I promise not to shoot you, will you do my hair?'

'Seriously?'

'Yes.'

'You're insane.'

'So they say. Do we have a deal?'

Eve frowns. Finally she nods, lays down the Glock, rolls up her sleeves, slips her watch into her pocket, and reaches for the shampoo.

Touching her is strange. And running her hands through her slick, wet tresses is stranger. Eve washes Villanelle's hair as if it's her own, caressing her scalp with dreamily circling fingers, probing and pressing and inhaling her biscuity, gardenia-scented smell. And then there's the fact of Villanelle's nakedness. The small, pale breasts, the lean musculature, the dark crest of pubic hair.

Testing the water temperature on the back of her hand, Eve rinses Villanelle's hair with the shower head. If you know that you're being manipulated, she tells herself, then you aren't. Inside her, something has shifted. Something has tilted her world on its axis.

When she's done, she drapes a towel over Villanelle's head, twists it into a turban and picks up her Glock. 'So what do you really want from me?' she asks, jabbing the end of the barrel into the base of Villanelle's skull.

228

'I put some champagne in the fridge. Could you open it for us?' Villenelle yawns, baring her teeth. 'I unloaded that thing, by the way. And the Sig.'

Eve checks both weapons. It's true.

Abruptly standing up, Villanelle stretches, revealing unshaved armpits. Then she reaches across to the medicine cabinet, takes out a pair of scissors, removes her gloves, and starts cutting her fingernails into the grey bathwater.

'I thought you were worried about forensics?'

'I'll deal with it. And talking of forensics, I could really use some clean pants.'

'Knickers?'

'Yes.'

'Couldn't you have brought some with you?'

'I forgot. Sorry.'

'Jesus, Villanelle.'

When Eve returns, Villanelle is wrapped in a towel, gazing at herself in the mirror. Eve throws her the pants but Villanelle, absorbed in her reflection, doesn't notice, and they land on her wet hair. Frowningly, she lifts them off. 'Eve, these are not very pretty.'

'Tough. They're all I've got.'

'You have only one pair?'

'No, I've got lots, but they're all the same.'

For a moment, Villanelle appears to wrestle with this concept, then she nods. 'So will you open the champagne now?'

'If you tell me why you're really here.'

The midwinter gaze meets hers. 'Because you need me, Eve. Because everything has changed.'

*

Leaning against the wall in the living room with a glass of pink Taittinger champagne in her hand, Villanelle looks poised, efficient and feminine. Her dark blonde hair is slicked back neatly from her forehead, and her outfit – black cashmere sweater, jeans, trainers – is chic but forgettable. She could be any smart young professional woman. But Eve can sense her feral aspect, too. The potential for savagery that beats like a pulse beneath the urbane exterior. It's a barely perceptible murmur, right now, but it's there.

'Have you got any nice dessert in the fridge?' Villanelle asks. 'Something that will go with this champagne?'

'There's ice-cream cake in the freezer compartment.'

'Can you get it?'

'You fucking get it.'

'Eve, *kotik*, I'm your guest.' She takes her Sig Sauer from the waistband of her jeans. 'And this time the gun's loaded.'

Wordlessly, Eve does as she's been asked, and then, turning back from the fridge, sees Villanelle raise the pistol and turn towards her. Her mind emptying, Eve sinks to her knees and squeezes her eyes closed. A long silence roars in her ears. Slowly, she opens her eyes to discover Villanelle's face inches from hers. Eve can smell her skin, the wine on her breath, the scent of shampoo. With shaking hands, she gives Villanelle the frozen cake.

'Eve, listen. I need you to trust me, OK?'

'*Trust* you?' Slowly, Eve stands. Villanelle has put the automatic down on the dining table. It's within easy reach. One good lunge, and . . . she's hardly even formed the thought when Villanelle catches her across the face with a stinging backhand slap. Breathless with shock, Eve staggers towards the sofa and sits down.

'I said. I need you. To trust me.'

'Fuck you,' Eve mouths, the side of her face throbbing painfully.

'No, fuck you, *suka*.'

They stand there, face to face, then Villanelle reaches out a hand and touches Eve's cheek. 'I'm sorry. I didn't mean to hurt you.'

Probing her teeth with her tongue, tasting blood, Eve shrugs.

Villanelle gathers up the glasses and champagne bottle, and deposits herself beside her on the sofa. 'Come on, let's talk. For a start, how was the bracelet? Did you like it?'

'It's beautiful.'

'So . . . what do you say?'

Eve looks at her. Notes how Villanelle mirrors the way she sits, the way she carries her head and neck, the way she holds her glass. If she blinks, Villanelle blinks. If she moves a hand or touches her face, so does Villanelle. It's as if she's learning her. As if she's occupying her, inch by stealthy inch, slithering into her consciousness like a snake.

'You killed Simon Mortimer,' Eve says. 'You almost hacked his head off.'

'Simon . . . Was that the one in Shanghai?'

'You don't *remember*?'

Villanelle shrugs. 'What can I say? It must have seemed like a good idea at the time.'

'You're insane.'

'No I'm not, Eve. I'm just you without the guilt. Cake?'

For several minutes they sit there in silence, spooning ice cream, chocolate chips and frozen cherries into their mouths.

'That was heaven,' Villanelle murmurs, putting her bowl on the floor. 'Now I need you to listen to me very carefully. And before I forget' – she pulls a dozen 9mm rounds from her jeans pocket and hands them to Eve – 'these are yours.'

Eve reloads the Glock, and, uncertain what to do with it, pushes it into the back waistband of her jeans, where it lodges uncomfortably.

'That's probably not a good idea,' says Villanelle. 'But whatever.' Taking her phone from her pocket, she retrieves an image and shows it to Eve. 'Have you ever seen this man?'

Eve peers at it. He's about thirty, lean and sunburned, wearing a khaki T-shirt and the sand-coloured beret of the Special Air Service. The photographer has caught him in the act of turning, his eyes narrowed in annoyance, with one hand raised, perhaps to shield his face. Behind him are the unfocused outlines of military vehicles.

'No. Who is he?'

'I know him as Anton. He used to command E Squadron, who handle black operations for MI6, and now he's my controller. On Thursday he ordered me to kill you.'

'Why?'

'Because you've got too close to us, and by us I mean *Dvenadtsat*, the Twelve. When Anton gave me the order, I was in a private hospital in Austria. He came to see me in my room, and when he left the hospital, he drove away with this man. That's Anton on the left.'

The image is tilted and poorly framed, but clear enough. It's taken from inside a building, looking down on a snowy car park. Two men are standing by the passenger door of a silver-grey BMW. The left-hand figure, in a bulky black jacket, has his back to the camera. Opposite him, clearly recognisable in an overcoat and scarf, is Richard Edwards.

Eve stares at the image for a long while without speaking. Inside herself she feels the collapse of all her certainties, like an iceberg imploding into the sea. This man, who just hours ago was pouring her prosecco in a pink linen shirt, and telling her that she was 'born for the secret life', has agreed to, and perhaps even demanded, her death.

Tikhomirov guessed. That moment when she asked him whether Richard had mentioned their suspicions about Yevtukh's disappearance. Just for a second, the FSB officer's eyes widened, as if he'd suddenly understood something that had eluded him for ages. That's when he asked her about the canary. She pictures the bird, singing in its cage, far underground. The deadly, odourless gas wreathing through the seam, and the canary silent now, a stiff little mess of feathers.

'I need to make a call,' Eve tells Villanelle, and, searching the detritus of her bag for Chloe Edwards's card, she calls the number. It rings for almost ten seconds, and then Chloe answers. She sounds as if she's been asleep.

'Chloe, it's Eve. I wanted to ask you something about our conversation this afternoon. Confidentially.'

'Oh hi, Eve. Yeah, um . . .'

'That Russian guy you were talking about.'

'Uh-huh.'

'Was his name by any chance Konstantin?'

'Er . . . Yeah! I think it was. Wow. Who is he?'

'Old friend. I'll introduce you one of these days.'

'That'd be cool.'

'Just don't mention to your dad that I called, OK?'

''Kay.'

Eve disconnects and lays the phone gently on the table. 'Oh, God,' she says. 'Oh my God.'

'I'm sorry, Eve.'

She stares at Villanelle. 'I thought I was hunting you down for MI6, but in reality I'd been set up by Richard to test the Twelve's defences. I was the canary in their mine.'

Villanelle says nothing.

'Every time I discovered anything I'd report it to Richard, he'd pass it on to the Twelve, and they'd patch the vulnerability. All I've been doing, all these weeks and months, is making them stronger. Jesus wept. Did you know?'

'No. They don't tell me things like that. Of course I knew you worked for Edwards, but it wasn't until I saw him with Anton in Austria that I understood how you'd been set up.'

Eve nods, coldly furious with herself. She's fallen for a classic false flag operation, constructed, like all the best deceits, around her own vanity. She thought she was so clever, with her intuitive leaps and her left-field theorising, whereas in truth she was just a skilfully manipulated dupe. How could I have been so obtuse? she wonders. How could I not have seen what was happening right before my fucking eyes?

'You liked it though, didn't you?' Villanelle says. 'Playing the secret agent in your secret Goodge Street office with your secret codes, which weren't secret at all.'

'Richard flattered me, and it worked. I wanted to be a player, not just some paper-pusher at a desk.'

'You are a player, sweetie. Any time I was bored, I'd log on and read your email. I love that you spent so much time thinking about me.'

234

Looking at her undrunk wine, Eve feels a vast weariness. 'So what happens now? I know this sounds weird, but why haven't you shot me or whatever, like Anton said?'

'Two reasons. When he ordered me to kill you, I realised that it was because you'd found out too much about me. Which meant that I'd be the next one to die.'

'Because you were compromised?'

'Exactly. The Twelve don't take any chances. I saw that with Konstantin, who you obviously know about. He was my handler before Anton. They thought he'd talked to the FSB, which was bullshit, and they . . . had him killed.'

'At Fontanka.'

'Yes, at Fontanka.' She looks pensive. 'And now one of my people has been arrested in Moscow.'

'Larissa Farmanyants. Your girlfriend.'

'Lara, yes, although she wasn't so much a girlfriend in the holding hands and kissing sense. With us, it was more just sex and killing.'

'Well, the FSB have got Lara now. She's in Butyrka.'

'*Putain*. That's bad. They'll definitely interrogate her, so I'm doubly burned as far as Anton's concerned.'

'What does that mean?'

'It means that he'll have me killed, as soon as he can. I imagine his plan is to wait until I've finished with you, then deal with me.'

'You're certain about this?'

'Yes, and I'll tell you why. I know that Lara was arrested, because she managed to send me an emergency message. And then when I saw Anton earlier today he spoke about Lara, but didn't say a word about her being arrested. He knew that I'd know what it meant.'

'You said there were two reasons you haven't killed me. What's the second?'

Villanelle looks at her. 'Really? You haven't worked that out yet?'

Eve shakes her head.

'Because it's you, Eve.'

Eve stares at her, the complexity, strangeness and sheer enormity of the situation suddenly bearing down on her. 'So what happens now? I mean, what . . .'

'What do we do? How do we get out of this alive?'

'Yes.'

Villanelle begins to pace the room, her movements as fastidious as a cat's. Occasionally she darts a glance at a book or a photograph. Catching sight of her reflection in the mirror over the fireplace, she comes to a halt.

'You need to understand two things. First, that the only way of surviving is if you and I work together. You have to put your life in my hands, and do exactly, and I mean *exactly*, what I say. Because if not, the Twelve will kill you, and me too. There's nowhere to hide, and no one you can trust to protect you except me. You have to take my word for it that this is true.'

'And the second thing?'

'You have to accept that your life here is over. No more marriage, no more flat, no more job. Basically, no more Eve Polastri.'

'So . . .'

'She dies. And you leave all this behind. I take you into my world.'

Eve stares at Villanelle. She feels as if she's in free-fall, weightless.

236

Villanelle hitches up the sleeves of her sweater. Her hands are strong and capable. Her eyes, all business now, meet Eve's. 'The first thing we have to do is convince Anton that I've killed you. Once he thinks you're dead, we've got a very short breathing space before he comes after me. We have to misdirect him, and whoever he sends. Then we disappear.'

Eve closes her eyes. 'Look,' she says desperately. 'Let me contact someone I know in the police. DCI Gary Hurst. He was involved in the Kedrin investigation. He's a good guy, and completely straight. He'd put us under full close protection, and I'm sure you could do some sort of a deal, testifying against the Twelve in exchange for immunity. I'd much rather go that route.'

'Eve, you still don't get it. They have people everywhere. There's no police cell, no prison, no safe house that they can't get to. If we want to live longer than twenty-four hours, we have to disappear.'

'Where to?'

'Like I said, another world. Mine.'

'And what do you mean by that?'

'I mean the world that's all around you, but which is invisible if you're not part of it. In Russia we call it *mir teney*, the shadow world.'

'Surely that's the Twelve's domain?'

'Not any more. The Twelve are the establishment now. You know what the assassination department is called? Housekeeping.'

Eve stands up and starts to walk around in tight circles. She's still in free-fall, plummeting down some endless lift-shaft. She can feel the barrel of the Glock rubbing sweatily in the cleft of her buttocks. Pulling the gun from her waistband, she holds it loosely in her right hand. Villanelle doesn't move.

'Niko would think I was dead?'

'Everyone would.'

'And there's no alternative?'

'Not if you want to stay alive.'

Eve nods, and continues to pace. Then, quite suddenly, she sits down again.

'Give me that,' says Villanelle, gently taking the Glock.

Eve narrows her gaze. 'What happened here?' she asks, reaching out and touching the scar on Villanelle's lip.

'I'll tell you. I'll tell you everything. But this isn't the time.'

Eve nods. Time rushes almost audibly past her ears. There's the world that she knows, the world of work, alarm calls, email, car insurance and supermarket loyalty cards, and there's *mir teney*, the shadow world. There's Niko, who loves her, and is the kindest and most decent man she has ever met, and there's Villanelle, who kills for pleasure.

She looks into the waiting grey eyes.

'OK,' she says. 'What do we do?'

On the dining table, Villanelle places the medical supplies from Whitlock and Jones, and from her backpack takes a bin bag, a tin of Waitrose dog food, a white porcelain cup, a plastic belt, a tin of modelling wax, a small glass dropper of spirit gum, a fountain pen, a packet of hair-grips, a face powder compact, an eye-shadow palette, a comb, several condoms, her Sig Sauer automatic and suppressor and Eve's Glock.

'OK, the first thing I need is some of your hair. I'm going to pull it out.' She does so, Eve winces, and Villanelle smiles.

238

'Now I need a dark sheet. Darkest you've got. Quickly, while I set everything up.'

Taking herself to the bedroom, Eve returns with a folded dark blue bedsheet, which Villanelle places on the table with the other items. She's turned the TV on, and is streaming a noisy Japanese cop show. 'Sit,' she orders Eve, pointing to the sofa. 'Pull up your sleeve.'

A little apprehensively, Eve does as she's bidden. From the table, Villanelle takes a cannula, a hollow blood collection needle. The cannula has a twistable port and a clear PVC transfer tube attached. Villanelle feeds the open end of the tube into a condom, holding it tightly in place with an elastic hair-grip. Taking the plastic belt, she tightens it around Eve's bicep until the vein in her forearm is bulging, and then, surprisingly gently, slips in the cannula and opens the port.

'Squeeze your fist,' Villanelle tells her, as blood flows through the PVC tube and begins to fill the condom. After a few minutes, it holds two-thirds of a pint of Eve's blood, and Villanelle turns off the port, and detaches and knots the condom.

Picking up the Sig Sauer, Villanelle walks to the centre of the room, then, holding the sagging condom over the carpet, she fires a single, downward-angled shot into its dark, distended belly. There's a wet smack, and an outward burst of blood. From the centre of the carpet, a shining red spatter fans outwards towards the window, shading into a myriad of fine droplets which gleam on the floor and furniture and walls.

Villanelle regards her work with a critical eye, then moves back to Eve. Taking a pinch of modelling wax, she rolls it into a marble-size ball, flattens it, and glues it to Eve's fore-head with spirit gum. Then taking the cap off the fountain pen, she presses the circular end into the low mound of wax, cutting a neat hole through to the skin. With the face powder, she blends the wax into Eve's forehead, fills the hole with black eye-shadow, and surrounds the raised area with bruise-coloured purple.

'You're going to have such a pretty entry wound,' she tells Eve. 'But now I need more blood. It's going to leave you feeling a bit weird, OK?'

This time she takes two condoms of blood, another full pint.

Eve is very pale. 'I think I'm going to pass out,' she whispers.

'I've got you,' Villanelle says. Placing an arm around Eve's shoulders and another under her knees, she lays her on her side on the carpet, with her head at the epicentre of the blood spray. Carefully spread-eagling her limbs, she places the Glock in her right hand. 'Don't move,' she says. 'I've got to work fast before the blood clots.'

Eve flutters her eyelids in response. She's swimming in and out of consciousness now. The room is shadowy and insubstantial and Villanelle's voice is muted, as if it's coming from far away.

Villanelle drops the porcelain cup into the Waitrose shopping bag, and swings it against the dining table so that it shatters, Then, opening the dog-food can, she empties its contents into Eve's hair, at the back of her head, and care-fully arranges half a dozen of the larger pieces of shattered porcelain in the gelatinous mess. Satisfied with the compo-sition, she pours the first condom of blood on top, dotting a scarlet forefinger into the cosmetic entry wound. The contents of the second condom form a dark lake behind Eve's head.

'OK. Look dead.'

This takes very little effort on Eve's part.

Taking out her phone, Villanelle photographs her from various angles and distances, checking the pictures until she's satisfied. 'Done,' she says eventually, and performs a little dance of pleasure. 'That looks so *great*. The jelly in the dog food is just perfection. Now I'm going to clean you up. Don't move.'

She runs the comb through Eve's hair, dragging out the already congealing blood and offal. Then, having put the Waitrose bag over Eve's head, and propped her up against the sofa, she scrapes the porcelain fragments and the remainder of the dog food from the carpet with a kitchen spoon, depositing it in the tin, and the tin in the rubbish bag. With it go the cannula and tube, the remains of the condoms, the comb, the eye-shadow and powder, the spirit gum and wax, the belt, the pen and the hair-grips.

Taking the hair she's pulled from Eve's head, Villanelle sprinkles it in the congealing blood, which she then smears across the carpet with a swipe of her hand. She peels off the latex gloves and drops them in the bin-bag then pulls on a new pair. 'Your turn for a bath,' she announces, scooping Eve up in her arms.

Lying semi-conscious in the warm water as Villanelle rinses her hair, Eve feels a vast sense of peace. It's as if she's between lives. Half an hour later, dried and dressed in clean clothes, she sits on the sofa drinking sweet tea and eating slightly stale chocolate digestive biscuits. She's crushingly tired, her skin is clammy, and the smell of blood is thick in her nostrils. 'This is the definitely the weirdest I've ever felt,' she murmurs.

'I know. I took a lot of your blood. But look what I'm sending to Anton.'

Eve takes Villanelle's phone. Notes with awe her own chalk-white features, half-closed eyes and gaping mouth. Just above the bridge of her nose, there's a purplish crater around a blackened 9mm entry wound. And at the back of her head, a chaotic horror of skull fragments, the bone shining whitely through the red, and a slick porridge of destroyed brain matter.

'Fuck. I really did die, didn't I?'

'I've seen headshots up close,' Villanelle says delicately. 'It's accurate.'

'I know. Your friend Lara blew an old man's brains out in the metro, aiming for me.'

'I'm really shocked she missed. And then to be picked up by the FSB and thrown into Butyrka. That's such a shitty day's work.'

'Aren't you upset about her?'

'Why do you ask?'

'Just wondering.'

'Don't wonder. Get your strength back. I'm going to tidy up and pack the car.'

'You've got a car?'

'It's a van, in fact. Give me that mug and biscuit wrapper.'

'Can I take anything with me?'

'No. That's the thing about being dead.'

'I suppose it is.'

242

Five minutes later, Villanelle surveys the flat. The place is as she found it, except for the bloody tableau in the main room, which looks just as she planned. She's particularly pleased with the clotted red-brown smear on the carpet, suggesting a bled-out corpse dragged away by the legs. As to what narrative will be constructed around this, she doesn't care. She just needs time. Forty-eight hours will do it.

'OK,' she says. 'Time to go. I'm going to wrap you up in this sheet, cover you with a folded rug and carry you out over my shoulder.'

'Mightn't people see?'

'Doesn't matter if they do, they'll just think it's someone moving their stuff. Later, when the street's full of police cars, they might see it differently, but by then . . .' Villanelle shrugs.

In the event, it's accomplished very quickly, and Eve marvels at Villanelle's strength as she lowers her, apparently without effort, onto the floor of the panel van. Mummified in the blue sheet, with Villanelle's rucksack jammed beneath her head, she hears the van's rear doors close and lock.

It's not a comfortable journey, and the first half-hour is made worse by a succession of speed bumps, but eventually the road levels out and the van picks up speed. For Eve, it's enough just to lie there, seeing nothing at all, in a state that's not quite wakefulness and not quite sleep. After what might have been an hour, but might equally have been two, the van comes to a halt. The doors open, and Eve feels the sheet unwrapped from her face. It's dark, with a faint wash of street lighting, and Villanelle is sitting on the tailgate of the van, her rucksack over her shoulder. Leaning inside she unbinds Eve from her winding sheet. Outside it's cold, and smells like rain. They're in a car park beside a motorway, surrounded by the dim forms of heavy-goods vehicles. An illuminated shack announces CAFÉ 24 Hrs.

Villanelle helps Eve out of the van, and they pick their way over the puddled ground. Inside the café, beneath the lunar glow of strip lights, a dozen men are silently addressing plates of food at plastic-topped tables as Elvis's 'Are You Lonesome Tonight?' issues from ancient wall-mounted speakers. Behind a counter a woman in a rockabilly bandana is frying onions on a hotplate.

Five minutes later, steaming mugs of tea and two of the biggest, greasiest burgers that Eve has ever seen are placed in front of them.

'Eat,' Villanelle orders. 'All of it. And all the chips.'

'Don't worry. I'm starving.'

When they leave, Eve feels transformed, if a little nauseated. She follows Villanelle across the car park, and then, mystifyingly, along a darkened path towards a sparsely lit residential block. At the foot of a tower, Villanelle inserts a key into a steel-fronted door. They climb an unlit stairway to the third floor, where Villanelle opens another armoured door, and turns on the light. They're in an unheated studio flat, furnished with bleak austerity. There's a table, a single chair, a military canvas-topped camp bed, a khaki sleeping bag, a cloth-covered wardrobe with a hanging rail full of clothes, and a stack of metal storage boxes. Insulated black-out curtains prevent the escape of light.

'What is this place?' Eve asks, looking around her.

'It's mine. A woman needs a room of her own, don't you think?'

244

'But where are we?'

'Enough questions. The bathroom's there, take what you need.'

The bathroom proves to be a concrete cell with a toilet, a basin and a single cold tap. A plastic crate on the floor holds a jumble of toiletries, tampons, wound dressings, suturing kits and painkillers. When Eve comes out, the sleeping bag has been unrolled on the camp bed and Villanelle is field-stripping and cleaning her Sig Sauer at the table. 'Sleep,' she says, not looking up. 'You're going to need all your strength.'

'What about you?'

'I'll be fine. Go to bed.'

Eve wakes into a cold and unidentifiable twilight. Villanelle is sitting at the table in the same position, but she is wearing different clothes and slowly scrolling through maps on a laptop. Slowly, wonderingly, Eve's memory recreates the events of the previous day. 'What's the time?' she asks.

'Five p.m. You've been asleep for fifteen hours.'

'Oh my God.' She unzips herself from the sleeping bag. 'I'm starving.'

'Good. Get ready and we'll go and eat. I've put out new clothes for you.'

They step outside into a desolate, twilit landscape. Eve looks about her. It's the sort of place she's driven past countless times without really seeing. The building they've just left is a condemned tenement block. Metal shutters cover doors and windows, security notices warn of patrolling guard dogs, wild lilac bushes have grown through the forecourt's littered tarmac. *Mir teney*, the shadow world.

245

When they leave the café the drizzle has become rain. On the motorway, the traffic is unceasing, zipping by in a grey, vaporous spray. Eve follows Villanelle past the building where they stayed the night, to a graffiti-tagged row of garages. The end garage is secured with a galvanised steel roller-door and a heavy-duty coded padlock, which Villanelle unlocks. Inside, it's dry, clean and surprisingly spacious. A hydraulic motorcycle repair bench runs along one wall; against the other, a shelved unit holds helmets, armour-panelled leather jackets, trousers, gloves and boots. Between them a volcano-grey Ducati Multistrada 1260 waits on its stand, fitted with locked panniers and top-box.

'Everything's packed,' Villanelle tells Eve. 'Time to get dressed.'

Five minutes later she wheels the Ducati out of the garage, and waits while Eve pulls down and locks the roller door. The rain has stopped, and for a moment the two women stand there, facing each other.

'Ready for this?' Villanelle asks, zipping up her jacket, and Eve nods.

They put on their helmets, and mount the Ducati. The whisper of the Testastretta engine becomes a murmur, the headlight beam floods the darkness. Villanelle takes the slip road slowly, allowing Eve to find her balance and settle tightly against her. She waits for a gap in the traffic, the murmur builds to a snarl, and they're gone.

Acknowledgements

To Patrick Walsh at Pew Literary, unreserved thanks. The same to Mark Richards at John Murray and Josh Kendall at Mulholland; I couldn't hope for finer or more supportive editors. Tim Davidson's surgical experience was invaluable, forensic psychologist Tarmala Caple gave me vital insights into psychopathy, and for correcting my Russian, thank you Olga Messerer and Daria Novikova.